Alex & Jackie

Feathered

being a fairy tale

Also by
Tom Weston

The Alex and Jackie Adventures:
First Night: *being a Ghost Story*
The Elf of Luxembourg: *being a Love Story*

And

Fission: based on a true story

Tom Weston

Alex & Jackie

Feathered

being a fairy tale

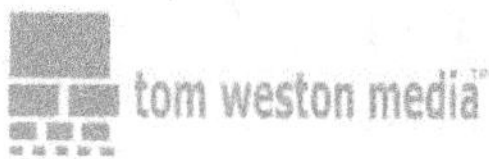
tom weston media

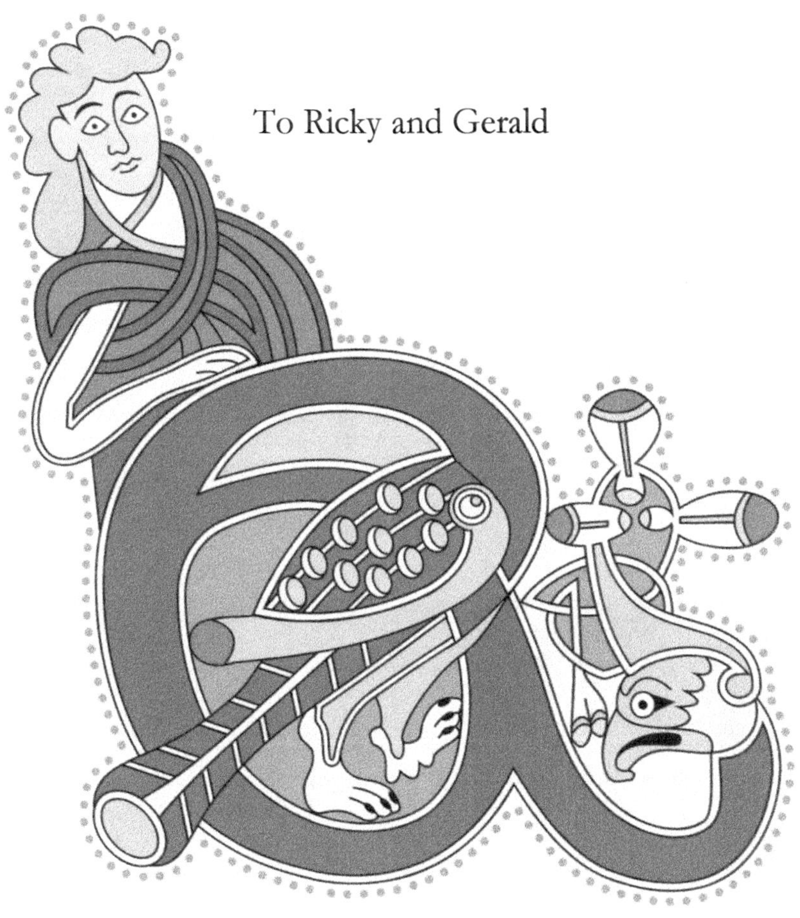

To Ricky and Gerald

CONTENTS

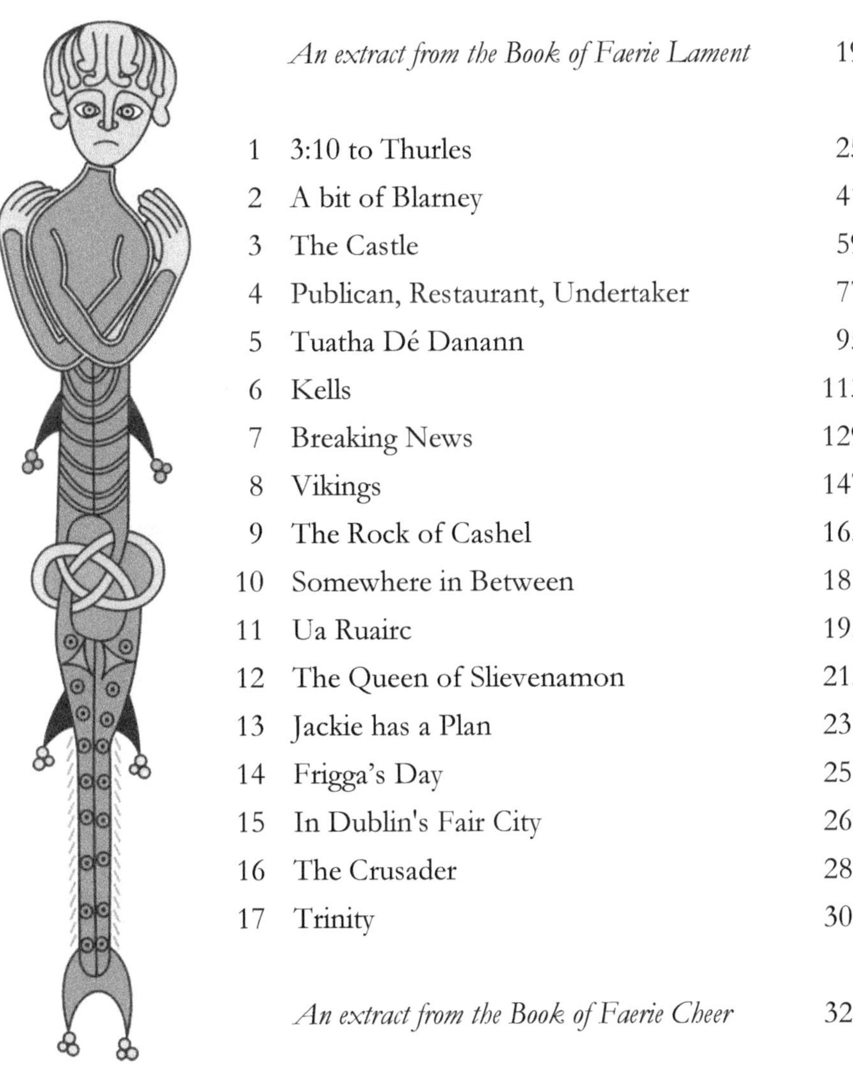

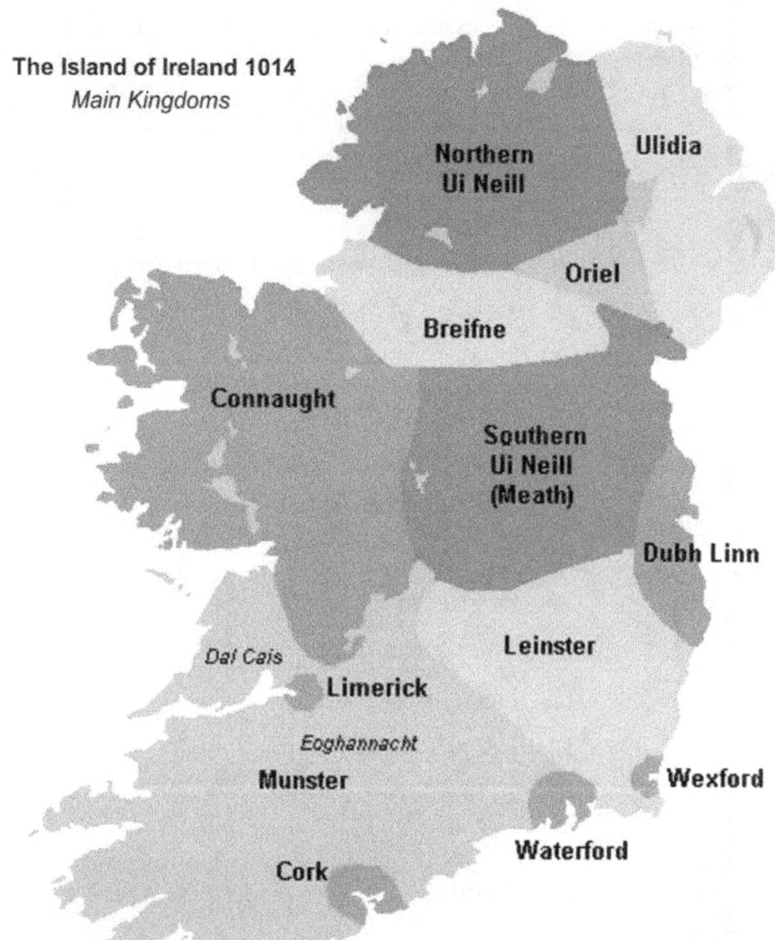
The Island of Ireland 1014
Main Kingdoms
Northern Ui Neill
Ulidia
Oriel
Breifne
Connaught
Southern Ui Neill (Meath)
Dubh Linn
Leinster
Dal Cais
Limerick
Eoghannacht
Munster
Wexford
Waterford
Cork

Author's Note

However, it is the common opinion of antiquaries that why it is Eire is from the name of the queen of the Tuatha Dé Danann who was in the land at the time of the coming of the Clann Míleadh into it: Eire, daughter of Dealbhaoth, was her name, and it is she was wife to Mac Gréine who was called Ceathúr who was king of Ireland when the sons of Míleadh came to it.

Foras Feasa ar Éirinn (The History of Ireland),
Geoffrey Keating, c. 1634

Tuatha Dé Danann

To some, the word, *fairy,* conjures up children's stories of the Brothers Grimm, Hans Christian Andersen and Walt Disney; and for a more serious, weighty, grown-up, appreciation of mythology, we should use *faery* instead. I won't make a case for one versus the other, but it seemed to me that neither did the Irish story tellers who I met. They interchanged these labels and others such as the Fay People, the Good People, and the Wee Folk; and within those classifications, you'll find Pookas, Leprechauns, Banshees, Sheoques, Merrows, Cluricaun, Ganconagh, Leanhaun Shee and others. If my incorrect use of labels hurts anyone's sensibilities, please forgive me; a rose by any other name would smell as sweet.

Nevertheless, there are references in this book to the *Tuatha Dé Danann* (people of the goddess, Danu) and that is a label which I use deliberately, for it is impossible to fully appreciate the role of the fairy in Ireland without first understanding that the country's history and mythology are as much intertwined as a Celtic knot. Ireland's ancient history is a blur of invaders and tribal conflict. At some time, one such tribe became mythologized as the magical Tuatha Dé Danann; and the mythology of the Tuatha Dé Danann is so superimposed on the real history of Ireland that attempts to separate fact from fiction would make both considerably less entertaining. Every nation has its history and mythology, but in Ireland they are not mutually exclusive, and I believe Ireland is the richer for it.

Vikings

The first Viking raid on Ireland took place around 795 and they stayed for four centuries. Kells Abbey was often sacked during this period, but somehow the monks managed to protect the national treasure known as the *Book of Kells*. To survive the long winter months, the Vikings established coastal settlements. The fortress of Dublin Bay was established in 852 and Dublin remained under Viking control until the Norman invasion of 1169.

The real Sigtrygg Silkbeard was king of Dublin in 1014, at the time of the real Battle of Clontarf, which also featured the real Brian Boru. In this book, Silkbeard's son, Prince Oleif and prospective daughter-in-law, Estrid, are fictional characters. Also in real life, the Icelandic poet and historian, Snorri Sturluson, lived from 1179 to 1241. I have a fictional character of the same name. This is a happy coincidence.

Fethard

In the county of Tipperary, under the shadow of Mount Slievenamon, is the medieval walled town of Fethard, famous for its thoroughbred horses and the celebrated McCarthy's Hotel.

The Temple Castle and Gatehouse Pub in this story are fictitious, but I drew my inspiration from the real pubs and towers of Fethard; most particularly, Court Castle and the Castle Inn on Watergate Street, where I've enjoyed an excellent pint of Guinness or two with equally excellent companions.

Acknowledgments

Many thanks to Tim Robinson of the Fethard Historical Society for your time, hospitality, and tour of Court Castle.

A big hello to Theresa and Willie of the Cozy B&B, which inspired my fictional Teolaí B&B, and whose breakfast is second to none.

Thanks also to the citizens of Fethard and Dublin for your warmth, good humor, and great stories.

Most of all, thanks to Carmel Trimble and her family for taking care of me during my visits to Fethard, and for sharing tales of childhood adventure at the Castle Inn. This book is for you.

Alex & Jackie

Feathered

being a fairy tale

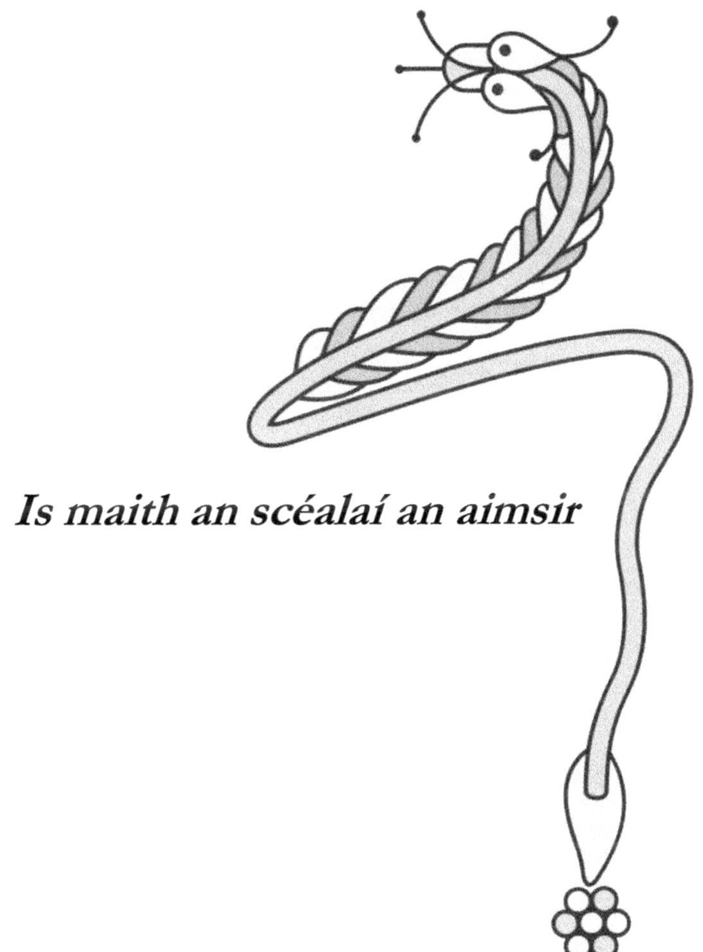

Is maith an scéalaí an aimsir

Time is a good storyteller

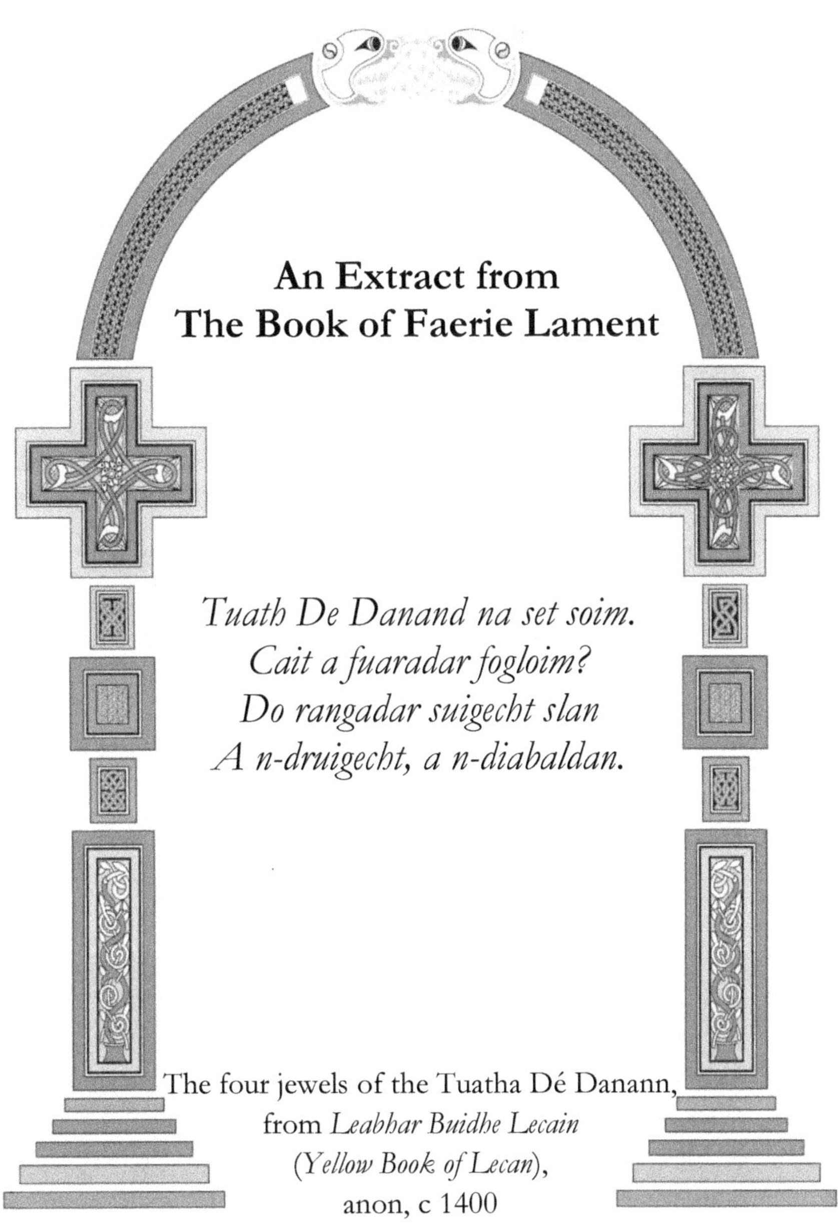

An Extract from
The Book of Faerie Lament

Tuath De Danand na set soim.
Cait a fuaradar fogloim?
Do rangadar suigecht slan
A n-druigecht, a n-diabaldan.

The four jewels of the Tuatha Dé Danann,
from *Leabhar Buidhe Lecain*
(*Yellow Book of Lecan*),
anon, c 1400

An extract from the Book of Fairy Lament

Author's Note: The *Book of Faerie Lament* tells of the last great battle of the Tuatha Dé Danann, the *Battle of Clontarf*, which took place in 1014. It was at that battle that the renowned Irish king, Brian Bóruma mac Cennétig (Brian Boru) met his end; although the Tuatha Dé Danann did not overly concern themselves with the human aspect of the battle, for their quarrel lay with the Norse gods.

This extract is from the English language edition produced by Professor K. S. Penbrooke of Boston in 1855. Professor Penbrooke worked from the Latin transcript of the book, created by the Benedictine monks of the Altmünster Abbey in Luxembourg in 1423, and who possessed the only known copy of the original medieval Irish manuscript. How the book arrived at Altmünster is not documented. The book survived the destruction of the Abbey in 1542, and was transferred to the replacement Neumünster Abbey, but alas, was ultimately lost in the fire of 1684. With the original work now destroyed, and as no other manuscript has been found to contain this story, the accuracy of the translation cannot be verified.

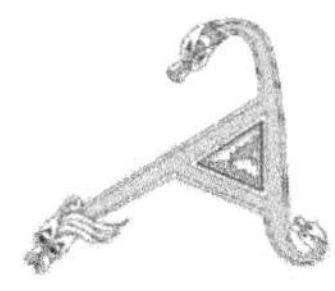**A**nd with the coming of the Norsemen, these Sidhe or Tuatha Dé Danann assembled for counsel at that secret place called Brug Maic ind Oc, the Castle of the Son of the Young, also called the Enchanted Palace of the Three Trees, whereupon they were greeted by Queen Eeviin of the Grey Rock, beautiful beyond beauty, pure beyond pure.

"Welcome! – Welcome, the children of Danu – Welcome the children of Nuada Airgetlám, bane of the Fir Bholg – Welcome to the children of Lugh Lámhfhada, woe of the Fomóraig – Welcome North and South, East and West – All welcome from the shapeless mountain – All welcome from the shipless sea."

So greeted Queen Eeviin in song, as was the custom and language of the Sidhe at that time, for rough, hewn words as spoke by men were as ashes in their mouths, unbearable and unbecoming to their noble birthright.

"Welcome to the three Gods of subtle art, Creidhne son of Tuirill Biccreo, Goibniu son of Tuirbe Trágma, and Luchta of Brighid born.

"Welcome to the poet masters of the four cities, fair and strong – bring forth the jewels of the Tuatha Dé Danann – From golden Murias, under the sea of tears, bring forth the sacred Cauldron of Dagda, so that we may be restored.

"And from snow covered Failias, where artful Morfessa did sing more joyful verse, bring forth the Lia Fail, herald of kings, yet silent these many days."

Failias, Findias, Gorias and Murias; these were the names of the cities where the ancient Sidhe learned their dark wonder and guile. The cities of wizards they were also named. Morfessa, Esrus, Semias and Uiscias were the wizards called.

And the eternal Cauldron was brought before the Tuatha Dé Danann, from which all drank until their bellies were full and their wounds healed. Then the Lia Fail, the sacred stone, was next placed before Queen Eeviin, in silence still, but doomed to sing of the new king of low born men.

Sang Queen Eeviin next of the Spear of Lugh. From bejeweled Gorias it came. From the hand of nimble Lugh, guided by the gods, its aim was ever true. None can abide its strike and live, save for its master to whom it can do none harm.

And the Tuatha Dé Danann did marvel at the Spear and praise it in the songs of the Battle of Magh Tuiredh, where Lugh defeated Balor Evil Eye and threw down the Fomóraig.

Then Queen Eeviin lay command on them that from Findias, city of the white flame, they bring forth the bright Sword of bold Nuada, that none can resist when in combat drawn.

"Dark queens and unfaithful kings, unwise warriors and base beggars have ever sought to wield it and ever received our laughter and our scorn," sang Queen Eeviin and again commanded them to bring forth the Sword.

And a silence befell the throne room of the Enchanted Palace. And the guardians of the Sword looked to the ground or to their companions, whereupon Queen Eeviin again commanded of them to fulfill their sacred charge.

"Majestic and Terrible Queen," they cried, "woe and sorrow is our fortune, for we were deceived in our care. Treachery upon treachery! Waylaid upon our journey, the jewel of which you sing, the shining Sword of Nuada is stole away to the city of the Danes."

"Oh, bugger!" sang Queen Eeviin.

"Fecking Vikings! [#1]" sang the Tuatha Dé Danann.

And in her rage at such offense, Queen Eeviin called upon the Sidhe to rise up against the invader. And they took up their lances of blue flame and their shields of diamond white. And the wild Púca were commanded to be their dread, black steeds of war. And as a mist across the land turned aside the gaze of cowering men, who at

An extract from the Book of Fairy Lament

the trumpet blast, barred their doors and trembled in their beds, the Tuatha Dé Danann rode out to compel battle upon their foe.

Lines 154-329, *The Book of Faerie Lament*,
anon, circa 1187, translated by K. S. Penbrooke, 1855

#1. With all due respect to Father Ted's more liberal interpretations of the word, feck is an old Irish verb which means to steal.

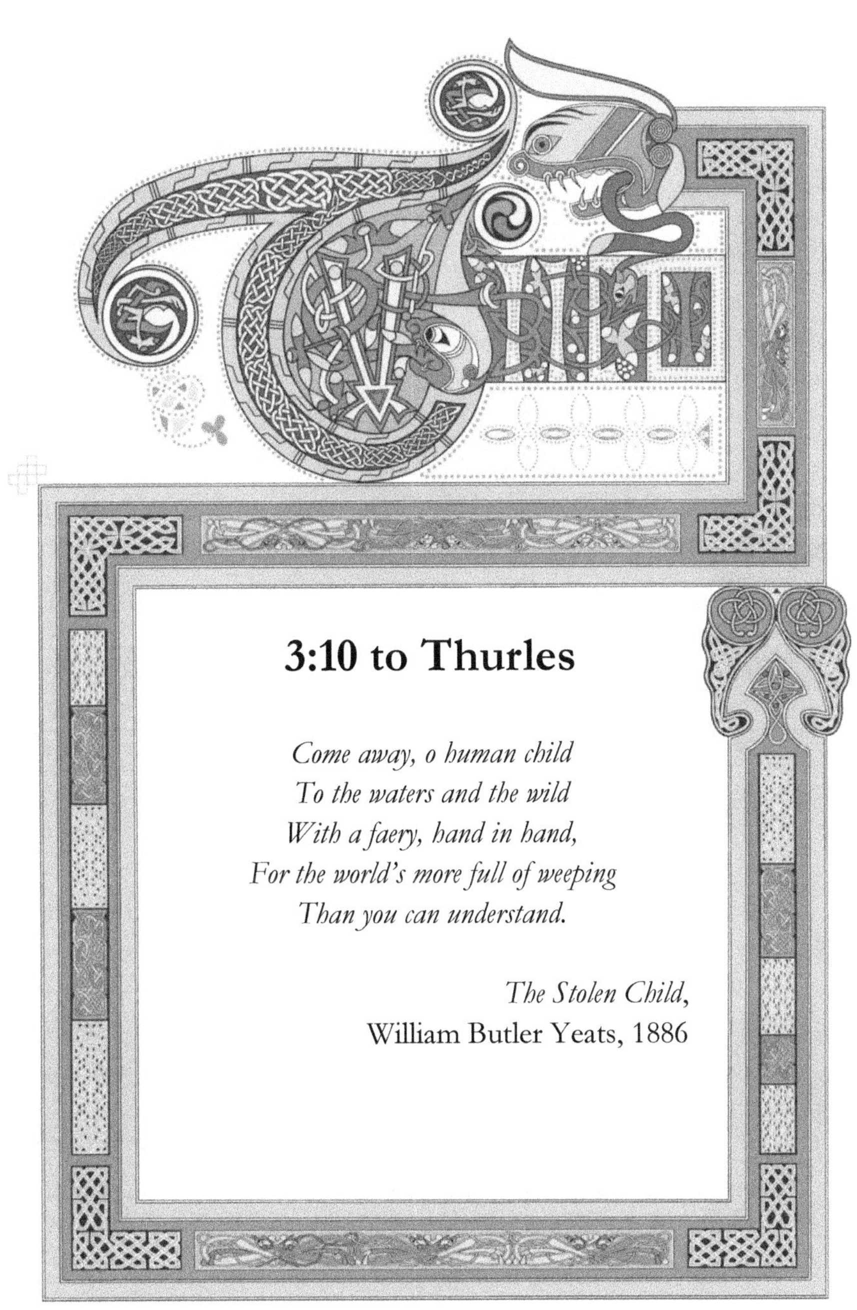

3:10 to Thurles

Come away, o human child
To the waters and the wild
With a faery, hand in hand,
For the world's more full of weeping
Than you can understand.

The Stolen Child,
William Butler Yeats, 1886

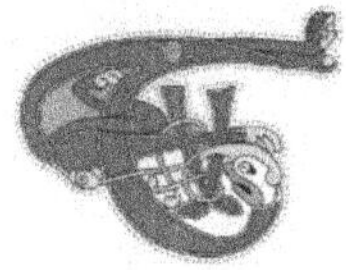 **"T**á sé ag cur báistí!"

"What?" sighed Alex at the interruption to her fitful attempts to sleep.

"Tá sé ag cur báistí," repeated Jackie. "It is raining; it's Gaelic for it is raining."

Alex, from the aisle seat, pressed across her sister and looked out the plane window. "It is quite clearly not raining," she said.

"No, not out there. *Tá sé ag cur báistí*, in the in-flight magazine, it's in the magazine." Jackie pointed at the appropriate spot on the page.

"And so?"

"Well, there's an article about Irish phrases to learn for when you visit Ireland. *It is raining* seems to be a popular one; might come in handy."

"Don't you think that the Irish would know it was raining without any help from you?"

"In fact, it says that it's not the only Gaelic expression for *it is raining*; it depends on the rain, whether it's a heavy downpour or just a drizzle and so on. Dad says that it rains a lot in Ireland."

"And this is useful to me how?"

"Just saying."

"Especially when it's not . . . tá sé . . . whatever that Gaelic says. Look out the window; it's a beautiful, bright, blue, sunny day with not a cloud above us."

"That's because the clouds are below us; we're at 30,000 feet."

Alex looked down. "Not a cloud below us, either; just water and some ships. I rest my case. Now let me rest."

Jacqueline Nicole O'Rourke, Aka Jackie, aged 14, blew her sister a raspberry and returned to the article. "Although it seems the Irish don't speak much Gaelic anymore. That's a pity now that I can converse fluently in it. I wonder how many words they have for umbrella?"

"As many as it takes," groaned Alex.

"Are you sure?"

"Yes, I'm sure."

"Well, I'm from San Diego and you know what they say."

"What?"

"It never *báistís* in Southern California."

"Are you going to be like this for the whole trip?"

"For eleven days and ten nights, to be exact. But it would be a whole lot simpler if I had a Babel fish."

"It would be a whole lot simpler if you just kept quiet."

The plane which carried the sisters was a Luxair flight from Luxembourg to Dublin. The water below them was the treacherous English Channel, just about to skulk around the Cornish coastline and invade the Irish Sea.

A flight attendant pushed the refreshments cart down the aisle, his comments delivered effortlessly in French, German, or English, to match the native tongue of the passengers, until he stopped beside the sisters.

"Something to eat?" asked the flight attendant, in English.

"What do you have?" replied Alex.

The flight attendant recited the list of sandwiches on offer and Alex decided on the jambon-fromage on baguette. Jackie concurred and the flight attendant handed them each a box.

"To drink?" added the flight attendant.

"Just some water, please," replied Alex.

"Je voudrais un verre de crémant," said Jackie, who had learned from her Uncle Jim that the bubbly fire water was traditional when flying with Luxair.

"Knock off the French," requested Alex. "It's not fooling anyone; you're not Joan of Arc."

Jackie's French did not fool the flight attendant.

"Sorry," he smiled sympathetically. "Just before boarding, your aunt gave us strict instructions not to serve you anything with alcohol in it."

"Horse Feathers!" groaned Jackie.

"Busted," laughed Alex.

"Okay, then, just water, please," said a disappointed Jackie.

The flight attendant obliged, poured the water, and moved on down the aisle.

"How did she know?" pouted Jackie.

"Who, Aunt Anne? Aunt Anne worries about everything, and therefore plans for everything. And of course, she knows you pretty well by now."

Jackie brightened. "But it won't be Aunt Anne in Ireland, will it. It will be Aunt Róisín; and Aunt Róisín doesn't know us at all. She hasn't seen us since my christening."

"I'm sure the aunts have talked to each other; aunts always talk. I hope Aunt Róisín doesn't fuss like Aunt Anne."

"And it's not crémant in Ireland; it's Guinness."

"And good luck getting your hands on any of that. Knowing our family; everything will be under lock and key, and they'll be watching you like hawks."

Jackie slumped down in her seat and sipped her water.

"No problem, I'll ask the fairies."

"Fairies?"

"Yes, it's Ireland; it's full of fairies."

"You're full of fairies!"

"You have no imagination, that's your problem. You're okay with elves and ghosts and vampires, but you don't believe in fairies. You're a snob."

"I just don't believe that Tinker Bell will greet you in Dublin with a glass of Guinness," said Alex - full name, Alexandra Caroline O'Rourke, who was two years older than her sister, and assumed that she therefore possessed two years more smarts; if by smart she meant cynicism.

"It's a *pint* of Guinness."

"Whatever. They won't let you drink it. I'm sure Mom and Dad warned them about you."

"I don't think it's fair that they sent us on this grand tour of Europe but won't let us live like the locals. We're missing half the fun," Jackie complained. "Still, it was nice of them to give us this great vacation."

"They weren't being nice," said Alex. "They wanted to get rid of us for the summer, so they could enjoy their vacation without your whining."

"Then I should whine more often," said Jackie.

The captain interrupted their argument to announce that they had started their approach to Dublin Airport. Jackie peered out the window, hoping to see landfall but she failed. The waves of the Irish Sea below her also became obscure, as clouds started to appear and thicken. The plane descended into the clouds and for a few moments the blue sky turned to cotton white, and then to slate grey. The plane then exited the clouds, which now rose up and raced away from them.

Under the clouds, it rained.

Jackie peered down. Hazy land formations appeared, but quickly resolved themselves into the shapes of the smaller group of islands that dotted the coast.

"Oh, look," said Jackie. "I think that one's Craggy Island."

Alex looked out. "Doesn't look very green; isn't Ireland supposed to be green?"

"That's Dublin you're looking at; it's a city. It's got buildings and things. How many green cities do you see?"

"The Emerald City on the Wizard of Oz, that was green. Even the witch was green there."

"But, Dorothy, look over there, that bit's green."

"That's a golf course; it's supposed to be green. Even in San Diego the golf courses are green."

Beyond the city and the golf courses, and out of sight of the Luxair passengers, the rest of Ireland, of course, boasted of the picturesque, postcard green much loved by the tourists. The landscape comprised a patchwork quilt of hews: of shades of green, with flecks of brown and red to break up the monotony; but mostly green.

"Tá sé ag cur báistí," said Jackie.

"Welcome to Ireland," smiled Aunt Róisín.

"And you're welcome to it," frowned the tall, lanky, 15-year-old youth beside her, christened Matthew but who answered to the name of Mattie, and who was Aunt Róisín's son, and therefore Alex's and Jackie's cousin.

"Don't listen to Mattie," said the still smiling aunt. "He's just upset that I dragged him away from the soccer field. He's soccer mad."

"*Pitch*, Mam, soccer *pitch*."

"Americans call it soccer, but I heard that over here it's called football," said Jackie.

"And how would you know?" asked Alex.

"It's called football," said Jackie. "Because it was one of the games played on foot by peasants as opposed to those played on horseback by the nobles. I refer of course, to the Scottish Act of 1424, when football was banned and offenses punishable with a fine of four pence."

Mattie's mouth began to drop open before it turned into a huge grin. "Oh, you're good, Cousin, you're very good," he laughed.

Jackie smiled and curtsied.

"But you're wrong. In England it may be called football, but in Ireland football refers to the Gaelic sport, and soccer is just . . . soccer."

Alex shook her head in an attempt to disown her sister.

Aunt Róisín frowned at her son. "He's football mad as well. Mattie, be polite to your cousins."

"Sorry, welcome to Ireland," said Mattie. "I mean it, welcome, Cousins."

"Now, let me get a good look at you," said Aunt Róisín. "My, haven't you both grown since I last saw you."

"I should hope so," said Mattie. "They were only babies then."

"So were you," said Alex.

"No," said Aunt Róisín, "This one was never a sweet, little baby; he's many things - mostly trouble, always hungry – and always a burden to his poor mother."

"She loves me, really," said Mattie, dourly.

"Anyway, let's be going, we have a train to catch," said Aunt Róisín. "Have all your bags? Let Mattie carry that large case. What's that?"

"This is Lämmy," said Jackie, referring to the small stuffed toy in the shape of a lamb, which she held under her arm. "He's come all the way from Luxembourg to visit his Irish cousins."

"Lamb, eh? Don't let Jeff see him," said Mattie. "He'll end up in a pot."

"What kind of pot?" asked Alex.

"We'll explain later, dear," said Aunt Róisín. "But for now we have to be on our way to Heuston Station. Come on, this way to the taxi stand."

Mattie tugged the larger of the two suitcases away from Alex; and aunt and cousin quickly headed for the airport exit. The sisters followed at a slower pace.

"Where do you get this nonsense?" Alex whispered to Jackie. "You don't know anything about soccer; you've never even seen a game."

"I've seen David Beckham."

"That was an Emporio Armani underwear advert. But the Scottish Act of 1424? Where did that come from?"

"It's amazing what you can read in the in-flight magazines, if you stay awake," answered Jackie.

"Come on, girls," shouted Aunt Róisín. "We have a train to catch."

Aunt Róisín did not usually succumb to extravagances such as taxis, but with four passengers and the luggage, she reasoned it made enough economic sense to fit within the budget.

On the twenty-minute ride to Heuston Station, Aunt Róisín kept up a continuous commentary as she pointed out the landmarks. "And this is Phoenix Park – did you know it has the largest Viking cemetery outside Scandinavia – look closely and you'll see the deer . . . there's the zoo . . . and now, we're crossing over the River Liffey . . .

Those chimneys over there, that's the Guinness factory . . . of course, you'll see more of Dublin when we return at the end of your visit, next week."

Jackie, who never wanted to miss a thing, stared out the window. Her head bobbed up and down, and turned to and fro, in the manner of an excited puppy. Could she have stuck her head out of the window, she would have.

Alex, immune to the charms of the scenery which Dublin had on display, reclined in her seat, switched on her phone, and began to exchange text messages with her friends from San Diego. She resented that the airlines forbid this harmless activity while in the air. To make her wait hours between texts displayed an unconscionable barbarity.

Mattie and the taxi driver chatted about soccer and football, as the driver, who had taken his cue from Aunt Róisín's narrative, randomly changed the route on a whim, sometime to give the trip more visible appeal, sometimes to avoid the traffic which ebbed and flowed around them and more often than not, to the untrained eye, resembled improvised street theatre.

They arrived at Heuston Station; a model of sleek, shiny, automated, efficiency inside a Victorian shell. Aunt Róisín paid the driver and bundled the family to the main concourse, separated from the platforms by a series of gates. Ticket and vending machines, juice bars and assorted shops lined the perimeter; and on its north side, the Galway Hooker pub and carvery served large helpings of roast beef to fortify the passengers for their imminent journeys.

As Jackie looked around and absorbed the atmosphere, she noticed that behind the foreground noise of the busy train station, she could hear singing; not overly insistent or performed for the sake of an audience, but as if someone mindlessly hummed a tune while their attention ran elsewhere. She realized that she had first noticed the singing at the airport, but with the excitement of the reunion with her relatives and the enforced haste to the taxi stand, she had not really paid attention to it.

Jackie looked around for the source of the sound but found none. Yet the singing seemed ever-present; an undercurrent of vibration on which every other sound carried. Like the sound of the ocean tide as it washed over the beach, or the eternal siren call of Manhattan which lulled its residents to sleep.

No one else seemed to pay attention to it; perhaps because of its permanency; it had become part of the fabric of life, taken for granted and generally unnoticed by the locals. But Jackie had noticed it – the very first thing . . . well, okay, the second thing – first, she had noticed the rain, which came from every direction, even up from the ground as well as down from the sky if that proved possible. And then next, she noticed the singing. It broke through the mist and carried on the rain drops, in rhythm and counterpoint to the changes of the weather. Jackie could not see the singers, nor understand the language, but for some reason, she believed she recognized the perpetrators – she knew who sang . . . the fairies.

Fairies? Granted, in Jackie's scant 14 years of life, she had taken many grandiose flights of imagination, but she did have a track record in these things: ghosts, elves, and vampires. Why not fairies?

"Cute, little, Tinker Bell creatures with gossamer wings," imagined Jackie. Except that the song sounded poignant and fragile rather than cute, whatever it meant.

Jackie looked to her sister to see if Alex had also detected the song. Alex just hammered away with her thumbs at the screen of her phone, deep in an exchange of texts with a boy named Chris, who corresponded from thousands of miles away in San Diego, California.

Jackie looked at Aunt Róisín and Cousin Mattie. Aunt Róisín's attention lay focused on the large, electronic departure board for platform information. Mattie returned her gaze, but simply acknowledged her with a languid smile. She looked at the disordered horde which zigzagged across the concourse before her, to and from the platforms, and in and out of the shops and bars. Obviously, no one heard the song but her. She tried to make out some of the words. Even if their gist currently eluded her, perhaps if she consigned them to memory, she could find out what they meant later. Jackie concentrated and tried to tune out the secondary noise; that made by humans and machines. She heard . . .

"Thurles, Platform 2," said Aunt Róisín, "Come on, Mattie, girls, hurry or we won't find a space for the luggage."

As the 3:10 to Thurles passed out of Dublin and into the Irish countryside, the signal on Alex's phone became unreliable and so she gave up on additional texts and decided to join in with the conversation.

"So, what's going to happen to Jackie's Lämmy when we catch up with Jeff? Something gruesome, I hope. You spoke about some kind of a pot?"

"Oh, yes, Jeff, I'd forgot," said Aunt Róisín, of her other son and Mattie's identical twin brother, older by a few minutes. "No, it's just when Jeff is not playing soccer or Gaelic football, like his brother, he's in the kitchen cooking something. He's a bit of a dab-hand at the culinary skills; so much so that he's taken over not just cooking for the family, but for the pub as well. We can't stop him. But sometimes his dishes are a bit more exotic than those usually found on a pub menu. I think he's going through an experimental stage."

"And he likes to experiment on us," added Mattie. "So, I would keep a close watch on Lämmy there, if I was you. If he goes missing, keep away from Jeff's Lämmy stew."

"Still, he's keen," continued Aunt Róisín. "The customers tease him, but they never turn down what's on offer; and they always clean off their plates. That's why he didn't come with us to greet you in Dublin. He and his dad are holding down the fort."

"Literally," said Mattie.

"Yes," said Jackie with glee. "You live in a castle, don't you? That's so cool. I can't wait to see it. What's it like?"

"You'll see it soon enough, so we'll let you decide for yourselves," said Aunt Róisín. "But don't expect too much. We live in the pub, the Gatehouse. The rest of the castle is in a terrible state of decay, I'm afraid; crumbling walls and rooms that are open to the elements. Most of the castle is unsafe now and not accessible anymore. The pub is the only habitable part of it today."

"Tell me about the fairies," pleaded Jackie.

"The Good People? What do you want to know?" asked Aunt Róisín.

"She wants to know if Tinker Bell is Irish and hands out pints of Guinness to the tourists," said Alex.

"Oh, no," said Aunt Róisín. "Our fairies are nothing like that; and it's disrespectful to talk of them in those terms."

"Best not mock the fairies," said Mattie. "At least, not in front of Mam."

"Just because they aren't real, doesn't mean people shouldn't believe in them."

"No, Mam."

"We like to hedge our bets."

"Even today?" asked Alex. "Fairies seem so, like . . . well, fairy tales . . . for the kids."

"Yes, even today. Not long back, near Newmarket-on-Fergus, in County Clare, they were building a bypass; and the planned path of the road meant that they would have to knock down a fairy tree; very disrespectful."

"There were protests," added Mattie. "Workers refused to carry out the order."

"The fate of the tree was debated in the Dáil, our government," continued Aunt Róisín. "Then wiser heads prevailed, and they rerouted the road to spare the tree."

"At the cost of many millions of Euros," said Mattie.

"Politics is one thing, but fairies are serious business," said Aunt Róisín.

"Hear that, Alex," said Jackie. "Don't mess with the fairy trees."

"We've got our very own fairy tree," said Mattie.

Jackie's eyes and smile widened simultaneously. "At the bottom of the garden?"

"Close," said Mattie.

Aunt Róisín smiled.

"Tell me more," pleaded Jackie.

"Where to begin," said Aunt Róisín. "Our fairies are not what you think; there is a great deal of history to them."

"That's okay. I'm studying to be a fairyologist."

"Fairyologist?" said Alex. "Oh, please!"

"It's going to be my major at college, with a minor in pixie dust."

The train raced by the small station of a town called Portlaoise. A distracted Aunt Róisín looked puzzled and briefly wondered if they had boarded the wrong train, for the timetable listed Portlaoise as a scheduled stop. She quickly dismissed the oddity as well within the vagaries of the Irish rail system and thought no more of it.

"Fairies!" pleaded Jackie again.

"First, what do you know already?" said Aunt Róisín. "Then perhaps I can fill the gaps or correct your misconceptions."

"Well, I already know about the singing. Tell me about that."

"What singing?"

"The singing I heard . . ."

The train came to an abrupt, shuddering halt in the middle of the countryside, with no station in sight.

"We appear to have stopped," said an elderly woman sitting a few rows down from the family. "Why have we stopped?"

"Could be bandits," said the elderly man who sat next to her.

"The engine driver missed Portlaoise," answered a middle-aged man, seated a few rows behind them.

"That was silly of him, wasn't it?" said the woman.

The train remained stationary for several minutes before it began to move again, but in reverse.

"We're going back to Portlaoise," said the man. "The driver must have had a change of heart and he's decided to go back to pick up the passengers."

"Well, isn't that good of him," said the woman.

Alex and Jackie tried to suppress their smirks.

"Now, girls," scolded Aunt Róisín. "It's only good manners to go back. Good manners go a long way."

"Unlike this train," said Mattie.

Alex and Jackie failed to suppress their smirks.

With the praise of the passengers ringing in his ears, the driver returned the train to Portlaoise station. Passengers boarded and the train and the conversation resumed, but no matter how hard Jackie tried to press her topic of choice, there seemed an endless supply of distractions and diversions; as if the Good People objected to the impertinence. Jackie gave up. All talk of fairies would have to wait for another time.

The final leg of the sisters' journey took them south from Thurles to Fethard, home to the Irish branch of the Tree O'Rourke. They drove through rolling countryside filled with horses, notably the noble thoroughbreds for which the region was deservedly famous. The rain pounded out a steady beat against the much abused and weary family car, and the worn windshield wipers squeaked back in retort, but did not diminish Aunt Róisín's enthusiasm as she resumed her commentary of local landmarks.

"Just like the singing," thought Jackie. "They don't notice the rain, either."

"Not far now. That ahead, on the other side of Fethard, is Slievenamon, the Mountain of the Women," said Aunt Róisín, as she pointed through the mud-streaked windshield to the murky, grey, bulky mass, covered in low clouds. "Now if you really wanted to know about the fairies, that mountain could tell you a tale or two."

"Mountain of the Women?" asked Alex.

"The Feimhin, of fairy origin. When Fionn mac Cumhaill, leader of the Fianna, wanted to take a bride, he went to the top of Slievenamon and decided that he would marry the first woman to greet him. A woman named Gráinne was the first to reach the summit and, although she was repulsed by him, for he was old, her father consented to the marriage, and plans were made for the two to wed. Fionn's bravest warrior, the young, strong, and handsome Diarmuid Ua Duibhne went hunting for boar to bring to the wedding feast and met a witch in a forest. The witch tried to seduce him. When he refused her advances, she placed a magic spot on his forehead. Any woman who saw the spot would fall in love with him."

"Let me guess," said Alex. "This Gráinne saw the spot and fell in love with him."

"Now the most loyal Diarmuid had to fend off Gráinne's advances," said Aunt Róisín. "But the lovestruck Gráinne wouldn't take no for an answer, and she placed a geis on him."

"A geis?" said the sisters.

"A spell. Gráinne and Diarmuid eloped, with Fionn in hot pursuit. But evenually Fionn forgave them, and Gráinne and Diarmuid married."

"And they all lived happily ever after," said Mattie.

"Like King Arthur and Lancelot and Guinevere," said Jackie.

"Well, that story also has its roots in the Celtic mythology."

"We use Slievenamon to forecast the weather," said Mattie. "The saying around here is, 'when you can see Slievenamon it is about to rain. When you can't see it, it's already raining.'"

They entered the medieval, walled town of Fethard via the R689. Aunt Róisín pointed out the houses of Moyglass, where the father of the notorious outlaw, Ned Kelly, was found guilty of stealing two pigs and deported to Australia.

At the town square, Aunt Róisín turned left on to Watergate Street and parked the car opposite the Gatehouse, much to the annoyance of the geese who squatted there and were forced to scatter. The square, apple-crumble, grey towers of the castle stood before them. Alex wondered whether the word, *foreboding*, was adequate. Jackie wondered whether she could get to the battlements.

"Come on in and meet the rest of the family," smiled Aunt Róisín. "Don't worry about the bags, Mattie will bring those, won't you Mattie?"

"Yes, Mam," replied Mattie.

They entered the pub, festooned on the outside with window boxes and hanging baskets of carnations and the blue and yellow ribbons of County Tipperary. Behind the bar stood Uncle Bob and Cousin Jeff.

"Girls, girls, at last," cried Uncle Bob. "Welcome home."

Uncle Bob and Jeff moved from behind the bar to hug the sisters.

But Alex and Jackie only indifferently returned the warm welcome offered by their uncle and cousin, because something else had instantly demanded their attention. For there in the center of the pub, right, smack, bang in the floor in front of the bar, stood a tree — a real, living, budding tree.

A bit of Blarney

Blarney; he has licked the Blarney stone; he deals in the wonderful, or tips us the traveller. The Blarney stone is a triangular stone on the very top of an ancient castle of that name, in the county of Cork in Ireland, extremely difficult of access, so that to have ascended to it was considered as a proof of perseverance, courage and agility, whereof many are supposed to claim the honour, who never atchieved the adventure; and to tip the Blarney, is figuratively used for telling a marvellous story, or falsity.

A classical dictionary of the vulgar tongue,
Francis Grose, 1785

"It smells really good," said Alex.

"As long as it also tastes good," replied Jeff, as he ladled the Irish stew into a bowl and placed it before her.

"He always says that," said Mattie. "He's never let us down yet."

"And I don't want there to be a first time."

"My first Irish stew," said Jackie. "I'm sure it tastes as good as it smells."

"I thought I'd start you off with something traditional, as this is your first visit."

"There's nothing traditional about your cooking, brother," said Mattie.

"But Irish stew is, isn't it?" asked Alex.

"Not the way he cooks it."

"What's wrong with the way I cook it?"

"Nothing, brother, you won't see me complain. On the contrary, your best yet I think; it'll go over well in the bar."

Alex and Jackie sat with Mattie at a large wooden table in the kitchen at the back of the pub. Jeff moved with haste between the stove and table with the bowls of the piping hot stew and baskets of oven-fresh bread. Aunt Róisín and Uncle Bob tended to the customers in the bar.

Jeff's physique appeared every inch identical to twin Mattie, perhaps an inch taller, but the similarity ended there; for Mattie, in spite of the teenage angst, reveled in the funny story or punch-line, as did many of his countrymen, but Jeff seemed eternally serious and single-minded of purpose, and insisted that his name was Geoffrey, never Jeff, a demand which everyone ignored completely. He sat down with the final bowl of stew before him.

Alex tested the stew. "Oh, yes, it tastes amazing. I knew it would. The beef is so tender and flavorsome."

"It's not beef; it's lamb," said Mattie.

"Oh, no," cried Jackie.

"What's the matter," asked Jeff. "Don't you like lamb?"

"No, pay no attention to her," said Alex. "She's got this toy, Lämmy the lamb; Mattie said you'd cook him."

"Well, Mattie's wrong as usual," said Jeff. "At least not for this dish, because it's mutton, not lamb. Lamb's too young; it needs adult sheep. Your little Lämmy would be much too tender for a hearty stew. It needs a strong meat which will become tender through the cooking process, but doesn't disintegrate; otherwise you've got soup not stew. It's the same with the French and coc au vin. Younger is not necessarily better. A good dish is often ruined by people who think a better and more expensive cut of meat would make it taste better. Age has its place, even at the table."

"It tastes just great," said Alex. "What else is in it?"

"Traditionally, it should just be potatoes, but I've added a few other things: carrots and onions, a few herbs and spices, some red wine."

"And some Guinness," added Mattie.

"Guinness? Woo hoo!" cried Jackie. "See, Alex, I told you."

"Oh, you won't get drunk on the stew, if that's what you hope," said Jeff. "All the alcohol is cooked out. But the Guinness adds a nice, malty texture to it, I think."

"I agree," said Jackie. "From now on all my Irish stew must have Guinness in it."

"But I detect something else in the pot this time, brother," said Mattie. "What have you done to it?"

"My secret ingredient," admitted Jeff. "And a pinch of star anise, not much mind, just a hint."

"See, told you he likes to experiment. He's a mad scientist."

"What's the secret ingredient?" asked Alex.

"Then it wouldn't be a secret," replied Jeff. "Now, eat up before it gets cold."

The girls ate up and peppered their cousins with questions between mouthfuls of the stew.

"What's it like living in a castle?" asked Jackie.

"Hard work, that's what it's like," said Jeff. "Take that stove for example; it's not only used for the cooking, but to heat the tank for the hot water. Someone has to come down and light it early every morning before anyone else gets up."

"But it's so romantic."

"It's cold and damp and drafty."

"Then it's gothic romance; that'll just suit Alex; she's a Goth."

"We don't really live in the castle," said Mattie. "Only the pub is livable now. The rest of the castle is boarded up and off limits."

"Oh, don't ever tell Jackie that something is off limits," said Alex. "She takes that kind of thing as a challenge."

"What's with the tree?" asked Jackie.

"Thought you'd like that," smiled Mattie.

"Is it a real fairy tree?"

"Don't know."

"But what's it doing in the middle of the room? Did you build the pub around it?"

"It wasn't always there, it just grew. Before our time. Back in the days when great, great . . . how many greats, Jeff?"

"Three."

"Great Grandfather Aedan; when he ran the Gatehouse. One day the Tree just sprouted, broke the slate, and came up through the floor. You'd have thought it impossible, but here it is to this day."

"Doesn't it need the sun?"

"Apparently not, nor water neither. It gets the occasional drop of alcohol spilled on it when a regular has had too much to drink, but mostly we let it alone and it lets us alone."

"Don't you have to cut the branches? If it grows any more, it'll break through upstairs and the roof, and out the windows."

"No, it has a mind of its own. When it reached the rafters, it stopped. Now it just is, and we let it be."

"You never thought of chopping it down?"

"No, we must be a bit careful with trees in this country. And it's good for business; the locals would never forgive us if anything happened to it."

"Me too; I'd never forgive you. It belongs right where it is: in the bar, in the pub, in the castle; just right. But the rest of the castle is off limits you say?" reflected Jackie.

"Off limits," repeated Jeff.

"Is there a chance you can show us the off-limits bits?"

"Not a chance in the world."

"Especially when Mam and Dad are not elsewhere occupied," winked Mattie."

"Oh, that kind of off limits," said Jackie.

"Jackie, no, don't even go there," warned Alex. "You've got us into enough trouble recently."

"No point in stopping now then."

"I was wrong about you," said Mattie. "I said you were good. I meant bad, very bad."

"Thank you," Jackie curtsied.

"Jeff, can you find a pot big enough to put my sister in?" asked Alex.

"Mattie is just as bad. It's the O'Rourke curse; it affects all the younger siblings; makes them mad."

"When can we explore?" asked Jackie. "After dinner?"

"Listen, Dora, no, no, no!" pleaded Alex.

"Dora?" asked the boys.

"Dora the Explorer, Boots the Monkey, Swiper the Fox . . ."

The boys remained puzzled.

". . . Don't you get that cartoon here? For the little kids? Look, it'll take far too long to explain."

"And it's something you watch, is it?" asked Jeff.

"Just forget it."

"Well, it's probably best not to explore with the light failing: there's no electricity, no light bulbs, and lots of dodgy steps." said Mattie.

"Hear that, Jackie? No light and dodgy steps; you know how you are with dodgy steps in the dark."

"Tomorrow then?" said Jackie.

"Tomorrow I believe we've got plans."

"Blarney Castle, to kiss the stone," said Jeff.

"Oh, I've heard of that; kiss the Blarney Stone and receive the gift of the gab," said Jackie.

"You talk too much already," said Alex.

"No point in stopping now then," repeated Jackie.

"Yes, stop now," insisted Jeff. "And eat your stew. I've got tea cake for dessert."

"Does the house have internet?" asked Alex. "I'd like to check my email."

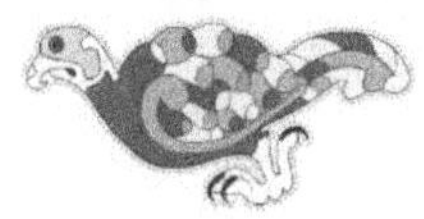

The plans for Blarney Castle were postponed for a day as various relatives and friends turned up to welcome their American cousins. Everyone seemed to be a cousin or an aunt or an uncle – even those who were not related - So many that Alex and Jackie started to speculate that they must be related to everyone in Ireland. The visitors came in a constant stream through the day. They brought little gifts of sweets and lucky shamrocks, knitted scarves, jars of strawberry preserve and Tipperary pennants.

Aunt Róisín pulled out the family album, a great big tome, dating back to when the camera had been invented. The first, grainy, black and white picture featured Great, Great, Great Grandfather Aedan, as he stood proudly beside the Tree.

Jeff worked back and forth between the kitchen and the bar, with plates of sandwiches and pastries, and cups of tea for the aunts who felt it too early to drink anything stronger, and the uncles who feared their stern reproaches. Braver men toasted Alex and Jackie in the bar and kindly offered to drink the sisters' share of the alcohol, seeming as how they were both too young to partake.

"I hope Jeff is looking after you?" asked a cousin named Teagan, who with her husband, Terry, ran a guest house in Fethard called the Teolaí B&B.

"Absolutely," answered Jackie. "He's a great cook."

"You're not wrong there," said Terry. "If it wasn't for Jeff's cooking, there's many a man wouldn't come within a mile of the Gatehouse, given Bob's reputation for quarreling," he joked loud enough for his host to overhear.

"Hey, I heard that," protested Uncle Bob. "Another word and you're banned, Terry O'Carolan."

"Are you saying your son's not a fine chef? I know some tease that he's wasting his time playing in the kitchen, but you should be sticking up for the boy."

"I'm not going to argue with you," laughed Uncle Bob.

"Jeff, I don't care what the others say," grinned Terry. "You turn out the dishes and you can always count on me to clean my plate."

"And if you set a place for me at your table, you can always count on me being there for breakfast," answered Jeff.

And indeed, everyone agreed that Jeff's cooking was as fine as could be, but the breakfast served by Teagan and Terry at the Teolaí B&B was second to none.

And Alex and Jackie agreed that their relatives in Fethard seemed extremely cheerful, witty and friendly, and hardly ever quarrelsome.

"Welcome to Blarney Castle," said Uncle Bob, this time assigned to baby-sitting duty as Aunt Róisín stood sentry at the Gatehouse.

They approached the castle grounds from the car park by the Woollen Mills; a walk which took them along a tree lined path. The sun had not fully penetrated the morning mist, and it lay on the trees as if spun by the universe's largest spider, the large square castle tower not so much rising up as lurking in the background.

Usually, Jackie would rise to the occasion and dash ahead of the family, stoop to inspect the petals of a single flower, or pepper her uncle with question after question; that sort of thing. But this morning, she displayed a little less zest than usual and appeared somewhat bleary eyed, following two nights of disturbed sleep. The sisters shared the attic at the top of the pub; reached via a cramped, spiral, stone staircase. The round, wooden room enticed her with its creaky floorboards, beamed ceiling, and arrow slits for windows. Two smallish beds faced each other from opposite sides of the room.

On an occasion such as this, Jackie would have happily chatted away to her sister until sleep took her, but Alex remained pre-occupied with texts from America, responded less than usual and replaced her customary, *'shut up and go to sleep, Jackie'* with an incessant tap-tap of her fingers on the screen of her phone. And Jackie's plans for her nights in Ireland to overflow with dreams of fairies went unfulfilled.

However, Jeff's insistence on a full Irish Breakfast before they started for Blarney proved ample compensation, and Jackie had tucked into the fried eggs, bacon, sausage, and black and white pudding with gusto, as the more cautious Alex had merely picked at the edges of some soda bread.

"Who's up for some stone kissing?" asked Uncle Bob.

"Sounds positively disgusting," said Alex.

"Voted the most unhygienic tourist attraction in the world," said Mattie.

"Then I'm sure Jackie will be right there."

"Yes, please, count me in," said Jackie.

"One legend has it that the Blarney Stone first appeared in the book of Genesis, as Jacob's Pillar," said Uncle Bob, as he read from the tourist literature. "Brought to Ireland by the prophet, Jeremiah, where it was taken by the Tuatha Dé Danann and renamed the Lia Fáil."

"Tuatha Dé Danann, who are they?" asked Jackie.

"They would be some of those fairies you've been asking after," said Mattie.

"The legend continues," said Uncle Bob. "The Lia Fáil, the Fatal Stone, was an oracle stone which predicted the kings of Ireland."

"Like Harry Potter's sorting hat," said Jackie.

"I didn't know Ireland had a king," said Alex.

"Not since . . ."

"Not since Brian O'Neal had his head chopped off by the Normans in 1260; last Gaelic king anyway," rescued Jeff. "The others are just pretenders."

"So how did the stone end up as a tourist attraction?" asked Alex.

"One story is that when the Gaelic tribe, the Dál Riata, colonized Scotland, they took the stone with them, where it became known as the Stone of Scone, or the Stone of Destiny, the coronation throne of the Scottish kings," said Uncle Bob. "It was then captured by Edward I of England and taken to Westminster Abbey. But a piece of the stone remained in Scotland until it was given to Cormac Laidir McCarthy by Robert the Bruce."

"Cormac McCarthy built Blarney Castle," explained Mattie. "But some of the timeline is wrong according to the historians."

"And that's the problem with legends," said Jeff. "The facts get in the way."

"But you should never let facts get in the way of a good story," said Jackie.

"McCarthy was involved in a lawsuit which he was certain to lose, when he came across a woman who was drowning in a river, and he rescued her. The woman turned out to be Clíodhna, and in gratitude, she told him that if he kissed the Stone, he would gain the gift of eloquence," said Uncle Bob. "He did as she advised and won his lawsuit."

"Clíodhna? You have so many names; it's hard to keep up," complained Alex.

"Another one of the fairies," said Mattie. "Clíodhna, the Queen of the Banshees."

"Oh, I know all about Banshees," said Jackie. "They're the ones that howl in the nighttime. Alex is a Banshee."

"Ooh, cutting," said Alex. "Did someone not get a good night's sleep?"

"As a matter of fact . . ."

"Now, girls, let's get on," said Uncle Bob. "Now, where are the stairs?"

"Stairs?" asked Alex.

"Yes, the Blarney Stone is set into the wall at the top of the castle; stone and wooden steps all the way to the top."

"Is there an elevator?"

"No, but you're young with sturdy legs; you can manage the . . . er, how many steps, Jeff?"

"One hundred."

"One hundred steps to the top."

"I suppose so."

"You'll like this," said Mattie. "The Stone is set into the battlements. To kiss it, they dangle you over the side."

"By your ankles," added Jeff. "Upside-down."

"In that case, I'll stay here," said Alex.

"Alex doesn't like being dangled upside-down by her ankles; it's a girl thing," said Jackie.

"You don't have to kiss the Stone," said Uncle Bob. "But you should still come up; the view is wonderful."

"No, thanks, I'll stay down here and wait for you. I'll be okay, honest," said Alex.

"Well, I don't want to make you do anything you don't wish."

"I'll stay with Alex," volunteered Jeff.

"Oh, no, you all go, I'll be fine," said Alex.

"I've already kissed the stone, so I'll not miss anything. Dad, you and Mattie take Jackie. I'll show Alex the gardens and we'll meet you back here."

"Are you sure?"

"I insist."

"Well, if that's settled," said Uncle Bob. "Jackie, do you have any objections to being dangled upside-down by your ankles?"

"I've always wanted to try it," said Jackie. "It's usually Alex who gets to do all the cool stuff."

"So, you don't like heights?" asked Jeff.

"No," said Alex. "It's not my favorite thing. Stupid, isn't it."

"Oh, no, not at all; we all have something we're afraid of."

"Not Jackie."

"Even Jackie. Although she's a lot like Mattie; he can be a bit reckless at times."

"She always gets me into trouble. What are you afraid of?"

"It's more who than what."

"Who are you afraid of, then?"

"Me! I have this apprehension of doing the wrong thing."

"Then everyone will stare at you. Fear of embarrassment, I have that."

"No, it's not that. It's more . . . it's more that every time I have to do something, I worry that I will make the right choice, like it's really, really important that I make the right choice."

"Why?"

"I don't know."

"Expect you will when you get it wrong. In the meantime, which way?"

"Er . . . look, this way to the Poison Garden; do not touch, smell or eat any plant."

"Better keep Jackie away from here, then."

Alex and Jeff followed the path to the Poison Garden, where plants such as wolfsbane and mandrake sulked in cages, as if prisoners of war. Scull and crossbones warnings decorated the cages.

"In the old days, most of these plants were considered medicinal, not poisonous," said Jeff.

"In California, I think some of them still are," laughed Alex.

"Wolfsbane is supposed to be good for keeping vampires away."

"Trust me, it won't work."

"Also called monkshood; just a touch can cause paralysis. They used to use it as an anesthetic."

"But it has such pretty blue flowers."

"Dad told me the pretty ones were the dangerous ones. Come on, this way to Rock Close, that's very pretty."

Jackie, Mattie, and Uncle Bob walked the hundred, winding steps to the top of the castle. Jackie skipped ahead, indefatigable and revived after her slow start to the day by the thought of the brand-new adventure which awaited her at the top. Mattie kept pace. Uncle Bob's heart raced, and he almost regretted his decision not to stay at ground level with Alex and Jeff.

"The word, *Blarney*, was given its current meaning by Queen Elizabeth I," gasped Uncle Bob. "When a later lord of Blarney, Cormac Tiege McCarthy, used his eloquence to postpone the hand-over of the castle to her commander, The Earl of Leicester."

At the top of the steps, they joined the other tourists who lined the perimeter of the castle. Jackie took in the view of the surrounding countryside.

"To the south is Cork; and over there to the east is the Comane bog," said Uncle Bob. "It used to be full of wolves at one time."

Jackie cast her gaze downwards to the gardens and walkways of the castle grounds. "Oh, look!" she said. "There's Alex and Jeff." She shouted. "Woo hoo, hey, Alex! Jeff, up here, hello."

But Alex and Jeff did not hear her.

Jackie's impatience and excitement grew as the family slowly shuffled toward the head of the line and her appointment with the Blarney Stone, until at last, a friendly guide said, "You're next."

Alex and Jeff trod the path to Rock Close. Although the Castle gardens teemed with people, the only sound they heard was the echo of their own footsteps on the leafy trail. The oak and yew trees hemmed them and formed a canopy overhead, through which the sunlight danced and sparkled, and cast angel-rays before them, which they could almost but never touch, as elusive as the rainbow's end.

Then a second sound reached their ears, a gentle, syncopated rhythmic welcome, which informed them that they approached the Water Garden. And soon enough, the leafy carpet turned to moss and ivy, and Alex saw the two waterfalls and the Wishing Steps.

"If ever Jackie wanted to see fairies at the bottom of the garden, this would be the place," said Alex.

"There is something magical about this spot," agreed Jeff. "People come here to kiss the stone. Then they leave and never see this; it's a shame. Come on let's pay a visit to the Witch's Kitchen."

"Can we get a soda there?"

"Doubt it, but you might get a wish. The Blarney Witch lived in a cave now called the Witch's Kitchen. The owners permitted her to live there and collect firewood for her cauldron, provided she granted wishes to them and their guests. It's said that some days, just before sunrise, you can still see the embers from her fire and her shadow on the walls of the cave. One of these rock formations around here is supposed to resemble her. She's trapped inside it. Come on, down the steps."

Alex started for the Wishing Steps, roughly carved in the rock, which formed the natural passageway to the Witch's Kitchen, but Jeff stopped her.

"No," he said. "You have to walk them backwards, with your eyes closed."

"What for?"

"Because that's the way the Witch did it when she was carrying firewood. Only if you can follow in the Witch's footsteps, will she grant you a wish."

"I don't know; those steps look a bit uneven."

"Come on, I'll look out for you and catch you if you trip."

"I still don't know."

"Don't you trust your cousin?"

"Is that a dare? You sound like Jackie."

"It's not a dare. It's a tradition."

"Well . . . okay."

Alex turned her back to the Wishing Steps and closed her eyes tight shut.

"Now, move one of your feet back and down until you feel the next step . . . good, now next step . . . there, easy."

Alex moved back and down and tentatively reached for each step, as if the inches between her foot and the solid rock seemed more a mile of uncertainty. But Jeff gave gentle words of instruction and encouragement, and counted down the steps until she reached the end.

"There you did it; make a wish, but don't tell anyone what you wished for, or else it won't come true."

Alex opened her eyes. "Perhaps I'll save it for a rainy day."

"See, you made it look easy. I would imagine you've done it before," said Jeff.

"Making wishes," answered Alex. "Yes, once or twice."

"This is so disappointing," said Jackie, when she discovered that prospective suitors to the Blarney Stone no longer proved their worth by dangling precariously upside-down from the battlements; and that strong iron bars now prevented the unfortunate from plummeting headfirst to their deaths.

"No, safety regulations and all that," said Uncle Bob. "Still up for it?"

"Oh, yes, please."

"All loose items out of your pocket?" asked the assistant. "Mustn't let things fall over the wall. Ready? Now sit down and reach backward for the handrails."

Jackie sat down with her back to the Stone, and with the arms of the assistant for support, she leaned back. At first the handrails seemed out of reach, but the strong-armed assistant tugged her out toward the edge.

"Ah!" giggled Jackie, as her viewpoint changed from horizontal to vertical and she instantly forgot the safety measures which surrounded the stone. The clouds rushed over her head, accompanied by the sudden surge of adrenaline which overwhelmed her body.

She felt the handrails with her fingertips and grabbed them tightly, as if her life depended on it.

"Tilt your head back," said the assistant.

Jackie did as instructed. The battlement wall came into view. She leaned farther back. The ground below came into view. She tried not to panic. The Blarney Stone floated an inch from her nose. One last tip of her head and an outstretched neck and her lips touched the Stone.

In the fraction of an instance before the assistant jerked her back to the real world, while she still kissed the Stone, and an impossibly short time for it to have happened, Jackie heard a voice sing.

"Welcome to the Daughter of the Ua Ruairc.
Welcome to the Child of the Charm."

Her vision would not come to focus, as if a mist surrounded her. Out of the corner of her eye, she could see the assistant, but knew he had not sung the words. She searched for and found Uncle Bob and Mattie and through the blurry haze saw them grin at her, as if in slow motion.

Then she returned to reality. Mattie helped her to her feet.

"And now you have the Gift of Eloquence," said Uncle Bob. "How does it feel?"

"A bit dizzy," said Jackie.

"The experience can induce a touch of vertigo; that will pass quick enough."

"I thought I heard something, someone singing. Did anyone else hear singing? No? It was definitely singing."

They shook their heads.

"Probably the blood rush to the head," said Mattie.

"Come on," said Uncle Bob. "Let's go find your sister."

"Before Jeff cooks her something from the Poison Garden," said Mattie.

"Now there's an idea," said Uncle Bob. "Who's up for a spot of lunch?"

Jackie looked around the parapets in one, last, futile attempt to locate who sang to her. The tourists shuffled along in line, as they waited patiently for their turn to kiss the Stone. Some chatted, but none sang. She saw Uncle Bob and Mattie already headed for the steps which led back to ground level. She shrugged her shoulders and followed them.

They found Alex and Jeff by the Sacrificial Altar, although to the girls it looked like any other rock, and Jackie found disappointment once again when she discovered that it did not drip with blood.

"Got here just in time," said Mattie. "Jeff was about to offer Alex to the gods."

"I was about to find Alex a soda," said Jeff.

"That's why we came looking for you," said Uncle Bob. "Jackie's kissing adventure may have taken it out of her a little. Thought we'd go find some refreshments."

"Jackie, you okay?" asked Alex, as the big, protective sister in her came to the fore.

"Sure, Sis," said Jackie. "You know me; you can't keep a good girl down."

"Give me some of that newfound eloquence."

"Er . . .," said Jackie. She thought for a moment. "Don't think it worked . . . I thought I heard singing."

"That was probably Dad," said Mattie. "He's always humming a tune no one else can recognize."

"Hey, I can always beat you at the old karaoke," objected Uncle Bob. "Remember, I once won first prize for my Elvis Presley impersonation. I got a cup for it."

"Because it was New Year's Eve and he was the only one in the Gatehouse who was sober," said Mattie to the girls. "What was that one you used to sing to us as babies, Dad? That one about Blarney."

"Richard Milliken, *the Groves of Blarney*," said Jeff.

And in the gentle, lyrical, pure voice of a tenor, Uncle Bob sang.

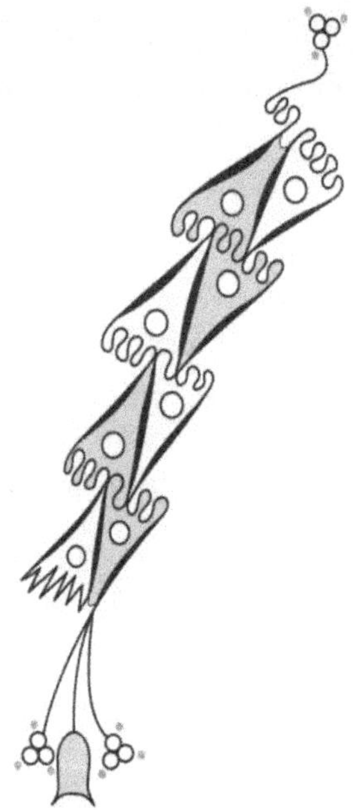

The Groves of Blarney
They look so charming,
Down by the purling
Of sweet silent streams,
Being banked with posies
That spontaneous grow there,
Planted in order
By the sweet rock close.
'T is there's the daisy
And the sweet carnation,
The blooming pink,
And the rose so fair;
The daffodowndilly,
Likewise the lily,—
All flowers that scent
The sweet fragrant air.

The Castle

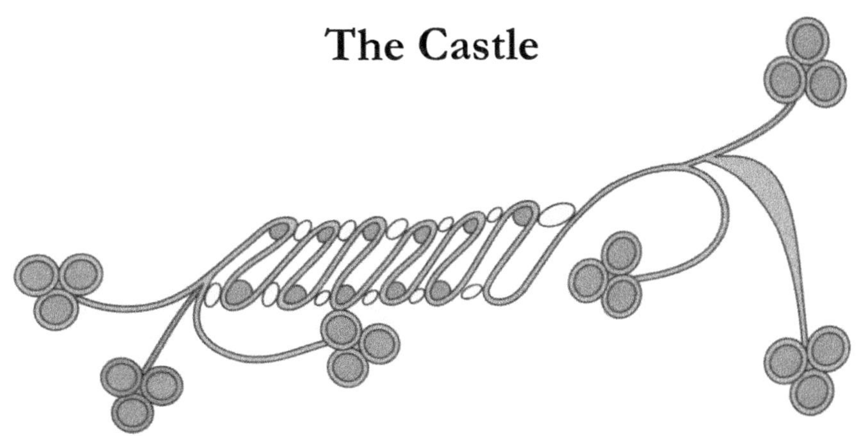

At a short distance to the east of this Church there is a square castle measuring on the outside forty two feet by thirty three feet; it is four stories high and built of limestone. Its windows are all of a quadrangular form and built of chiselled limestone.

The Parish of Fethard,
John O'Donovan, Sept 17th 1840

Back at the Gatehouse, Aunt Róisín and Uncle Bob worked the bar. Jeff wanted to showcase his culinary expertise and served up apple planked salmon for dinner. Afterwards, Aunt Róisín gave permission for Alex and Jackie to sit in the bar, provided they didn't upset the locals. They sat in a corner, partly shielded from view by the Tree. A television above their heads broadcast the horse races from Leopardstown.

"Several of the races feature local horses," explained Mattie. "It's a major business around here. So, there's a lot of interest in the races. Like to see a local filly do well."

"There's nothing the locals love so much as their horses," said Jeff.

"And their fairies, I hope," said Jackie.

"We put them on a pedestal all of their own," said Mattie.

"Do the horses have fairies? Fairy horses?"

"Of course, oh, wait a minute, there's Seán Murphy, he'll tell you a thing or two about fairies," said Mattie, pointing out the elderly man accepting a pint of Irish Red from Uncle Bob. "Seán, Seán, over here."

Seán Murphy ambled over. "And a good evening to you, Mattie, Jeff. Who have we here?"

"This is Alex and Jackie," said Mattie.

"Ah, the cousins from across the pond, says your dad. And hello to you, Misses."

"Hello," said Alex and Jackie.

"Seán is an authority on fairies. The girls want to know about the Púca," said Mattie. "Jackie fancies she can ride on one."

"Oh no, keep away from the Púca," warned Seán. "No one can ride the Púca except Brian Boru himself."

"So, the Púca are fairy horses," asked Jackie.

"They are shape shifters," said Seán. "Mostly they take the shape of a wild, black horse with a long, flowing mane, sulfur on their breath, and fire in their eyes. They race around the countryside, kick down fences, and trample the crops."

"That doesn't sound very friendly," said Alex.

"None of the Good People are what you'd call friendly, but the Púca are the war horses of the Tuatha Dé Danann. They are meant to strike fear into the hearts of their enemies."

"Tuatha Dé Danann? They seem to get around."

"So, you know of them? They are the Good People, the ancient and magical rulers of Ireland, the faerie. What have you heard about the faerie?"

"Fairies are little people with wings, except for the Leprechauns of course, they have a pot of gold." said Jackie. "Fairy horses should be little horses with wings as well."

"Fairies, yes, F.A.I.R.Y - The Fay Folk, no. F.A.E.R.Y. There's a difference. Have the boys been filling your heads with nonsense? I expect that from Mattie, but Jeff should know better."

"Nothing to do with me," objected Jeff.

"I blame Peter Pan," said Seán. He shook his head. "And Disney too, I blame Walt Disney."

"So, there aren't any little, magical people with wings?" asked Jackie.

"Only in the movies, Jackie," said Alex. "I did try to tell you."

"The Good People are shape shifters," said Seán. "They can be taller than us, they can be smaller than us; whatever suits their purpose. But they are very cunning and sometimes flattering. If they wanted to be little people with wings then they would, but mostly that is a Victorian fancy."

"So first, the Blarney Stone didn't work, and now no Tinker Bells, strike two!" sighed Jackie. Then she brightened. "But Leprechauns, what about them?"

"Leprechauns, yes, Leprechauns."

"With pots of gold?"

"If you can catch them."

"And Banshees?"

"Hopefully, you won't be hearing the Banshee's wail. You don't want her bringing death to your door."

"And the singing?"

"What singing?"

"Jackie says she can hear singing," said Mattie.

"Ever since I got here, but no one else can hear it," said Jackie.

Seán Murphy tilted his head to one side to listen. "No, nothing. What is the song?"

"I don't know; I can't make it out."

"Well, that could be the faerie; you can't rule it out. They have a strange sense of humor. But humans are nothing more than an amusement to them. I wouldn't take it personally."

"Most likely it's the plumbing," said Mattie.

Through the pub door came an elderly woman, small and white haired, precise, and slow, as if every step required enormous concentration, which it did.

"Hello there, Mary," said Seán Murphy. "We don't usually see you in here except on a Saturday night."

"Oh, hello there, young Seán," answered Mary O'Keefe. "No, just had a bit of a fright. I thought I'd get a little something to steady my nerves."

"Mary is our oldest customer," whispered Jeff to the girls. "Her nerves often get the better of her."

"Come and join me and the boys," said Seán. "I'll get you a little something and you can tell us what's wrong."

Mary waddled toward them. Mattie offered her a seat and Seán returned with a glass of whisky.

"Oh, thanks, thanks, Seán, very considerate of you," said Mary.

"Now get that down you and tell us what's wrong," said Seán.

Mary took a tiny sip, as if the whisky were precious gold. "I was in Rob Roy's," she started. "Getting a bit of tea."

"Rob Roy's is a local store, what you would call a convenience store," whispered Jeff. "The owner is named Rory, but the locals call him Rob Roy because his prices are so outrageous. Sometimes he changes the sell-by dates on the produce, when he thinks he can get away with it."

"What's up with Rob Roy then," asked Seán.

"He's been robbed!"

"Rob Roy's been robbed?" laughed Mattie.

"No man deserves it more," said Seán.

"Oh, don't laugh," said Mary. "I was there when they came in, two of them." She took another sip of whiskey, closer to vapor than liquid. "They had helmets on and hurly sticks; threatened to hit Rob Roy over the head."

"Oh, dear, Mary, I hope you are all right."

Mary sipped. "Oh, yes. They took the content of Rob Roy's till and made off on a bicycle."

"They wouldn't have got far on a bicycle."

"She probably means motorbike," whispered Jeff.

"No, they didn't get far. The Gardaí caught them over by St. Johnstown," said Mary.

"Police," whispered Jeff.

"Oh, that's all right then," said Seán. "Drink up, Mary, I'll get you another."

"The Gardaí took them away in cufflinks," sipped Mary.

"Handcuffs," whispered Jeff.

Later in the attic bedroom, after the pub had closed and the family had retired for the night, Alex finally confronted her sister.

"Are you okay?"

"Sure."

"Well, I worry. You did get a nasty bang on the head when we were in Luxembourg; and we never got it checked out properly."

"I feel fine."

"No headaches or blurry vision,"

"No."

"If there was, you'd tell me, right?"

"Alex, what's with the twenty questions?"

"What about the singing?"

"That's just my imagination, that's all. You said I have an overactive imagination."

"Can you hear the singing now?"

"No," Jackie lied.

"And you don't recognize the song?"

"Alex, what is this? You don't usually care about me except to yell at me."

"Well, given our recent history, we know anything is possible. We have to look out for each other."

"I'm okay, honest."

"Well, if you're okay."

"Yes, let's go to sleep, I'm tired. Goodnight."

"Goodnight."

Alex turned out the light. Jackie reclined and closed her eyes, but before long, she heard the familiar sound of Alex's fingers tapping at her phone. The click, click, click and the singing fought for dominance in Jackie's head, and sleep lost. She lay in bed and stared in the darkness at the ceiling. The patter of rain on the slate roof added to the symphony of sound. She sighed, got out of bed and reached for her gown and slippers.

"I'm going down to the kitchen to get a glass of water," she said. "Do you want any?"

"No thanks," answered Alex, as she continued to type and mutter a few words under her breath.

Jackie wrapped the gown tight around her and began to descend the stone, spiral steps to the kitchen. Once there, she retrieved a glass from a cabinet and turned on the tap at the sink, allowing the water to run for a few moments until the glass felt chilly. Even the water seemed to sing to her.

Shadows bounced around the kitchen walls. A nightlight provided a pale and adequate glow, but not enough to account for the shadows. Jackie looked for the source of the light and saw that it came from the crack in the door between the kitchen and bar. The light continually grew, receded, and sparkled.

"Either someone has left the television on or . . ." Jackie stopped mid thought. The cautious, pragmatic, dispassionate thing for a girl to do at this point would have been to take her glass of water and return to the security of her bedroom. And so naturally Jackie, who possessed none of these qualities, moved toward the bar door.

The playful light stopped briefly, as if its source sensed Jackie's presence, but then it began again. Jackie opened the door just wide enough to peer around it into the bar. The light vanished, leaving the bar without light, except for that provided by the orange glow of an outside streetlight.

Jackie's eyes adjusted to the conditions. She could see the Tree between her and the window. She took a breath and held it . . . nothing more . . . then as she made to draw another breath; she saw a spark of white light from the other side of the Tree . . . and then a glow, about the size of a tennis ball.

Jackie edged the distance between the kitchen door and the Tree, as slowly and methodically as if she had been Mary O'Keefe. The sparkle of light would stop occasionally but did not go out. Jackie inched around the Tree . . . And then she saw it and she froze in her tracks.

Alex continued to tap away at her text messages, interrupting herself occasionally to curse the limitations of the technology and to wonder whether Chris in San Diego was really worth the effort anymore, when she realized that Jackie had not yet returned from the kitchen. It had been a while . . . too long, and Alex decided to follow in her sister's footsteps down the spiral staircase. She found Jackie in the bar, sitting on the floor, in the dark, by the Tree.

"Jackie, what are you doing?" she whispered.

Jackie looked up. "Oh, hi, you just missed him," she said.

"Missed who?"

"His name is Lämmy."

"Jackie, Lämmy is the name of your toy lamb."

"Yes, I know; what a coincidence. Of course, that's not his real faery name, but I couldn't pronounce that anyway."

"You've been talking to a fairy?"

"F.A.E.R.Y. There's a difference."

"You've been talking to a F.A.E.R.Y?"

"Yes . . . No, that's wrong. I talked; he sang. The Faerie don't talk, that's too human, and so they sing."

"He told you that?"

"Yes, you should have seen him; such a pretty thing. But you scared him off when you came clattering down the stairs."

"I didn't clatter." Alex sat down next to her sister. "This fair . . . faery, what did he look like?"

"A little, tiny, white horse, about the size of your hand."

"A horse?"

"With wings."

"That Seán guy said they don't look like that."

"Well, Lämmy does. And a horn, like a unicorn's."

"Let's go back upstairs and talk about this."

"You don't believe me."

"Let's go back upstairs."

"Okay, I don't think he'll come back tonight anyway; you scared him away. It's all right if you don't believe me."

"It's not that I don't believe you. After what we've been through, I'm prepared to believe anything."

"But?"

"Well, Dad says that the simplest explanation is usually the correct one. We know you had a knock on the head in Luxembourg. Maybe you banged it again when you kissed the Blarney Stone."

"No, my head is fine. Why can't my explanation be the simplest one? It seems obviously simple to me."

"But to see a fairy, and it's exactly like you've always imagined it to be, and its name is Lämmy? That's a lot of coincidences."

"Come back down with me tomorrow night and you'll see for yourself."

"It's a deal. Now let's get back upstairs."

"So can we see the castle now, please," asked Jackie, no worse for her nighttime escapade.

Uncle Bob and Aunt Róisín had left the Gatehouse in the early morning to run some errands. Mattie and Jeff stayed behind to keep the sisters entertained.

"I suppose you won't quit asking until we give in?" replied Mattie.

"You suppose right."

"Help me with the breakfast dishes and I'll think about it."

Jackie swept up their plates from the table and ran to the kitchen sink.

"Go steady with that china," ordered Jeff.

"Sorry," sang Jackie, and she and Mattie reached the sink and began to argue about who should wash and who should dry, splashed water at each other and laughed.

"Jackie seems very upbeat this morning," Jeff said to Alex.

"That is her usual state, believe it or not," replied Alex.

"Not much keeps her down?"

"Oh, not much. She means it; she really won't stop pestering you until you give in and show her the castle."

"Then I suppose we'd best get it over with sooner rather than later, before the ancient parents get back. Though, as you've already been warned, there's really not that much to see. Mattie, grab the key to the shed." Jeff stood up. "Come on."

"We're going exploring, we're going exploring," sang Jackie.

Jeff headed to the door which led from the kitchen to the courtyard. The others followed. The wall to their left contained a large, arched, wooden, double door, about fifteen feet from the ground.

"Strange place for a door," said Alex. "No one can reach it."

The boys said nothing but led the sisters across the courtyard to a stone building with a rusted, tin roof and an equally rusted, tin door, held shut by a large, rusted padlock.

"This use to be the stables," said Jeff, while Mattie removed the padlock and shouldered the door open. "Now we use it as a storage room."

Mattie entered the stable, pushed closely by Jackie.

"Careful there," warned Mattie. "There's junk all over the place to trip you."

"Sorry," sang Jackie.

Mattie took a long step ladder which stood propped against the stable wall, turned and shooed Jackie back out to the courtyard. He then took the ladder and placed it against the floating door in the wall.

"There used to be stone steps," explained Jeff. "But they were crumbling and dangerous. And as we would have local kids climb over the wall to explore the castle, we had to remove the steps as a safety measure. So now we have to get into the main castle via the ladder."

"And this is safer than the stone steps, how exactly?" asked Alex.

"I'll go up first and open the door, then you and Jackie, then Mattie last."

"To catch you if you fall," said Mattie.

"Gee, thanks," said Alex.

Jeff climbed the ladder and perched at the top, while he removed the padlock and pushed at half of the double door. With a groan of hinges, the scrape of wood against stone, and the kicking up of dust, the door moved, and Jeff hopped from the ladder into the opening. He disappeared from view for a moment, but then popped his head back through the door.

"Okay," he said. "Ladies first."

Jackie sprang to the ladder and briskly climbed, which caused it to wobble.

"Wo, steady there!" said Mattie. "Let me hold it." But Jackie had already reached the top step and sprang lightly through the doorway. "You next, Alex."

Alex hesitated.

"Don't worry; I'll keep the ladder from moving. Just take it one step at a time and make sure you have a good grip before you go to the next step."

Alex reluctantly obeyed and started to climb. Inch by inch and step by step, as Jackie or the Three Stooges would have said, Alex worked her way to the top of the ladder. Once there, she realized that she had performed the easy part, for now she had to relinquish her vice-like grip of the ladder and step across to the doorway. Something her flesh found unable to do, even if her spirit was willing, which it wasn't.

Jeff held out a hand. "Here, take hold and I'll pull you in," he said.

"I don't think I can," said Alex. "Maybe I'll just go back to the kitchen and wait for you there. You can show Jackie the Castle. I'll be all right."

"Take my hand. You won't fall, I promise."

"I can't"

"Still don't you trust your cousin?"

"Is that a dare?"

"It's a tradition."

"Well . . ."

Alex took one hand from the ladder and waved it in the general direction of Jeff, who caught it with a hand of his own and moved the other to her arm.

"You've got to let go of the ladder, otherwise we'll be here all day."

"Er . . ."

Alex loosened her grip on the ladder and Jeff hauled her to the safety of the doorway. Before she could regain her composure, she found Mattie at her side.

"You need to work on your climbing skills," he laughed.

"She used to be really good at it," said Jackie. "At home, when she sneaks out at night there is no stopping her."

"Can we just get on?" complained Alex.

"Welcome to Temple Castle, built by the Knights Templar of St. John, but for five generations, in the possession of the O'Rourke family," said Mattie. "Your tour today begins here in the guardroom. Note the fine perpendicular windows of the late gothic period, without the glass of course, which survived the cannons of Oliver Cromwell, but not the slings and arrows of generations of bored schoolboys; and the Hammerbeam roof . . ."

The girls looked up. A bird flitted across the dilapidated ceiling, half open to the sky.

". . . Home, of course, to one of the finest collections of nesting starlings in all of Ireland. This way to the battlements."

Mattie led the way to the corner of the guardroom, where another stone, spiral staircase led up; and before long, the sisters gazed out across the battlements, over the medieval walls of Fethard.

Despite the mist, but also because of it, the countryside reflected the lush green which Alex had anticipated on her arrival in Ireland. Here stood the Ireland of the tourist postcard: the undulating patchwork quilt of fields and hedgerow, dotted with horses, cattle and the white stoned farmhouse; framed by the babbling, chattering Clashawley river to the fore, engorged by the recent rain and in full flow; the crosses of the Augustinian Abbey to the east; the walls, chimneys and sloped roofs of the town to the west; and finally, in the distance to the south, the smooth, rising mass which was Slievenamon; still cloud covered and barely visible through the moist air.

"Go careful," said Jeff. "The battlements are difficult to walk at the best of times; more so when they are wet."

They moved east along the wall, down some steps, and across the inner courtyard to the square shaped keep.

"Or what's left of it," said Mattie. "We are standing in the Great Hall."

Glass remained in many of the windows, some original lead-lined stained-glass featured coats-of-arms, some clear glass from later repair work; although clear was a relative word, for decades of neglect had allowed the grime to build and the light from outside had lost most of its potency by the time it had penetrated to the center of the hall. The dust-filled air draped heavy around them, almost as if it were a lace curtain which they had to push aside in order to pass. On the west wall, a great, stone fireplace dominated, wider than a barn door, taller than a man, and carved with figures of oaks and horses. Jackie ran to the center of the fireplace and peered up into the darkness of the chimney.

"Santa Claus would have no problems getting down here," she said. "You guys must have got lots of presents."

"In the days when the castle was occupied, there was always a fire burning," said Jeff. "It's hard to keep the place warm. In the end, it just cost too much."

"But it's still so romantic. I wish I lived in a castle."

"You would have been a servant girl, working in the kitchen all day," said Alex.

"I would have been Cinderella; and you would have been my ugly stepsister. What's that up there?"

High on the east wall, a balcony overlooked the hall.

"That's the Minstrel Gallery," answered Jeff. "This hall was used for banquettes and dances. The musicians would play from up there."

Jackie danced around to imaginary music, stirring up the dust from the floor. "Can we go up?"

"Sure, but stick to the stone. We don't know how safe the floorboards are any more."

They climbed the staircase in the north-east corner of the hall, until they reached the Minstrel Gallery. Through the arrow slits which followed the staircase, they caught glimpses of the town and the Holy Trinity Church of Ireland (not to be confused with Fethard's Holy Trinity Parish Church).

"I think what's great about it is," said Jackie. "All these spiral staircases everywhere; you never know what's around the next bend. The great unknown, that's what's great."

"That's great, Jackie," sighed Alex.

They stopped at the Minstrel Gallery, though the stairs continued up.

"What's up there?" asked Jackie.

"That would have led to the sleeping quarters, first the master's chambers and above that the servants'," said Jeff, "But we can't go any farther, the way is blocked."

"How about down? Does the castle have a dungeon?"

"What kind of a castle would it be if it didn't have a dungeon?" said Mattie. "Iron maidens, manacles, racks, red-hot irons."

"There's none of that," said Jeff. "It was mostly used for storage, not torture. I think it's called a cellar. But that's blocked as well."

"Secret passages? You've got to have secret passages," pleaded Jackie.

"What kind of a castle would it be if it didn't have secret passages?" said Mattie.

"And as a matter of fact, there is one," said Jeff. "Well, at least one; there may be others that are still secret. Come on."

Jeff led them back to the Great Hall and the fireplace.

"Not the fireplace," groaned Alex. "That would be such a cliché."

"Clichés notwithstanding," said Mattie. He walked into the fireplace and turned a blackened iron ring which was attached to the fireplace on its north side. The outline of a door appeared, about four feet in height. Mattie ducked his head and entered the passageway. "Mind your heads," he yelled at them.

"I'm not going in there," objected Alex. "It's like, totally dark."

A light appeared.

"I'm not going in there," objected Jackie. "It's like, not totally dark."

"How did you do that?" asked Alex.

"The ancients knew a trick or two," said Jeff. "Granddad installed electricity."

They followed Mattie into the passage. Jeff closed the door behind them. More spiral steps led down to a long tunnel, which ran east. A string of light bulbs, hung from a wire which ran the length of the tunnel, provided dim but sufficient illumination. Mattie was already moving down the tunnel. Jeff and the girls followed.

After a minute or so, another staircase appeared in the gloom, and they stopped. The rubble of broken stone, cement and old plaster dust blocked any farther exploration of the passage to the east.

"The passage continues all the way to the Abbey," said Jeff. "Or it used to: it collapsed when they were doing some road work on Watergate. So, this is as far as we can go."

"So now what do we do?" asked Alex.

"Here, we go up again," said Mattie.

At the top of the stairs, the stone wall framed a small wooden door, similar to the one in the fireplace of the Great Hall. Mattie worked the latch of a door and with some effort, pushed it open. He ducked his head and stepped through it. Jeff and the girls followed.

On the other side of the wall, they stood in a small rectangular shaped room with shelves on three sides and an oak door on the fourth. Boxes, cans, jars, and bottles lay stacked on and under the shelves. The small door through which they entered also had shelves.

With the door closed and flush with the wall, its presence proved almost impossible to detect.

"Oh, my God!" said Jackie. For she and Alex recognized that they had arrived back at the Gatehouse, and now stood in the kitchen pantry.

"And this concludes the tour," said Mattie. "Any questions?"

"Yes, I have one," said Alex. "If we had a secret tunnel all along from here to the Great Hall, why did you make me climb that ladder?"

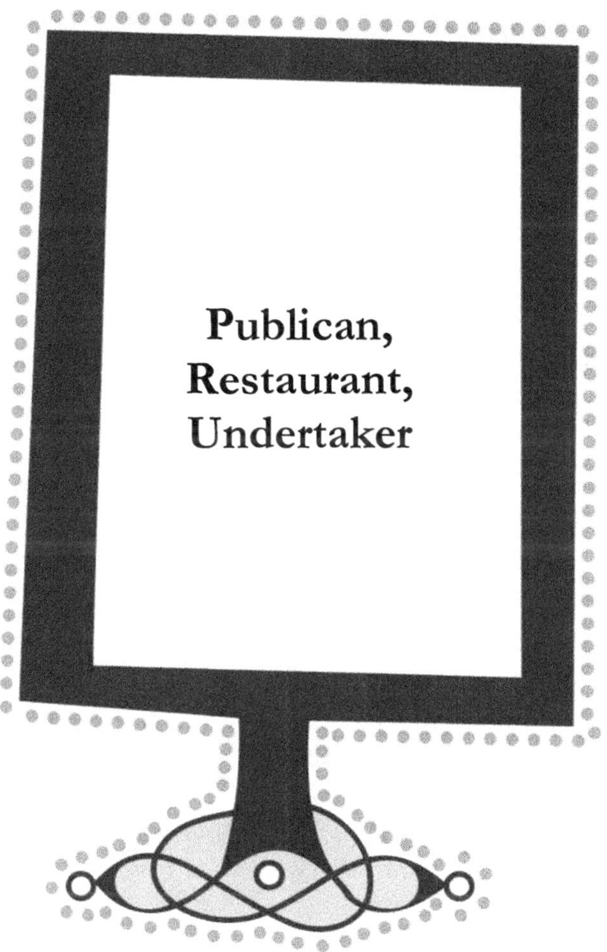

The Church of the Holy Trinity was erected many centuries ago by the Catholics for the Canons Regular of St. Augustine and dedicated to the Most Holy Trinity. It was connected, it is supposed, with the present Abbey by an underground passage.

Tipperary Annual,
Richard M. O'Hanrahan, 1913

 **"L**et's start at the Abbey," said Jeff.

Uncle Bob and Aunt Róisín had returned to open the Gatehouse for the lunchtime locals and insisted that the sons show their American cousins around Fethard.

"Is this the same abbey with a tunnel to the Gatehouse and Castle?" asked Jackie.

"The very same."

"Are you going to throw history at us?" asked Alex.

"As much as you can take before your head explodes."

"In that case, let's skip it and go to the mall instead."

"Mall? This is Fethard, not Dublin. We've got some shops on Main Street."

"Well, where's the nearest Louis Vuitton?"

"Louis who?"

"Vuitton! You know, style, fashion . . . handbags!"

"Sorry, but you'll probably have to go to Dublin for that as well."

"But if you can't hang out at the mall, what do you do for entertainment?"

"There's the youth centre near Main Street."

"And football and soccer," added Mattie. "There's always that."

"I don't play soccer," said Alex.

"And she doesn't do youth centres," whispered Jackie to Mattie. "Or art, or music, or movies, or Ferris wheels, or anything. She's what we Americans call a snob."

"And we don't go shopping for handbags," countered Jeff.

"Sorry, I don't mean to be rude. I guess it's the Abbey after all," Alex sighed. "Just keep the history stuff to a minimum; me and history don't mix."

"This way," said Jeff. He turned and walked across Burke Street towards Abbey Street.

Alex followed sheepishly.

Jackie and Mattie grinned at each other and dawdled along at the rear.

"Do you like history?" Mattie asked Jackie.

"I like all the stuff that Alex hates, which is everything," said Jackie. "I especially like old movies."

"We sometimes have old movies at the youth centre; Charlie Chaplin, Laurel and Hardy. The little ones love Laurel and Hardy."

"Oh, I do too! *That's another fine mess you've gotten me into*; Alex is saying that to me all the time."

"Come on, Ollie, Jeff and Alex are getting away."

The Augustinian Friars came to Fethard in 1300, and despite the lack of a shopping mall, decided to stay and build an Abbey at the east end of the town. Over the centuries its fortunes waxed and waned, and the Abbey saw dissolution under Henry VIII, when the friars disguised themselves as peasants and laborers to fool the authorities; and suffered indignity under Cromwell, when he used the Abbey as stables for his army's horses. And now, except for the restored chapel and the old mill and bakery, which stood hard by the Clashawley River, the Abbey lay mostly in ruins.

Inside the chapel, only half its original size because of the instability of the tower which once stood at the entrance, Mattie and Jeff dropped some small coins into a collection box and lit candles.

"A prayer for those who've gone before," explained Jeff. "Sort of a tradition."

"Jeff and me were christened in here," said Mattie. "And Mam and Dad wed."

"Did you sneak in and out through the tunnel to avoid the mobs?" asked Jackie.

"No, it was blocked long before our time. We thought about excavating it, but that would be a lot of dirt to shift."

"You could have been the Tunnel King, like in *the Great Escape*. Wish we had a secret tunnel back home, eh Alex."

"Oh, yes," said Alex. "It would beat climbing out of windows."

Around the chapel, medieval carvings grinned at them from their stone perches. Alex looked up at the ceiling. "Any hidden symbols in the rafters?" she asked.

"Don't know," replied Jeff. "Should there be?"

"Someone once told us it was something the builders did sometimes; to thumb their pagan noses at the Christian Church. They had to do it in secret though, so the Church wouldn't get angry."

"Our pagans and Christians have a much friendlier relationship. Come and say hello to Sheela."

"Who's Sheela?"

"This way."

Jeff led the sisters from the Chapel to the Abbey grounds. The grounds contained a small, wall-enclosed graveyard, overrun with Celtic crosses, as if they had sprung up through the grass with the weeds. In a notch in the north wall stood the Sheela na gig *(Sile na gCioch)*, a small, medieval statue of a naked women, and an ancient symbol of the fertility mother goddess. To find such pagan imagery openly associated with the Christian church may seem curious, but as the typical Sheela tended toward the grotesque, even by medieval standards, the Church used the Sheelas as a warning to women what would happen to them if they succumbed to the sin of lust.

"Meet Sheela," said Mattie.

"Hello, Sheela," said Jackie.

"This is one of two Sheelas in Fethard; the other is in the town wall near Watergate Bridge," said Jeff. "The town used to have four Sheelas, but there's more thieves than just those who robbed Rob Roy. It's a shame that people do stuff like steal a Sheela."

"Why would anyone want anything so ugly?" asked Alex.

"Well, Chris . . .," began Jackie.

"Stop right there! Another word and I'll turn you into a Sheela."

"My lips are sealed . . . but I think it's kinda cute . . . and there is a resemblance . . ."

"Stop now!"

"But . . ."

"Stop!"

"I was only . . ."

"Now!"

Jackie pulled an imaginary zipper across her lips. It would silence her for a moment or two at most.

"The thing about Ireland," said Jeff. "Is that you really can't separate one thing from another; everything is all mixed together. Ireland is a bit of the Christian, a bit of the Pagan, a bit of the Faerie."

"And the weather," added Mattie.

"And the occasional dash of real history just to confuse you," continued Jeff. "But it all seems to come together nicely in the pot. Leave out any of the ingredients and we wouldn't be Irish."

"Like one of your recipes," said Alex.

"Mmnn mmmmmm mmm mmmmmmmm," said Jackie. The others stared at her. She opened her imaginary mouth zipper. "Don't forget to add the Guinness," she said.

"Cousin, I think you are developing an unhealthy obsession with our biggest export," said Mattie.

"Speaks the boy who lives in a pub."

"There's a difference between selling it and drinking it."

"And putting it in the stew?"

"Seems to me," observed Alex. "That your biggest export is your people?"

"Some truth in that," said Jeff. "And a shame it is."

"Oh, I don't know," said Jackie. "You gave the world St. Patrick's Day. You should see the shamROCK Party in San Diego, when we all become Irish for the day and hit the Gaslamp Quarter; lasts all day."

"Enough of that wickedness now," said Jeff. "Let's take a walk down by the river."

"You sound just like Aunt Anne."

The four cousins walked down to the Clashawley and then followed the footpath west toward the Cashel Road. To their right ran the river and the south wall of the town. Mattie encouraged the girls to wave hello to the second Sheela as they passed, which Jackie did both vigorously and vocally. The pair dashed ahead, as Jackie zigzagged amongst the tourist information signs and ordered Mattie to keep up with her, to explain it all and provide context; which he did with equal enthusiasm.

"Is there something you can put in her food to slow her down?" Alex whispered to Jeff.

"Doesn't work," replied Jeff. "I've tried for ages with Mattie. Best you can hope for is to let them run about until they're exhausted."

"Does that work?"

"Come to think of it, no. Mattie plays on the wing at soccer; he runs non-stop from start to finish. He's a handful for the opposition. I get exhausted just from watching him."

"You don't run non-stop? I thought everybody did at soccer."

"I play more of a central role, directing the action. It requires more brains than speed."

"So, you're the quarterback?"

"We don't have quarterbacks in soccer."

"At school, they make us try out for the soccer team. Everyone is always running about. I found the easiest thing is to fall over and pretend I've hurt my leg."

"Sounds like some professional soccer players I could name. But I would have thought Jackie would be good at running about, as much energy as she has."

"She falls over as well, but in her case she's not pretending. Coach Allen says she has the natural agility of Bambi on ice. Mom made us take ballet lessons when we were small. Jackie did a pirouette and broke a mirror."

"That's seven years bad luck."

"If only! The ballet instructor suggested that we were better suited to kung fu lessons."

"We have a game tomorrow; it's a cup tie. You should come and watch. You might learn to love soccer, even if it doesn't have quarterbacks."

"What's a cup tie?"

"We're playing against a team from Cork in the Irish Youth Tournament. It's the quarter final. If we win then it's the semis and after that the final is in Dublin."

"Will Jackie and me still be here by then?"

"The final is the same time as you're going back to Dublin anyway. But I forgot; you'll be too busy at Louis Vuitton to have time for the likes of us."

"Do you think you'll make it to the final?"

"I think we have a good chance."

"Tell you what, if you make it, I'll come and watch. If you don't, you can take me to Louis Vuitton. Do we have a deal?"

"Deal. In the meantime, you can browse the shops on Main Street. Turn right at the Fethard Ballroom and over Madam's bridge."

Main Street, Fethard, did not strike the sisters as likely to compete with 5th Avenue, New York or Champs-Élysées, Paris. At first glance, they failed to see the shops alluded to by Jeff. Sure, the bright purple hue of Burke's Bridge Bar on their left caught their eyes, but mostly Main Street consisted of houses as far as they could see.

Behind the Bridge Bar lay the manicured grounds and house of the girl's school, founded in 1862 as the Presentation Convent, but now called Nano Nagle, after the founder of the Order. A little farther to the north, by the Holy Trinity Parish Church (not to be confused with the Holy Trinity Church of Ireland) and along Chapel Lane stood the *Sparagoleith*, Fethard's only surviving medieval town gate.

Upon mention of the word, *school*, the sisters instinctively moved a few paces to the south. Even in Ireland, a school was still a school and to be avoided as much as possible.

"That's the parish school," said Jeff. "Back in the days of William of Orange, they banned Catholic schools and Catholic teachers."

"Banning school sounds like a sensible thing to do," said Alex.

"But it didn't stop anyone; the teachers and kids would gather for lessons in cow sheds or under trees in country lanes – Hedge Schools, they were called."

"So let me get this straight; school was banned, but the kids went anyway. Why would you go to school when you had a perfectly good excuse not to?" Alex believed one must always approach education with extreme caution.

On further inspection, Alex and Jackie realized that Main Street did indeed contain shops: an occasional antique shop or hairdressers which occupied the ground floor of a converted home, then a smattering of small, specialty shops. Sometimes the business would advertise itself with a sign which hung over the entrance.

"Publican, Restaurant, Undertaker," Jackie read aloud.

"This is the world-famous McCarthy's," said Jeff, as way of an explanation.

"Publican, Restaurant, Undertaker?" asked an incredulous Alex. "Really?"

"One stop service and convenience," said Mattie.

"Do they have a discount if you use more than one service?" asked Jackie.

"Don't laugh; in a small town such as this everyone has to wear several hats. Lonergan's Bar up the road has a Chinese takeaway at the back. And you'll see a bit more of McCarthy's this evening. We're giving Jeff a day away from the kitchen and coming here for dinner."

"As long as it's only dinner," said Alex. "I don't want their undertaker service, with or without a discount."

"Just dinner as far as we know," said Jeff.

"And where are these shops you've promised me."

"Come on; let me show you the video store, butcher's, newsagent, pharmacy, and post office."

"You're kidding, right?"

"I never kid."

"If you'd like more history, we can also show you the town hall and Holy Trinity Church, both of them," said Mattie.

"Now I know you're kidding," said Alex. "You are . . . Right? . . . Please tell me you're just kidding."

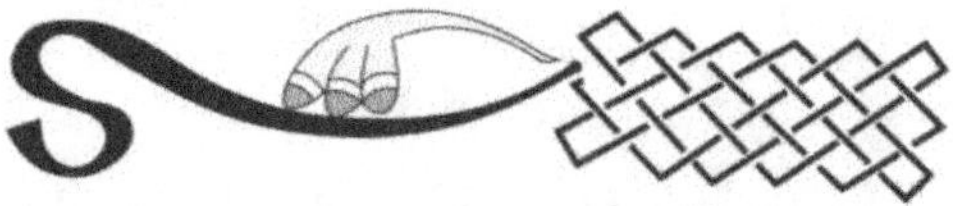

"Hello, Molly," said Aunt Róisín to the waitress at McCarthy's.

"Hello, Róisín," replied the waitress. "Jeff, Mattie."

"These are my nieces from America, Jackie and Alex."

"America, I've always wanted to visit. I have a sister in New York, do you know her? Ah, of course you don't! Welcome to McCarthy's."

"Thank you," said the sisters.

"Of course, Fethard doesn't quite meet the eye the way that New York does: Times Square and the Statue of Liberty."

"We went shopping on Main Street," laughed Mattie. "So, their trip to Fethard wasn't a total loss."

"Oh well, there you are then."

"I brought a belt," said Alex. "See."

Alex proudly displayed her belt; the buckle had an intricate design which featured two dragons trying to swallow each other.

A roar of heated debate came from the bar.

"I'll put you down the back; it's a bit quieter there."

The dining room at McCarthy's stood on the other side of the wall from the bar; and had a separate entrance. Usually, the noise from the bar did not carry through the wall to the restaurant, but today, the locals packed the bar to argue the merits of horses and jockeys, topics for which the inhabitants of McCarthy's had great passion.

Unlike many establishments which tried to mirror the vagaries of transient fashion, the pub had resisted change since Richard McCarthy had opened his doors to the public in 1850; but now, instead of epitomizing a relic from a bygone era, the dark, polished wooden walls, ceilings and floors appeared trend-setting, as if the fashions had gone on ahead only to circle around again and sneak up from behind.

A lighter touch prevailed in the dining room, where white tablecloths matched the color of the plaster walls, and the floral patterns of the curtains reflected in the little vases of flowers which adorned the tables.

"What's good tonight, Molly?" asked Jeff as they sat at the table.

"Some fine sole, fresh in today," she replied. "And the lamb cutlets are popular. Is Bob joining you?"

"No, he's minding the pub," said Aunt Róisín.

"Then I'll let you look over your menus and fetch some water for the table."

"Thanks, Molly."

"It's a shame you and Uncle Bob never get to go anywhere together," said Jackie.

"Business is business, but we shall both go to Dublin with you. We get some help in occasionally."

"Speaking of business," said Alex. "I don't understand why, if you own a pub, you would go to another pub in the same town?"

"Because in a community such as Fethard where everyone is a neighbor - I went to school with Molly - it helps to spread the wealth. You have to look out for your neighbors."

"It's only neighborly," said Mattie.

"But look at all the pubs," insisted Alex. "Aren't there too many? If there were fewer pubs, the Gatehouse would get more business."

"If we start shutting pub doors simply because of lack of business, where would that lead? And what if the Gatehouse was one of those whose doors and windows were shuttered?"

"That would never happen with the Gatehouse, you've got a castle."

"The loss of any business, even if it was a competitor, even if it brought more trade to the Gatehouse, would make the whole community a little poorer. If Fethard had less to offer then fewer people would come here and that would put more pressure on those who remained. It would be a downward spiral."

"I suppose so. I guess I'm not very good at business."

"There is business and then there is friendship. But if it's any consolation, friendship also has its advantages, such as the fact that we can dine here at a friend's house, and I can enjoy some excellent lemon sole, thank you, Molly."

Molly had returned to take their orders. The sisters followed their aunt's lead and also ordered the fish. Mattie satisfied his craving for steak, and Jeff, after quizzing Molly on the preparation of the redcurrant sauce, decided on the lamb cutlets.

"It's very good," Alex commented on the food. "But not quite as good as yours though, Jeff."

"They do a fine dinner here," agreed Jeff.

Jackie scooped up some creamy, smooth, white concoction from a side dish. She imagined it to be fairy ice cream as it melted in her mouth. "This is amazing," she said. "I've never tasted anything like it. What is it?"

"It's an Irish specialty," answered Mattie. "It's called the potato."

"This is potato?" questioned Alex in rare agreement with her sister. "No way!"

"Come on now; they have potatoes in the States."

"Not like this; they don't cook them like this."

"How are they cooked then?"

"We empty a box of potato flakes into a pan and add boiling water."

"What?" cried Jeff. "I know of at least 101 ways to cook potatoes, but boiling water and a box? You poor girls!"

"Okay," said Alex. "I now believe the pub and restaurant bit, but I still don't believe the undertaker bit."

"Don't believe us, then ask Molly," argued Mattie.

"Oh, yes," said Molly as she returned to clear the plates. "We'll bury you good and proper."

"After waking you good and proper."

"Over the years we've also been a hotel, baker, grocer, draper, and china shop, hackney car business; and a little bit of horse and carriage rental too."

"Don't forget ghost hunters,"

"I'm sure the ladies don't want to hear about our ghosts."

"Yes, we do," said Jackie. "We like ghosts."

"Well, for those who believe in that sort of thing, McCarthy's is said to have a ghost or two. We often get sightings reported by the customers."

"Some of them allegedly sober," said Mattie.

"Have you ever seen a ghost?" asked Jackie.

"Good Lord and Heaven forbid," replied Molly. "But then there's the warning of pending death, whenever a McCarthy dies."

"Like the Banshee?"

"No, not the Banshee as such, but a knocking at the front door. Three loud raps, as if death himself demanded entry. It happened when Beattie died. Three loud knocks on the door. Everyone in the bar heard it and instantly stopped drinking and arguing the horses. Three loud knocks, then the picture behind you fell off the wall."

Alex and Jackie turned to view the picture; it remained immobile. No one spoke. The silence took on a supernatural quality.

"Now, who's saved room for dessert?" asked Molly.

Filled with chocolate roulade, as recommended by Molly, the O'Rourkes departed McCarthy's. A gentle rain drizzled down on them. They had no umbrellas, but the warm evening air kept them comfortable, and they felt no need to hurry the short walk to the Gatehouse.

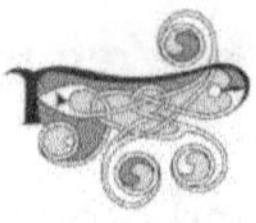

They arrived back at the Gatehouse, just before the heavier rain arrived. Aunt Róisín joined Uncle Bob in tending the bar. In the kitchen, Mattie turned on the TV and tuned in to a soccer match already in progress. Jeff tried in vain to explain the rules of the game to the sisters, but when they became completely befuddled by the offside rule, he gave up.

Jackie studied the clock on the wall. Time seemed to slow down. She knew that the pub would not fall into its nighttime stupor until Uncle Bob had served the last customer and the soccer match had ended. The day could not end soon enough, she sighed, so she could keep her appointment with the fairy horse, Lämmy.

"Extra time," said Mattie.

"What does that mean?" asked Jackie.

"Thirty more minutes and then, if it's still tied, penalty kicks."

Jackie groaned.

Alex gave a placid, indifferent shrug; she had promised to join in Jackie's vigil, but she did not look forward to it. Nothing good could come of it, she surmised. Either Jackie had suffered hallucinations, in which case she should have sought medical help for her sister, or worse yet, and the reason Alex had said nothing to the others, and not beyond the realm of possibility given their other encounters with the supernatural, Jackie really had seen a fairy.

She turned on her phone. She wanted to text someone . . . a lonely, miserable, pleading, HELP! . . . But decided against it. No one could help. Who could she text? Who could understand? She stared at her phone, hoping perhaps that it would ring with an answer to her dilemma. It didn't and she joined her sister in playing the waiting game.

"Goal!" cried Mattie.

The sisters looked up.

"There goes the penalties," said Jeff. "Not enough time on the clock to come back."

The referee agreed with Jeff and blew his whistle to end the match. The locals filed out into the rain and went home. Alex and Jackie said their goodnights, went to their bedroom, lay in silence, and listened to the muffled sounds of the pub; of Uncle Bob locking the front door; of Aunt Róisín instructing the boys in some matter which the girls could not ascertain; of goodnights exchanged and lights extinguished.

Then they lay on their beds and listened to the rain, until finally, as Alex had just about convinced herself that her sister had fallen asleep, Jackie whispered.

"Come on, everything is quiet now."

"Are you sure you want to do this? Maybe we should just get some sleep."

"You promised."

"Oh, all right then."

The dark made the stairs dangerous to walk, but the sisters did not dare turn on the lights. At least the stone steps did not creak. Halfway down, the night lights of the kitchen and bar crept up to meet them. This time no sparkly light cast shadows.

"Do you think we should get milk and cookies?" asked Jackie.

"Unless you're expecting Santa Claus, the answer is no."

They moved into the bar.

"There's nothing here," whispered Alex.

"Shush," said Jackie. "I'm trying to listen." She tilted her head and strained to hear the familiar singing but failed. "Maybe we're early, let's wait under the Tree."

Jackie sat down. Alex looked around the bar room and tried to think of something reasonable to say which would see them safely back in their beds, until a sharp tug on her dressing gown compelled her to the floor beside her sister.

"Ouch," she said.

"Shush," repeated Jackie.

Alex shushed. She fumbled in her robe pocket and retrieved her phone.

"What are you doing?" Jackie glared.

"I thought I'd send a few texts while we wait."

"Lämmy's not going to appear while you're texting, put it away."

Alex shrugged her shoulders but complied. She wondered if she could get away with whistling in the dark. The look on Jackie's face told her she could not.

And so, they sat on the floor, under the Tree, for what seemed hours, and waited for the fairy horse to appear. It did not. Alex stifled a yawn.

"Jackie, this is a waste of time. I'm tired."

Jackie said nothing.

"We've sat here half the night. We have to get some sleep."

Jackie sighed.

"Well, I've had enough. I'm going to bed. Are you coming?"

Jackie nodded. "I'm not sleepy, but you're right; Lämmy's not going to appear tonight. I can't hear the singing either. I'm sorry I've wasted your time."

"No problem."

They rose from the floor and their now stiff legs complained about the sudden rush of blood.

"I'll just get a glass of water to take up with me," said Jackie.

"Don't dawdle. It'll be light soon."

Alex went up the stairs and out of view. Jackie moved to the kitchen sink. Before she could turn on the tap, she heard.

> *"The child of woman wishes for song,*
> *But cannot sing in harmony.*
> *The child of man wishes for dreams,*
> *But cannot cast the spell of sleep."*

Then the song ceased.

"Alex, Alex!" Jackie whispered hard into the darkness, but Alex had already climbed the stairs to bed.

The song began again.

> *"And if the child so dares to see,*
> *And I will follow who follows me."*

"Jeff, Mattie, is that you trying to scare me?" A light grew behind her. She turned around and saw the fairy horse. "Lämmy, Lämmy, where were you?"

The tiny, white horse with gossamer wings turned and glided to the pantry.

"Lämmy, wait a minute, where are you going?"

> *"And I will follow who follows me."*

Jackie followed.

Tuatha Dé Danann

Hearken, ye sages without sorrow,
if it be your will that I relate
the deaths yonder, with astuteness,
of the choice of the Tuatha De Danann.

Lebor gabála Érenn (The Book of the Taking of Ireland),
Anon, Circa 11th Century

Jackie followed the fairy horse to the pantry. Once inside, she saw that the door to the secret passage had opened and light from below shone through. Continuing with its song, the fairy horse entered the passage. Jackie ran to the door. But as she reached the passage steps she halted; not out of fear but because she detected a new song. Several new songs, in fact, had joined the first. All different, all unique, but all came together naturally, as the colors of light combine to make white.

"Welcome to the Daughter of the Ua Ruairc;
Welcome to the Child of the Charm."

She heard above the general chorus; and she headed down the steps. The light in the tunnel did not come from the electrical genius of Granddad O'Rourke, but from a countless number of fairy lights, along the ceiling, floor, and walls, and strung with invisible wire. They glowed with the intensity of a thousand Christmas trees.

"Should have brought milk and cookies," she mused.

And she saw that the lights ran in two directions: For in addition to the passage to the Great Hall which she had walked earlier, the passage to the Abbey was now clear; the rubble which had blocked it gone or invisible.

The fairy horse moved in the direction of the Abbey and Jackie trailed behind. After a few paces the tunnel opened to reveal a large, circular space filled with an intensive brightness. The light at first blinded her. The fairy horse became nothing more than a hazy glow.

"Lämmy," she called, and the fairy horse returned to her side.

When her eyes had adjusted to the brightness, Jackie could see that the passage exited at the far side of the circle and continued east. But in addition, she stood at the intersection of this passage with others which ran along all points of the compass, all aglow with the magical light.

And in the circle, and along every tunnel, the fairies moved. Thousand of fairies: Some in the shape of horses such as Lämmy; some more balls of light and energy than any definitive outline; some shaped as tiny humans, male and female, but with wings. Little doll-like creatures just as Jackie had imagined them, fragile and beautiful. They swarmed around her but did not touch her.

Jackie held out a hand and they flew back a few paces. Jackie lowered her hand, and they moved in again, as if they mirrored her curiosity.

At the center of the circle stood the Tree; its twisted, tangled roots reached deep down into the earth; Its branches formed a canopy which filled the space; its silver leaves glinted as if stars in the night sky. The trunk of the Tree disappeared into the rock above her head and beyond that, she knew, into the bar of the Gatehouse.

The Tree occupied an island on a pool of silver water. An ornate bridge, suspended from the Tree's branches, connected the island to the passages. At each end of the bridge, and all around the island, stood torches of smokeless, golden fire.

And a few paces beyond the bridge stood a throne of white marble, carved with images of animals and trees, with green vines wrapped around it, and precious stones scattered at its base as if they fell from the Tree each autumn.

On the throne sat a woman of Jackie's size. She wore a simple, silken gown and a crown of yellow daises on her head. Jackie should have instantly seen the resemblance to Shakespeare's Ophelia as illustrated in countless Victorian oil paintings, but instead thought the woman reminded her of Princess Amidala from Star Wars.

"Welcome to the Daughter of the Ua Ruairc," sang the woman.

"Er, hello," answered Jackie, and wondered if a curtsy was in order.

"Approach us, Daughter of the Ua Ruairc, and do not be afraid."

Jackie walked over the bridge. The woman indicated a root beside the throne, which formed a stool.

"Sit with us, Daughter of the Ua Ruairc."

"Call me Jackie."

"Sit with us, Jackie of the Ua Ruairc."

Jackie sat.

"What's the Ua Ruairc?" she asked.

"You are."

"Oh . . . er . . . oh."

"The Ua Ruairc are known to us these many centuries of man. Speak with us, Jackie of the Ua Ruairc, as your ancestors once spoke."

"If you say so, miss . . . er . . .?"

"You speak with Eeviin, Queen of the Grey Rock."

"Are you a fairy?"

Queen Eeviin pouted at the insult. "We are Tuatha Dé Danann, the children of Danu, the children of Nuada Airgetlám, the children of Lugh Lámhfhada."

"That's a lot of children . . . er . . . Your Majesty."

"And you have many questions."

Queen Eeviin song washed over Jackie and immersed her with a beauty beyond words.

"How come I can understand you? You're not speaking – singing – English."

"You are a Child of the Charm."

"I don't understand."

"You have laid your lips on the Lia Fail and it has blessed you with the Charm."

"Do you mean the Blarney Stone?"

Queen Eeviin winced in pain. "The Lia Fail is a jewel of the Tuatha Dé Danann; it should not be spoken of in vulgar tongue."

"Sorry. So, when I kissed the . . . Lia Fail, it gave me the power to understand your song? Like the Babel fish."

"You may understand us. We do not understand you."

"The Babel . . . oh, never mind, it's not important."

"Few humans are blessed so with the Charm, but then you possess other gifts of song, do you not."

"How do you know about that?"

"You have heard us sing, we have heard you sing."

"I don't remember singing."

"You sing in your heart. Your song tells all. Yours is a song of the Otherworld. You have been where the Tuatha Dé Danann cannot go."

"I thought this was the Otherworld?"

"This is the dominion of the Sidhe. I sing of Magh Meall, the Plain of Joy, beyond Tír na nÓg, beyond the edge of death."

"And I've been there, have I?"

"Your song says it is so."

"Well, I sing a lot of things; sometimes I get the words mixed up. I wouldn't really . . ."

"What is your want, Jackie of the Ua Ruairc?"

"My want? Like in three wishes or something?"

"You are a Child of the Charm; otherwise, you would not be before us. We must honor you . . ."

Jackie went to speak, but Queen Eeviin raised her hand.

". . . Before you ask of us, you should be certain. You have many questions to which we shall give answers, but you may ask only one question in particular, for which we shall give honor."

"What question?"

"As a human there is much you will not understand of us; and yet to ask of us you must understand."

"We seem to be going 'round in circles. Can we start again?"

"We are Tuatha Dé Danann," sang Queen Eeviin.

"I got that bit, thank you," replied Jackie.

"I think not! How do we seem to you?"

"Well . . . er . . . you know . . . fairies, cute dresses, little horses with wings, lots of sparkly things."

"We appear before you as you imagine us to be, as in a dream."

"So, Alex is right; a little bang on the head and I've gone to hallucination land."

"To see the true nature of the Tuatha Dé Danann, you must first understand us; otherwise, your want is also an illusion and not the truth."

"What if I can't handle the truth?"

"Understand us better. You may ask of us."

 "So, let's start with, 'who are the Tuatha Dé Danann?'"

"We are."

"It's going to be a long night, isn't it?"

"We are Tuatha Dé Danann."

"How about you begin, with 'Once upon a time," asked Jackie.

"Once upon a time," sang the Tuatha Dé Danann.

From cold winter of the Great Flood did spring
The four sturdy ships over Mare Rubrum,
Decked with captains of the mighty Gaedil

Tuatha Dé Danann

And so we sailed unseen for countless days
In mist until we reached the Northern Light,
And four jeweled cities did welcome us,
Failias, Findias, Gorias and Murias praised
By the Tuatha Dé Danann.

Four wizards ruled over those lands of Ice
Esrus in Gorias, Morfessa Failias,
Semias in Murias and renown Uiscias,
They taught the arts of magic and delight
To the Tuatha Dé Danann.

The Tuatha Dé Danann sang in beautiful, unworldly harmonies. They did not sing in a language which Jackie could understand, if they even used language as we understand it, but their song formed images in Jackie's head which she could follow, although she found some of the imagery as complicated as a Celtic knot, and she hoped she wouldn't have to sit a test at the end.

They sang of their triumph over magic under the guidance of the magicians and, when the time came to leave the four cities, of the gifts they received from their hosts.

"But take with you our love and these treasures,
From Failias the Lia Fail, Stone of Kings,
By whose counsel are princes claims measured
And parent to the children of the Charm,
Listen wise Tuatha Dé Danann."

"From Murias take this cauldron of plenty.
That none of your race shall hunger or thirst,

Tuatha Dé Danann

Ever shall your guests proclaim the bounty
Of the table of hospitality
Of the generous Tuatha Dé Danann."

"Take this spear from fair Gorias, which released
By the hand of its owner can never
Be turned from its target of man or beast,
Or used harshly against the warrior
Of Tuatha Dé Danann."

"And princely Nuada, for you this sword
From the blacksmiths of Findias was it wrought
When drawn from its scabbard, none can avoid
Your might. With it shall you claim your birthright,
Nuada of the Tuatha Dé Danann."

Nuada Airgetlám to prove his worth
Before us all sat on the Stone of Kings
"Let the Lia Fail tell if by my birth
I be true king of any land or sea
And of the Tuatha Dé Danann."

"Hail Nuada Airgetlám," sang the Stone,
"Of the Tuatha Dé Danann true king."
"Then where is my kingdom? Where is my throne?"
Nuada sang. "To Ireland you must go."
"To Ireland," sang the Tuatha Dé Danann.

They sang with pride and joy at the remembrance of their early years, as one took joy in the birth of a child, and before the full-grown man could turn their joy to grief. They sang of happy times before time itself deprived them of their joy.

Tuatha Dé Danann

With wind at our backs to Ireland we sailed,
Over the black sea in black ships we came,
Our number hidden in a black cloud 'til
Down on the mountains of Conmaicne Rein
Landed the Tuatha Dé Danann.

Our magic held back the sun for three days
And three nights while with the Fir Bholg we stood
And parlayed for our share of that fair land
And a kinship 'tween us for common good.
"No!" cried the Fir Bholg to the Tuatha Dé Danann.

"War!" said the Fir Bholg and bade us battle
On Mag Tuired, where armies came to die,
Where two great armies stilled the breathing air
Until the ground shook with the battle cry
Of the Tuatha Dé Danann.

And slaughter raged for long days without end
On Mag Tuired, 'til the sons of Nemed
At last struck down luckless Eochu their king
And from the field the confused Fir Bholg fled
From the wrath of the Tuatha Dé Danann.

Still a warrior of the Fir Bholg, Sreng
The brave, refused to quit the death red field
And for honor fought with King Nuada.
And Sreng with one mighty blow broke the shield
And hacked of the arm of Nuada of Tuatha Dé Danann.

"Not all sweetness and light after all," mused Jackie. "Or are they just trying to scare me?"

Tuatha Dé Danann

Jackie dismissed the notion. The syrupy, cute fairies which fluttered around her and sang in such a poetic, poignant fashion couldn't possibly harm a fly, let alone invade a country and vanquish its occupants.

"No, they don't fool me. It's all bluff and bluster."

But one armed Nuada could rule no more.
And the leeches took seven years to heal.
Then Miach shaped an arm of silver steel
And with cunning attached it to the veins
Of Nuada of the Tuatha Dé Danann.

In Nuada's place, Bres was chosen king
From the marriage of Princess Eri and
Prince Elatha of the Fomoiaig land.
But wicked Bres was cruel and in scorn named
Tyrant of the Tuatha Dé Danann.

We rose to combat the evil of Bres,
Nuada Silver Arm once more our Lord,
And Bres fled to his Fomorian horde,
Where they plotted revenge and drew war plans
Against the Tuatha Dé Danann.

So the second battle of Mag Tuired
Raged as hard and long as the first had done,
With blood enough on either side to turn
Clover red from green and men grey from red
Hard fought the Tuatha Dé Danann.

For the Fomoraig, evil eyed Balor
Sire to Ethlinn of the Crystal Tower
Then Grandfather but foe to Lugh this hour

Tuatha Dé Danann

Came forth and burned all gazed on by his eye.
Perished many of the Tuatha Dé Danann.

But Lugh took the treasured spear of Gorias
And with it, Lugh Lamhfada drove the eye
Of Balor from his head, as prophesized,
And turned the eye upon the Fomoraig.
So went the day for the Tuatha Dé Danann.

But with victory we learned again that
With too brief joy come eternal sorrows,
And for today and for all tomorrows.
Nuada with those slain by Balor's eye,
Nuada, king no more of the Tuatha Dé Danann.

Unless of course . . . the poignancy came from a deep well of loss and the fairies were just shadows of their former selves. Jackie braced for the story yet to come - of the fall of the Tuatha Dé Danann. What had happened to the once powerful warriors to turn them into these pitiful creatures hiding in tunnels?

The three kings now shared the throne with three queens;
Banba, Fodla, Ériu of Ireland green.
But in Brigantium, King Breogán built
A tall tower and from the top did see
The green lands of the Tuatha Dé Danann.

"I will have that emerald for my crown
And so send my son, Ith", said King Breogán,
"To entreat with them to name a fair price."
But in reply the three kings struck Ith down
And war came once more to the Tuatha Dé Danann.

Tuatha Dé Danann

The Sons of Mil landed then on our shore
And met the three queens under flag of truce;
Bade by their husbands to barter for terms,
During which the Sons of Mil would anchor
At nine waves' distance from the Tuatha Dé Danann.

And the Tuatha Dé used our dark charms
To anger the sea and capsize their ships,
But Amergin Glúingel, the white-kneed Bard
Gave answer and returned the sea to calm,
And the Sons of Mil attacked the Tuatha Dé Danann.

Great loss for the Tuatha Dé Danann,
And three kings, by their own actions betrayed,
With no surrender, on the field lay.
No side could triumph, and no side would stay.
No quarter given to the Tuatha Dé Danann.

The three queens to Amergin sped away,
In counsel went to end the killing day,
And agreed to share Ireland equally
Between them and that Amergin would weigh
The spoils of Mil and the Tuatha Dé Danann

Clever Amergin; Amergin profound.
No one before did so cruelly confound.
For he split the kingdom in mirrored share
And gave the Sons of Mil all above ground
And all that lay below he allotted to the Tuatha Dé Danann.

With binding oaths which could not be undone
And with somber hearts as funeral drums,
Amergin led us to the Sidhe Mounds,

Tuatha Dé Danann

No more to walk out in the light of sun,
The Tuatha Dé Danann are a Fay people become.

Jackie expected that the fairies would sing of glory, grandeur, and heroic deeds, even at their fall from power. But instead, their loss came through greed, deceit and common trickery. And this hurt them above all. The sadness which permeated their song came from the knowledge that they were lesser creatures than they hoped, and that they had been lesser creatures all along, from the beginning, as if their victories and their heroism were merely illusions, that they were always Fay people. Jackie fought back the tears.

"On our parting, we must honor the Child of the Charm, as we would honor the Lia Fail itself," sang Queen Eeviin.

"So, I do get three wishes?"

"We are not the Jinn of the East. You cannot steal our treasure or magic. What is in your heart? How would you have us honor you?"

"I don't know. Can I think about it?"

"Reflection is always wise, Jackie of the Ua Ruairc."

"Maybe I could sleep on it? A good night's sleep would be welcome."

"Then sleep on it, Jackie of the Ua Ruairc."

"Wait a minute; no tricks."

"Tricks?"

"Well, fairies do have a certain reputation . . . sorry, no offence. A good night's sleep is not my wish, in case you were about to wave a magic wand and make it happen."

"I have no wand; and the Tuatha Dé Danann have no need to trick honest humans. We must honor the Child of the Charm and we cannot do that through deception."

"Okay, just making sure. I'm not thinking straight. Perhaps my mind is playing tricks."

"You are in ill health?"

"No, I feel a little tired. It's just that Alex is always texting and you're always singing. It's hard to ignore sometimes."

"Our song is one with nature. Would you have us cease?"

"Oh, no, no! Sorry, I don't mean to be rude."

"We understand you are tired. Leave us. Sleep well. Until you claim your honor, through the hours of the darkest night, we shall sing you a lullaby and you shall wake refreshed."

Jackie realized that she stood at the foot of the steps to the pantry. The fairies had disappeared. Lämmy the fairy horse had gone. The rubble which blocked the tunnel's passage to the abbey had reappeared, and the fairy lights replaced by the bare electric bulbs, which mercifully shone so as not to leave her in total darkness. She climbed the steps to the pantry.

"Jackie?"

Mattie's voice startled her.

"Oh, hi, Mattie."

"Jackie, what are you doing?"

"Oh, er . . . I, er . . . what are you doing?"

"It's my turn to light the stove . . . I saw the passage light. What were you doing down there?"

"Come quick and see."

Jackie ran down the steps. Mattie followed. There, of course, was nothing to see.

"They were here, Mattie, the fairies, they were here. Please believe me."

"Let's go to the kitchen. I'll make you a cup of tea."

"I don't want a cup of tea."

"But it's the law – whatever the problem, the solution is a cup of tea."

They returned to the kitchen. Jackie fell into a chair at the table. Mattie fetched a pot and two cups.

"You're not going to believe me, are you? You think I'm crazy."

"Tell me what you saw?"

"I saw the fairies. There was a horse. His name was Lämmy. And a queen; her name was Eeviin. But she wasn't small like the other fairies. She was as big as me and she sat on a throne under the Tree."

"And what did they say to you?"

"The Ua Ruairc, that's what Queen Eeviin called me. Daughter of the Ua Ruairc. Who are the Ua Ruairc?"

"You are."

"Now don't you start that; it was bad enough with the fairies."

"It's the old name for O'Rourke. The O'Rourkes have been in Ireland for centuries. You might have already known that. You sure you didn't read it somewhere?"

"No."

"Or see a documentary? Maybe Seán Murphy told you?"

"No, I swear. I first heard it at Blarney Castle when I kissed the Stone, then I heard it again tonight. Then they sang this long poem at me. They called themselves the Tuatha Dé Danann and they had kings named Nuada Airgetlám and Lugh Lamhfada."

Mattie frowned.

"What is it?"

"There is an old book, *Lebor gabála Éren*. In English, *the Book of the taking of Ireland*. It tells of our early history, including the story of the Tuatha Dé Danann."

"So do you believe me?"

"Not so fast; 'cause I definitely heard you talk to Dad and Seán Murphy about the Tuatha Dé Danann, but I don't remember them specifically mention Nuada or Lugh."

"So do you believe me?"

"Have you slept tonight?"

Jackie shook her head.

"Didn't think so. Look, I have to light the stove and get some coal. There's still a couple of hours before daylight. Go and get some sleep and we'll talk some more then."

"I'm not tired . . . funny, I was tired, but now I'm not. The fairies said they would sing me a lullaby."

"I think we should discuss this in the morning with Jeff; he's the expert on all things historical. Go on up now."

"Oh, all right, if you're not going to believe me."

Jackie pushed back her chair and crossed the kitchen to the staircase.

"But . . ." she turned and began.

"Go on up, we'll talk in the daylight. It's best not to speak of the fairies at this hour."

"Oh, okay."

Jackie climbed the stairs to the bedroom. She expected to find that Alex had fallen asleep, but the glow from Alex's phone and the occasional grumble, which emanated from under the blanket on Alex's bed, indicated otherwise.

"Alex, you awake?" asked Jackie.

From under the blanket came an indecipherable mumble.

"Alex, I want to talk to you."

Jackie snatched at the blanket and pulled it back.

There was Alex's phone, emitting a pale blue light, and softly beeping as its buttons were pressed. There was Alex's dressing gown, pulled tight and almost bursting at the seams, as if Alex had suddenly doubled in size. But the creature in the dressing gown and tapping at the phone was certainly not Alex. It was a pig. Jackie could tell the difference, even in the dim light.

Now, in all the movies Jackie had seen which contained a pig, and in all the stories she had read, there was a tendency to portray the pig as cute. She had never seen the attraction herself, and certainly didn't see it on this occasion.

Perhaps she was mistaken. Perhaps after all, pigs were cute, loveable, little creatures which didn't smell, grunt, or defecate, but on the whole, she reckoned, and as much as it pained her to admit it, she would have preferred to have found Alex in the bed and not the pig.

"Why does this keep happening to me?" sighed Jackie.

Kells

The great Gospel of Colum-Cille was wickedly stolen in the night out of the western sacristy of the great stone-church of Cenannas - the chief relic of the western world, on account of its ornamental cover. The same Gospel was found after twenty nights and two months, its gold having been taken off it, and a sod over it.

Annála Uladh (*The Annals of Ulster*), 1007,
translated by William M. Hennessy, 1887

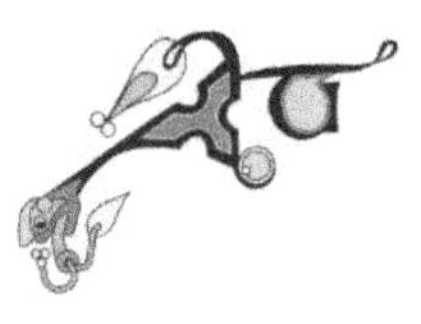 **A**lex's parents had often commented that her bedroom resembled a pigsty. And she had always considered them too judgmental and harsh. Now she awoke to find her bedroom categorically transformed into one of her parents' more expressive descriptions.

Two huge, unfriendly pigs stood at her feet and stared ominously. A chicken clucked at her ear. And the creature which just scurried away appeared to be a rat. She instinctively tried to scramble away from the animals but came up hard against a stone wall behind her.

She thought that perhaps a little scream would help.

"Aaahhhh!"

It didn't. The evil-eyed pigs still stared.

"Okay, don't panic," she thought, after she had panicked for several minutes. "Let's close my eyes and wake up again."

That didn't help either. The pigsty and its occupants remained. Alex tried to recall the sequence of events which led to this bizarre predicament. She could recall none.

"What do I remember?"

Her last memory was of a warm bed, where she lay as she wrote a scathing, sarcastic text to Chris back in San Diego. In retrospect, the text could have seemed hypercritical, but she had been tired and cranky, and felt that he deserved it. She had hit the send button. She must have fallen asleep while she waited for his reply.

Obviously, definitely, she no longer lay in bed. The bed had disappeared, along with Jackie's bed and all the other contents of the room. The bedroom had also disappeared. Given the unfamiliarity of the surroundings, she knew she was no longer in the Gatehouse. She remembered that when she had crawled into bed, she had still worn her dressing gown. It was also gone. Her slippers absent, mud squished through her toes. Her phone was gone. At least her pajamas remained.

She felt tired thanks to Jackie's stupid insistence that they stay up half the night to wait for a fairy horse called Lämmy, which never appeared. Now she instantly knew who to blame for her current predicament and decided that the moment called for another scream.

"Jackie, what have you done?"

The pigs glanced at each other and decided to retreat; their visitor also seemed unfriendly; and as they saw that she carried nothing of interest (i.e. food), they soon lost interest in her.

Alex sighed, pulled her knees under her chin, and bowed her head. Her pajamas lay oddly heavy on her. She tugged at them. They felt cold and wet. She looked around her new environment. Apart from the pigs and the rogue chicken, she saw puddles of brown water on the muddy brown dirt which served as the floor of the pigsty. An old, wooden, broken, often repaired fence with a gate in one corner abutted the wall and enclosed her and the pigs. A half-rotten, wooden, entirely inadequate, slated roof over her head did little to divert the path of the water. It splashed in the puddles, dripped on her head, and soaked her pajamas. The inconvenient rain, at least, felt familiar to her.

"Oh, God!" she moaned.

"An unusual place to kneel for prayer," said a voice. "Not of course do I believe that Our Lord would object, for he himself first appeared to us in a stable."

"What?" Alex looked up.

The pigs stirred and attempted little piggy smiles.

"We do have a stable if you prefer. You will find it a drier than the pigsty."

"What?" A confused Alex repeated.

"Forgive me; I have interrupted you in your penance. I shall withdraw and return to feed the pigs at another time."

The man behind the voice turned to walk away.

"No, no, wait," cried Alex. "Please don't go."

A sentiment echoed by the pigs.

The man turned again.

"May I be of service?"

"Who are you?"

"I am Brother Oswald."

"You're a monk?"

Brother Oswald nodded. The question could have seemed rhetorical, for unless Brother Oswald had tickets to a fancy dress party, the traditional habit, sandals, and bald spot were a dead giveaway. Had Alex possessed minute, detailed knowledge of the various religious orders (or access to Google) she would have noted that the habit and shaved head also identified Brother Oswald as a member of the Order of St. Columba. The sparsely populated Order eventually merged with the Benedictines, but old habits died hard.

"And how shall I address you, good Mistress?"

"I'm Alex."

"Hello, Mistress Alex. Have you travelled far?"

"I don't know; where am I?"

"You are on the Abbey grounds. I do not recognize you as from the village. You are a stranger to these parts. Where are your companions?"

"Who says I have any companions?"

"No one travels alone, except perhaps an ambassador of the Church, and I do not think you are a prioress or missionary. Your dress is also strange to me. Tell me of the design upon it? The pattern is most delicately woven. Is it the crest of your family?"

Alex checked her pajamas.

"Er, they're bunny rabbits."

"Most interesting. And your features also identify you as a visitor. Are you from Dublin?"

"No, I'm just visiting family."

"Are you from the Norse lands?"

"I'm from San Diego."

"Ah, yes, San Diego . . . I am not familiar with San Diego."

"Norse lands?"

"Denmark, Norway, Sweden, the Northern Isles. Your fair visage and golden locks are more common amongst the Swedes than with our own people."

"I'm not Swedish."

"Forgive me. Are you injured? I see you have no baggage. Were you robbed? The world is full of many scoundrels who prey on the helpless and innocent . . ."

"I'm not helpless." Alex snapped.

"As you say," calmed Brother Oswald.

"Just a bit confused about how I got here."

Brother Oswald opened the gate to the pigsty and entered. The pigs surrounded him and brushed against his legs. If they had been cats they would have purred.

"Indeed, I am also at a loss for an explanation," he agreed. "Perhaps you have hit your head and sustained an injury to your memory?"

"No, that's Jackie."

"Jackie?"

"My sister."

"Is your sister travelling with you?"

"She was. I don't know where she is now."

"If I may make a suggestion . . ."

"Yes?"

"I see that the fabric of your garments is soft and fine – and that may be the fashion for the people of San Diego – but they do not seem to offer much protection against the harsher elements of our climate."

"What?"

"Your clothes are wet; you will catch a cold if you stay out here with the pigs. May I suggest that you accompany me to the chapel?"

"Maybe I should just be going; sorry for the inconvenience."

"We can provide you with some warm clothes; and perhaps we will have news of your sister. Either way, I'm sure that Father Abbot will want to examine you; we do not get many visitors these days, what with the scoundrels who inhabit the forest and the peat bogs, the quarrelsome Ua Ruairc and the Goths."

"We've got some Goths at school; can't say I ever saw them cause trouble though, just sit around and mope most of the time. Jackie says I could be a Goth."

"And are you?"

"No, do I look like one?" Alex pouted. "Notice any black eyeliner or fingernails?" She presented her fingers for inspection.

Brother Oswald checked the color of Alex's fingernails.

"No, of course; you are from . . . where was that again?"

"San Diego."

"Ah yes, San Diego. As you see, my memory also fails me at times."

Brother Oswald held out his hand to assist Alex to her feet. She accepted gladly, as the rain-soaked pajamas and the mud combined to make her position on the ground uncomfortable.

"I must say for a visitor, you speak our language remarkably well," said Brother Oswald.

"I'm not speaking your language, you're speaking mine."

"That is a convenient accident."

"No, it's English."

"English? San Diego is in England?"

"No, it's in California."

"Ah, yes, California . . . I am not familiar with California."

"You don't get out much, do you?"

"Actually, I am the cellarer for the Abbey. I get out often - to purchase the provisions we cannot supply from our own land or industry."

"It was a joke."

Brother Oswald looked at Alex, as if he examined her for signs of a cracked skull, and then said, "Come, let me take you to Father Abbot."

They left the pigsty; Brother Oswald shut the gate behind them. Alex could see that the wall she had found at her back in the pigsty ran in a large circle around her. All around the circle, at the perimeter, stood small domed structures, forty or fifty of them, each of which could house several people. Alex thought they resembled igloos made of stone. In one segment of the circle stood some larger, square buildings, with windows and sloped roofs. Above one structure, smoke billowed from a kitchen chimney. In another segment, a round, bell tower stood as the tallest object for miles.

Alex and Brother Oswald crossed the open square to the largest of the buildings, the chapel, which occupied the center. As the two passed, monks briefly stopped their activity to stare. It could have seemed impolite perhaps, but years of training had still not prepared them for the sight of a girl in pink pajamas.

"Come back with our food," pleaded the pigs in vain.

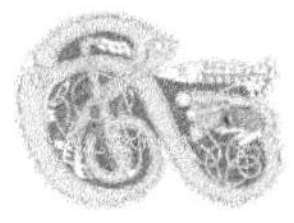

They entered the chapel and Brother Oswald led Alex to a small room off the entrance. With only a plain, wooden bench in one corner, and a writing table in the other, the room resembled a prison cell. Some unlit candles stood on the table and a small, high window provided the only light, and that was filtered and grey.

"Please be comfortable," said Brother Oswald. "I shall tell Father Abbot of your arrival."

He departed and closed the heavy wooden door behind him. Alex suspected that he may have locked her in the room, and she ran to the door. It opened at her touch. She peered out. Several monks milled around the cloister before her and the chapel to her left, but not Brother Oswald. She closed the door, crossed to sit on the bench and considered what to do next. She decided that she was already doing it.

After several minutes, each more tedious than the one before, Brother Oswald returned with some clothes.

"Here," said Brother Oswald. "I cannot vouch as to the artistry of the stitch, the guests of the Abbey generally provide for themselves, but you should be more at ease in dry garments. I shall wait outside while you change. I have informed Father Abbot and he asks to speak with you. When you are ready, I shall take you to him."

He handed Alex an ankle length brown tunic, hose for underneath, sandals, and a scarf.

"What's this for?" asked Alex as she held up the scarf.

"A kerchief to cover your head; is that not the custom of your home?"

"No, I don't do head covers; it's really easy for me to have a bad hair day."

"If you prefer to shave your head, I can fetch you a razor and a bowl of water."

"Er, I think I'll wear the scarf, thanks."

"As you wish."

Brother Oswald departed again.

Alex stripped from her wet pajamas and put on the hose and tunic. The coarse, woolen material scratched her skin so much that she considered a change back to the pajamas, but at least the tunic remained free of designer bunny rabbits.

She walked to the door and opened it. A second, smaller monk stood with Brother Oswald.

"This is Brother Dúngal . . ."

Brother Dúngal looked shyly at his feet, as if he had never before met a female and expected that a single glance would have a Medusa-like effect on him.

". . . He shall take your wet clothes to the kitchen to dry. Father Abbot is waiting for you in the sacristy."

Alex handed her pajamas to Brother Dúngal.

Brother Oswald nodded to Brother Dúngal, who took Alex's pajamas and exited the chapel. Brother Oswald then indicated that Alex should follow him, and they walked the length of the chapel, turned right and entered another small room, where another monk stood to greet them.

"Father Abbot, this is Mistress Alex," said Brother Oswald.

"Welcome, Mistress Alex. I am Abbot Máel Muire."

"Hello," said Alex.

"Brother Oswald tells me that you wandered into our grounds under trying circumstances. How can we be of assistance?"

"Well, er, if you've got a phone I could use, I could call my aunt to come pick me up and bring me some clean clothes."

"A . . . phone . . . pick you up? I'm sorry, your words are not familiar to me, but if you require us to send a message to your aunt."

"No phone? How about Wi-Fi?"

"Why, er . . ."

"No Internet either?"

"Perhaps if you could explain your meaning?"

"No, sorry, it would take too long, I'll just go." She briefly considered the embarrassment of a walk outdoors while she wore the unstylish tunic; then she compared that to the even greater embarrassment of a walk outdoors while she wore her pajamas. "Yes, if you could send a message to my aunt that would be great."

"And where may we find your aunt?"

"The Gatehouse on Watergate Street."

"I do not think I know of that street. Brother Oswald, are you familiar with it?"

"No, Father Abbot," said Brother Oswald.

"But you have to know it, it's just on the next block," objected Alex.

"Block? Again your words have no meaning for me."

"It's just a five-minute walk."

"Mistress Alex, the village is an hour from here."

"Wait a minute; is this the Abbey in Fethard?"

"This is the Abbey of Kells."

"Kells? How did I get to Kells?"

"That is what we are trying to determine."

"I was in bed; I couldn't have got here this fast. What time is it? Anyone got a watch?"

"Mistress Alex, you are obviously distressed. Perhaps you have a fever? We could take you to the infirmary."

"No, I'm okay," said Alex, as she made a mental note to strangle Jackie the next time she saw her. "Maybe I was asleep for longer than I thought. What time is it?"

"The day is just past the Terce."

"Now I don't understand you."

"Between sunrise and noon."

"Okay, and what day is it?"

"Today is Tuesday."

"Tuesday? It's supposed to be Saturday. I've missed three days! How can I have missed three days?"

"Calm yourself. Your memory will return."

"Okay, I know what's happened; it's still Friday night, I'm still in bed, and this is all a dream; and I'll wake up to the smell of a full Irish breakfast coming up from the kitchen. In the meantime, I'll stay calm and play along. So, I'm in Kells Abbey, am I?"

"Yes."

"And it's half past Terce or whatever."

"Yes."

"And it's Tuesday."

"Yes."

"What month is it?"

"The month is Eastertide in the twelfth year of the reign of the High King, Brian Bóruma mac Cennétig."

"Run that one by me one more time?"

"April in the year of our Lord, 1014."

"1014?"

"Yes."

"That's a thousand years ago."

"No, it's a thousand years hence."

"From what?"

"From the days when our Lord walked amongst us."

"This makes as much sense as a talk with Jackie."

"And who is Jackie?"

"Mistress Alex's sister, Father Abbot," answered Brother Oswald.

Brother Dúngal entered the sacristy, with Alex's pajamas under his arm.

"Yes, Brother Dúngal?" asked the Abbot.

"The Mistresses clothes, Father Abbot, they are dry," Brother Dúngal mumbled at the stone floor.

"Good . . . return them to the good lady, Brother, if you please."

Brother Dúngal fidgeted closer to Alex and extended his arms. Alex took the pajamas and smiled at him, not that he looked up to see it.

"Thank you, Brother Dúngal, you may return to your duties."

"Er, there are some men at the gate, Father Abbot," said Brother Dúngal.

"Men, what men?"

"Don't know, Father Abbot. Brother Fedelmid says they are demanding admittance. He thinks they may be Ua Ruairc."

"Ua Ruairc?" The Abbot frowned. The Ua Ruairc had a reputation as mercenaries. They usually came in the night to steal cattle and to take slaves, or to rob the Abbey of its precious treasures. "How many men?"

"Don't know, Father Abbot."

"Well, try to keep them at the gate. I shall be there in a moment. And have the brothers attend – but, gently; we do not want to alarm our visitors; just a small show of unity." He turned to Alex. "Forgive me; I must see what they want. The Ua Ruairc possess little patience. We shall continue our conversation later. In the meantime, Brother Oswald, perhaps the Mistress Alex would care to enjoy the warmth and hospitality of our kitchen."

Alex and Brother Oswald left the chapel and continued around the perimeter of the Abbey, en route to the Kitchen. Before they arrived, they passed one of the square, steep roofed buildings.

"This is our library," explained Brother Oswald.

"Nice," said Alex automatically.

"The Abbey has many sacred treasures, but we are blessed with our books."

"Books are good."

"It's not easy to protect them; the Ua Ruairc, Vikings, and petty thieves are a constant nuisance. Then there is fire and neglect.

Sometimes we find a book with a nest of mice inside it. Come let me show you."

They entered the library, not large or well populated by modern standards, but at a time when every book on the shelf was written and bound by hand, the monks could not afford to buy in bulk. But also, by modern standards, the books were huge, some several feet long, all bound in dark leather, some studded with jewels.

A smaller room, reached by a ladder, and lit by candles, lay above the library.

"That is the scriptorium; much of my brothers' time is spent in there, as they copy the great works. Not just the gospels, but other books of great import."

"Sounds exciting," Alex lied.

"Come and see."

Alex's hesitation yielded to politeness, and they climbed the ladder to the scriptorium, where several monks would usually occupy their time with the books, but because of the Abbot's summons, the room had a dearth of monks. The scriptorium consisted of a few desks. On most desks lay two books: an original and a copy at various stages of completion. On the nearest desk lay a single book.

"This is the Abbey's most prized possession," whispered Brother Oswald with reverential pride. "It is the Book of St. Columkille, by his own hand, as some believe."

"Do you believe that?"

"Who can say, but it is a wondrous book. When the holy relics of Columkille were transferred here by our brothers of Iona, the Book came with them. That was over 200 years ago when the Viking raids killed many of our brothers and threatened out sanctuary. It is a miraculous book. It has survived all attempts to steal it or destroy it, both here and on Iona. We rescued it from the great fire of Abbot Cellach mac Ailello, when the Vikings plundered the Abbey; and the great flood of Abbot Ferdomnach's time. And fire again in 880 . . . and again in 927 . . . and er, 932 and 948 and 967. But then we kept it from the danger of the flame . . . until 991, that is. But that was the last fire until 1003.

"It is usually kept safe in its shrine in the western sacristy of the chapel, but just last week, thieves stole the shrine. Fortunately, in their ignorance, they believed that the jewels encrusted in the shrine were of greater value than the Book, and so they tossed it aside when they made their escape. Yet, it suffered damage at their hands, which we must now repair; and it will remain here until a new shrine is built for it."

"What's it about?"

"It is a copy of part of the *Versio Vulgata* of St. Jerome, as he translated the Testaments from the Hebrew, Greek and Aramaic."

"Of course, it is; I knew that."

"You speak Latin?"

"Is that the same as German? I speak a little German, *eins*, *zwei*, *drei*."

"Perhaps you will know it better as the gospels of the four Evangelists?"

"Evangelists?"

"The great saints: Matthew, Luke, Mark, and John. Are you not of the Christian faith, Mistress Alex?"

"Oh, those evangelists, yeh, sure."

Alex politely glanced at the Book, then suddenly transfixed, gazed ever closer. She exhaled. She had never seen anything like it: She wondered if she dared to touch it. She could not tell whether the Book was real or an extension of her dream? Her finger caressed the page open to her, beautiful beyond her ability to describe it. She turned the page to find another, even more beautiful, she turned again, and again.

Every page flowed with designs and bright colors, faces, icons and animals, fantastical beasts and heavenly creatures knotted with intricate maze-like patterns which seemed as the outward manifestation of an invisible and infinite mystery. Even the text, each letter painstakingly crafted, seemed more art than literature. Alex found it hard to believe that the hand of man could produce such a book. It mesmerized and enticed her. The Book sang to her. Jackie would have said that it was a work of the fairies.

Then angry shouts from below broke Alex's spellbound state. Brother Dúngal popped his head over the ladder.

"Vikings, Brother, Vikings! We are overrun, come quick, come quick!"

"Come, Mistress Alex," ordered Brother Oswald. "We must get you to safety."

Brother Oswald roughly grabbed Alex and handed her to Brother Dúngal. She missed a rung on the ladder, but Dúngal caught and steadied her, and down they climbed. Brother Oswald followed with the Book of St. Columkille.

Once more on the ground floor, they went to exit the library, only to come to an abrupt halt at the horrible sight of carnage and mayhem: of monks who fled in every direction, chased, and tormented by men who brandished swords, clubs and axes. Some monks lay prostrate on the ground, struck down from blows received from their attackers, others fell to their knees to pray for deliverance, but most simply panicked and blindly fled in a desperate attempt at self preservation. A monk ran towards the library with a Viking in pursuit. In the monk's eyes she saw the look of abject terror, of a man on the precipice of existence. In the Viking's eyes she saw madness; no reason, no mercy, no humanity, just bloodlust.

"Not this way, not this way," begged Alex inwardly.

The monk halted and hesitated for a split second; and that proved enough time for the Viking to catch him and strike.

Alex raised her hand to her mouth to stifle a scream. The Viking moved away.

In spite of the apparent randomness of the proceedings, the Vikings acted as one, with organized precision. They corralled the monks, as if they herded sheep and drove them ever closer towards the pen. They did not intend to kill but to capture; yet they didn't mind if they caved in a few heads or stabbed a few hearts to ensure that their intentions were understood and unopposed.

"You must hide," cried Brother Oswald, grabbed Alex's hand, and retreated back inside the library. He let go of Alex and pushed at a desk. Once he had shifted the desk a few feet, he pulled at a slab of stone on the ground.

"Help me, Brother," he pleaded with Dúngal, and jointly they lifted the stone to reveal an underground room. "Quickly, inside!"

Alex obeyed and entered the cellar. Brother Oswald dropped the stone back on the opening, only to raise it again and toss the Book down to her. The Book hit her on the shoulder.

"Ouch!" she cried. "Watch what you're . . ."

The slab dropped a second time and an inky, black gloom immersed Alex. She could not see so much as the end of her nose, but she could hear, and that was worse. In the darkness, every sound was amplified and sharp; the cries and screams of the monks, the terrible curses and laughter of the Vikings. She knew that above her head, all was confusion and chaos. The screams echoed around the cellar.

"This would be a good time to wake up," she howled as she rubbed her bruised shoulder.

Breaking News

No child but must remember laying his head in the grass, staring into the infinitesimal forest and seeing it grow populous with fairy armies.

Essays in the Art of Writing, Robert Louis Stevenson, 1905

 **"Y**ou're pulling my leg!"

"No, I swear it's true; come look for yourself."

"A pig?"

"Yes, a pig."

"I don't know what you've heard, but we're not that gullible in Ireland," Mattie shook his head. "First the fairies, then this; now I've heard everything."

"Just come and see, please," insisted Jackie.

"Let me have a cup of tea and some toast first; don't think I can face a pig in the bedroom on an empty stomach."

Jackie fell heavily onto the kitchen chair. "Ooohh!" she added for emphasis.

"Calm down, Cousin," said Jeff, as he walked to the kitchen table with a pot of tea.

"I am calm; it's the pig that's upset."

Jeff sat down and poured tea into the cups. "Repeat it one more time, slowly," he said.

Jackie sighed. Mattie took a sip of tea. The television, tuned to the morning weather forecast, predicted a day of rain.

"Alex is missing . . . there is a pig in her bed . . . it is wearing her dressing gown . . . have I forgotten anything? No, don't think so; that's the whole story; will you believe me?"

Mattie took another sip of tea. Jackie sighed again. On the television, the weather forecast was preempted by breaking news.

"I'd like to believe you, I really would," said Jeff. "But there's just one thing about your story which doesn't add up. I don't often agree with Mattie, but I have to say this sounds like a joke. Strange sense of humor you Americans have."

"What doesn't add up? How do you know my story doesn't add up if you don't come and see for yourself?"

"Don't have to come and see – Morning, Alex. Sleep well?"

Behind Jackie, the pajama and robe wearing Alex appeared at the foot of the stairs and walked over to the pantry. Jeff and Mattie tried not to laugh. Jackie swiveled round. The television caption read, *'Live from Trinity College.'*

"Alex, what are you doing here?" cried Jackie.

"Getting a piece of soda bread, I'm hungry," replied Alex. She crossed to the table and sat down. "And thirsty; can I have some of that tea?"

Jeff poured.

"Alex, what did you do with the . . .?" Jackie began.

"Shush, Jackie," said Jeff seriously. "There's some big news on the telly."

"We report live from Trinity College," said the reporter.

"I had the strangest dream," said Alex.

"Officials confirm that the Library and the Kells exhibit are closed to all visitors."

"There were these pigs and some monks."

"And will remain closed, pending an investigation by the Gardaí."

"And one monk called Brother Oswald showed me this great big book."

"Although we cannot get anyone to go on record to confirm it."

"It was really old and beautiful and full of pictures."

"We can report, unofficially, that the Book of Kells is missing, believed stolen."

"And the funny thing is, when I woke up this morning, the book was in my bed. Jackie did you put the book in my bed?"

"Trinity has been home to the Book of Kells since 1661."

"You should see it, it's really beautiful, it looks like – it looks like that one there on the television – just like it."

Jackie, Mattie, and Jeff turned away from the television to face Alex.

"And then we were attacked by Vikings, and I had to hide . . . What? Why are you all looking at me?"

"There's a book in your bedroom like the one on the television?" asked Jeff.

"Yes, that's what I was saying. First there was this pigsty and then the monks showed me this book."

"And these . . . monks gave you the book last night?"

"Well, not exactly gave. We were being attacked by Vikings and I hid in a hole in the ground, and Brother Oswald threw the book down to me. It hurt my shoulder." Alex rubbed her shoulder. "Funny, but my shoulder really does hurt, I must have slept wrong on it."

"And the book is upstairs now in your bedroom?"

"That's what I just said. Which of you put it there?"

"And it looks just like the one on television?"

"Yes, I . . ."

Mattie and Jeff did not wait for Alex to complete her sentence. They leapt from their chairs and headed to the staircase.

"Did you see a pig?" asked Jackie.

"Yes, as I just said, when the dream started, I was in a pigsty. There were two pigs. Why?"

Jackie did not respond, but instead sprang up and ran after her cousins.

"Why is everyone behaving so strangely?" Alex asked no one in particular. She saw a pot of strawberry preserve on the table. "Oh, some toast and jam sounds good."

Alex rose from her chair and crossed the kitchen to the toaster.

Mattie and Jeff reached the bedroom; and sure enough the Book lay on Alex's bed. Jackie burst through the door.

"Oh, God, oh, God!" said Mattie.

Jackie looked around the room. "At least the pig is gone," she said.

"Will you shut up about pigs; this is serious. Jeff, what do you think? Do you think that's the Book?"

"What else could it be?" answered Jeff.

"But it can't be! Who would go to all the trouble of stealing the Book of Kells only to give it to Alex?"

"Er . . .," said Jackie.

"Shut up, Jackie, we're trying to think."

"Maybe it's fake. It has to be fake." said Jeff.

"Why would a fake Book of Kells show up here on the day the real one is stolen? That's one ginormous coincidence there."

"It can't be the real book; just look at it; the colors are too bright. That book isn't twelve hundred years old. And the real book is in four volumes. It can't be the real book."

"Er . . .," said Jackie.

"Shut up, Jackie."

"Did they say that all four volumes had been stolen?"

"I don't know."

"Er . . .," said Jackie.

"Jackie . . ."

"No, I won't shut up! Listen to me," ordered Jackie.

Jeff and Mattie stopped panicking and listened.

"That's better. Now then, let's everyone calm down," said Jackie. "If we look at this logically, there's only one, simple explanation: the fairies did it."

"That's your idea of logic, is it?" asked Mattie.

"Do you have a better explanation?"

"Yes . . . no."

"Okay, then let's all go back down to the kitchen. Jeff can make us some breakfast, and we can ask Alex what happened last night. It has to be the fairies."

"What's all this about fairies?" asked Jeff.

"Oh, that's right, you weren't there; it was just me and Mattie."

"Mattie, what's all this about fairies?"

"Jackie said she talked to the fairies last light. I wasn't sure if she was being serious, but I said we'd discuss it with you in the morning," said Mattie.

"And now it's the morning, so let's discuss it," said Jeff.

"Down in the kitchen," said Jackie. "We need to get Alex involved."

"Okay, but what shall we do about the Book?" asked Mattie.

"Leave it there, it won't disappear, but if it did, that would help." said Jeff.

"Okay, let's go down."

"Just check under the bed for pigs, first," said Jackie.

In the kitchen, Alex munched on toast. and sipped from her cup of tea. The television continued with live coverage from Trinity College, and Alex already suspected that the book in her bedroom and the book on the news were one and the same.

Jackie and the cousins returned.

"Care to share with me what this is about?" asked Alex. "And don't say it's Jackie's fault because I already know that."

Jackie and the cousins joined Alex at the table.

"We have to tell Dad," said Jeff.

"Are you mad," said Mattie. "We can't do that."

"Why not?"

"You know what'll happen: we tell Dad, he tells the Gardaí and they invite us 'round for questioning; we can't give any explanation how or why the most valuable treasure in Ireland ended up in Alex's bed; not ones to take no for an answer, Dad will stand trial, be found guilty and spend the rest of his life in prison; Mam will have to sell the Gatehouse; we'll have to leave Fethard and change our names."

"We have an explanation – the fairies did it," said Jackie.

"And they'll lock you up in an institution for the criminally insane," added Mattie.

"But you know they did," Jackie insisted.

"If the fairies did it, they can undo it."

"So, you believe me at last?"

"I don't know what to believe, but for the sake of Jeff and Alex, why don't you tell us exactly what happened last night before I found you in the pantry."

"After Alex went to bed, Lämmy appeared."

"Your toy lamb?" asked Jeff.

"No Lämmy the fairy horse."

"Fairy horse? I don't . . ."

"Just go with it," interjected Mattie. "Or we'll be here all day."

"Okay, Lämmy the fairy horse if you say so. I'm already confused, but please continue," said Jeff.

"Jackie told me that she saw the fairy horse under the Tree in the bar," explained Alex.

"Did you see it?"

"No, when I came down it vanished . . . according to Jackie. But I agreed to stay up with her last night in case it came back."

"And did it?"

"No, so I went to bed. Jackie was supposed to be right behind me."

"I was about to go up when Lämmy appeared," said Jackie. "We went down into the tunnel. It was all lit up with fairy lights and the fairies were all about; they called themselves the Tuatha Dé Danann and a woman sat on a throne under the Tree. She was called Queen Eeviin."

"Tree? Our Tree?" asked Jeff. "Are you telling me that our Tree sits on top of a fairy palace? But there's nothing down in that passage except rubble."

"They said I was a daughter of the Ua Ruairc."

"The Ua Ruairc? I've heard that name before. They were in my dream last night," said Alex.

"They said that because I kissed the Blarney Stone, they had to honor me. I just had to tell them what I wanted and claim my honor."

"I've kissed the Blarney Stone," said Mattie. "The fairies never gave me a wish."

"What did you ask for?" asked Jeff, ignoring his brother.

"I didn't - I said I wanted to think about it. Then I came up and Mattie was in the kitchen. Then I went upstairs and there was a pig in Alex's bed."

"Jackie, pigs don't just magically appear in people's beds," said Mattie. "If the fairies did it, they did it for a reason. Are you sure you didn't make your wish? The fairies can be very devious. They would try to trick you."

"No, I definitely did not make a wish. I was quite clear about that. I told them I was tired, and I'd like to . . . oh, oh no . . ."

"Oh no, what? What did you say?" demanded Jeff.

"I told them I was tired . . ."

"And?"

"I told them I needed to get a good night's sleep . . ."

"And?"

"Because I was tired . . ."

"And?"

"Because they were always singing . . ."

"And?"

"Because Alex was always texting – but I didn't make a wish, I swear."

"What did they say exactly?"

Jackie thought hard to remember the exact words. "They sang, 'Until you claim your honor, through the hours of the darkest night, we shall sing you a lullaby and you shall wake refreshed.'"

"Oh, Jackie, you idiot!" cried Mattie.

"What? What did I do?"

"What did she do?" added Alex.

"She told the fairies that you were the reason she was not sleeping well," said Jeff. "So, the fairies decided to help her out. The pig must have been a changeling."

"What's that?" asked Alex.

"Sometimes the fairies would steal a human child, usually a baby, and leave a changeling in its place."

"It's bad luck," said Mattie.

"You don't say!" said Alex. "Are you telling me that wasn't a dream I had last night?"

"I don't know. Tell us about it."

Alex recounted her adventure at Kells Abbey.

"Well, what do you think?" asked Jackie when her sister had finished.

"I think it's very bad luck," said Mattie.

"But there are some differences from the changeling stories that I've heard," said Jeff. "For a start, Alex was freely returned to us. 'Through the hours of the darkest night.' Whatever the spell, it only lasted the night. Usually with changelings, you're either stuck with them or you have to force the fairies to return the human."

"And now we're stuck with the Book of Kells," said Mattie. "What are we going to do about that?"

"I don't know. Did the fairies plan that Alex would bring it back or was it an accident?"

"Are you saying that I really was at Kells Abbey, and it really was the year of our Lord, 1014?"

"Could be," said Jeff.

"But there were Vikings, running around and killing people. I could have been killed," said Alex.

"Not necessarily," said Jeff. "You said everyone spoke English? They certainly wouldn't have done in 11th century Ireland. There's got to be some fairy magic in that . . ."

"Or a Babel fish," said Jackie.

". . . The fairies may have protected you."

"Is that a good thing?" asked Alex.

"It's just like *Back to the Future*," said Jackie. "What did the Ua Ruairc look like?"

"I don't know if I even saw them. What does it matter?"

"It matters because apparently the Ua Ruairc are our ancestors. This is heavy. Let's see if any family members have vanished from any photographs, because if you accidentally killed one of them, we might all disappear in a rip in the space-time continuum."

"It wasn't me doing the killing - Oh, God! Those poor people: I saw them getting killed. I think I'm going to throw up." Alex slumped in her chair.

"Show me this fairy palace." Jeff stood up.

"It won't be there," objected Jackie.

"Still . . ."

The four cousins walked to the pantry and descended to the tunnel. As Jackie predicted, no entrance to the fairy palace appeared and nothing flew in the air except for some dust.

"Told you," said Jackie.

They returned to the kitchen.

"So, what are we going to do, Jeff?" asked Mattie.

"Why do I have to be the decision maker?" replied Jeff.

"Because you're the oldest."

"That's no reason."

"What shall we do about the Book?" asked Alex.

"Best not do anything for now, except hide it."

"Shouldn't we just dump it somewhere, so the Gardaí can find it and return it to Trinity College?" asked Mattie.

"If the fairies did arrange for Alex to bring it back from the 11th century, they might not take too kindly to that. And as long as we've got it and not them, it might make for a good bargaining tool. Besides, we'll need to wait for night fall before we try to move it; we don't want to be caught red-handed with it. Alex, is there some place you can put it for now? We wouldn't want Mam or Dad to stumble across it."

"My suitcase; I'll put it in there," replied Alex.

"And then what?" asked Mattie.

"And then we have a soccer match."

"This is no time for soccer," objected Alex.

"We have to act normally. I don't think we can do anything else until tonight. Maybe then, the fairies will contact Jackie again. If not, we can spend the day thinking about how best to get rid of the Book. Jackie, you said you can hear the fairies singing. Can you hear them now?"

"Yes, I'm surprised that no one else can hear them."

"What are they singing?"

"I don't know, but they sound more cheerful than they did last night."

"They're up to something," said Mattie.

"No kidding, Sherlock," said Alex.

On the soccer pitch, beside the youth centre, a few lads of Mattie's and Jeff's age kicked a ball back and forth amongst themselves. As their manager, who had the key to the changing room, had not yet arrived, they wore street clothes. One player, a short but stocky boy called Andy, and whose body seemed to consist entirely of neck muscles, yelled insults at another boy named Tommy, who seemed the fragile and awkward male counterpart to Jackie.

"Come on, Tommy, run for God's sake," yelled Andy. "It's called a football, try kicking it sometime, preferably to one of your teammates."

Andy kicked the ball chest-high at Tommy, who flinched before the impact, and the ball hit his shoulder instead, and then bounced away from him and off the pitch.

"Go get it, idiot," yelled Andy.

Tommy ran to retrieve the ball. It bounced towards the path between the pitch and the changing room, where Mattie brought it under control and nonchalantly flicked it up to his knee, where he bounced it a few times before he caught it. Tommy arrived, out of breath.

"Hi, Tommy," said Jeff. "Remember what I said, control the ball with your chest to take the speed off it."

"Hi, Jeff, Mattie, yes, sorry, I, er, yes, sorry," said Tommy.

Mattie handed the ball to Tommy. "Go get 'em, tiger," he said.

Tommy turned and trundled back on the pitch.

"Come on Tommy, we're waiting," yelled Andy. "We haven't got all day; kick it."

Tommy dropped the ball and attempted to kick it to Andy. It came up several yards short, but Andy didn't react: Alex and Jackie had caught his attention.

"Look, boys, cheerleaders," he cried. "Jeff has found us some cheerleaders."

"Who's that?" whispered Alex.

"That's Andy Brennan," whispered Jeff. "He's probably going to walk over here and insult you. Don't take it personally; he does that to everyone."

"Inferiority complex, eh?"

"Don't think so; he's just a bit of a bully; likes to wind people up; just ignore him."

"What if I was to just kick the bully out of him?"

"Can you wait until after the match? We need him at left-back."

"It all depends on what he says next."

Andy swaggered to the side of the pitch.

"Hello, Girls," he said. "What you doing hanging around with these two losers?"

"Hello, Andy," said Jeff. "How's that knock you picked up in the last match?"

"Fine, Jeff, just fine. There'll be a few more with knocks today when the whistle blows."

"As long as it hasn't slowed you down; you seemed to be a yard or two off the pace at the end of the game, last week; and I hear their winger has some speed about him."

"Don't worry about me; that winger ain't getting 'round me today. After all, have to show the girls what a real player looks like; none of that tippy-tappy stuff what you and Mattie play."

"Cut it out, Andy. You'll do the team no good if you get a red card."

"Best behavior, I promise," Andy put his hand on his heart. "Wouldn't want to upset the girls; they'd probably faint at the sight of blood."

"Have you ever seen an axe split a man's head in two?" Alex asked as sweetly as if she merely enquired whether Andy preferred chocolate or vanilla ice cream.

"Have I what?" said Andy.

"The thing is, it doesn't look anything like it does in the movies; all those special effects and fake blood, not at all like the real thing."

"If you say so."

Jackie recognized her sister's methods, of how she would draw her victim near before she lashed out. Jackie had witnessed it many times. She knew that she had to interject before the volcano in Alex erupted.

"Hello, Andy, I'm Jackie," she breathed and slowly raised a hand for Andy to take.

"Er, hello," said Andy, caught off-guard by Jackie's engaging smile.

"Don't mind Alex, she just has a weird sense of humor."

"I like a girl with a sense of humor."

"And I like a boy with . . ." started Alex.

Jackie silenced Alex with a glance and pulled Andy closer. "How did you know I was a cheerleader?" she whispered.

"Well, er," blushed Andy.

"Is it the long blond hair?"

"Er."

"Or the American accent?"

"Er."

"Or is it because . . ." She leaned closer.

"Hello, Boss." interrupted Mattie.

Andy snatched his hand away and took a step back, as if he suddenly remembered the story of the frog in hot water.

"Mattie, boys, why are you all standing around? Come on, we have a game to win," said the man who had just come round the corner, and who went by the name of Ardan Fennelly.

"Can't get changed, the door is locked," sneered Andy, as he regained his sense of superiority.

"Less of your lip, Brennan," said Fennelly, as he removed the padlock from the changing room doors. "Come on boys," he yelled to the players on the pitch. "Team talk."

As Tommy and the other boys walked from the pitch, a bus pulled in to the car park and unloaded its passengers from Cork; the opposition had arrived. A car, which was already parked when the cousins arrived, also unloaded its one passenger - the referee. The opposition and referee walked towards the changing room.

"They're here," said Fennelly. "Come on, Jeff, let's get changed."

"We have to go and get changed," said Jeff to Alex and Jackie. "Have a seat." he pointed to the wooden bench which stood outside the changing rooms.

"Aren't you going to get changed as well?" asked Andy as he entered the changing rooms. "Into your cheerleading uniforms. Don't forget the pom-poms."

"Give us an F, give us an A," sang Jackie. "Give us a T, give us an H - E - A - D."

"That's not how you spell *Fethard*," said Mattie.

"We know," said Alex.

Had the sisters ever felt the least bit interested in sport, the game would still have disappointed them. Compared to US sports events, the game lacked pizzazz, showmanship, and any attempt at interaction with the fans. But that didn't seem to matter, for there were no fans. There was no stadium for the fans. There were no cheerleaders or marching bands; just the players, the referee, and the two managers, who did double duty as linesmen. Behind each manager stood the few players not selected to start the game. Alex and Jackie were the only spectators apart from a woman who observed the game for a time from the hill opposite.

"Can't even get a hot dog," complained Jackie.

Alex shrugged in agreement.

On the pitch, the ball moved between the two teams and ended up in the net occasionally. The managers yelled at the players. The players argued with the referee. Jeff, who wore the captain's armband, yelled at his teammates. Mattie, on the wing for his team, seemed to fair better than his counterpart did against Andy, who managed to avoid the dreaded red card, but also failed to draw blood.

The managers made changes; players went on the pitch; players came off the pitch. Tommy stood behind Fennelly and did not participate in the game, except to retrieve the occasional, wayward ball which came near to him. And as far as the sisters were concerned, the whole thing took far too long.

In fairness to the sisters, they did have other things on their minds. They had spent the match deep in conversation about the fairies and the Book of Kells, and what to do about both.

"What's going on, Jackie?" asked Alex. "Ghosts, elves, vampires . . . and now fairies. Why are we so popular with the supernatural all of a sudden?"

"Don't know. Maybe we're on some sort of magic social network, like Facebook for the paranormal."

"I don't remember adding friends. Remember Sergio said that we had a gift," said Alex, referring to an earlier encounter with an elf.

"The gift of revelation, whatever that is."

"I wish we didn't have it; it's scary. I just want to be normal."

"I could ask the fairies to take away the gift; I could wish for that."

"Something to consider. Had you decided what you wanted?"

"I thought about world peace, but everyone does that, it's so passé."

"Just be careful. You asked for a good night's sleep and look where that got us."

"We'll talk to the fairies tonight and get it all sorted out."

The referee blew the final whistle, and the players shook hands.

"Good work," yelled Fennelly, as the teams walked from the pitch and to the changing rooms. "But sloppy at times. You almost let them pinch it at the end. I want everyone here tomorrow at six o'clock for a practice session."

"Who won?" asked Jackie,

"We did," said Mattie. "Didn't you watch?"

"Were we supposed to watch?" asked Alex. "Sorry."

While Aunt Róisín and Uncle Bob pulled pints in the bar for the locals, the four cousins occupied the kitchen and made plans; or rather, didn't make plans, for they couldn't think of a single solution to their problem. Their mood fell to the morose. Even Jeff's excellent dinner of game hens in Mead failed to lift their spirits.

On the television, the story of the theft of the Book of Kells from Trinity College continued to dominate all channels, accompanied by everything that the sisters had never wanted to know about the Book: its creation, its removal from Kells to keep it from the clutches of Oliver Cromwell, its separation into four volumes from its original single form.

When closing time came, and Uncle Bob locked the pub door, the cousins made no pretense of retiring to bed, believing instead that to stay up together would rouse less suspicion. The senior O'Rourkes shrugged their shoulders, considered it normal teenage behavior, and let them get on with it.

And after some time, when the absence of light and sound from above them suggested that the senior O'Rourkes slept, they moved to execute a plan which they hadn't made. Nothing more than a suggestion to find the fairies came to mind; and so they went to the pantry and descended to the tunnel.

Jackie warned the others that she didn't think the fairies would appear if they all . . . if any of them but her . . . went down to the tunnel. She insisted she would go alone. They insisted she would not. They outnumbered her 3 to 1 and so carried the day, but they agreed to let her go first, and present a friendly face. Jeff followed next, and Mattie and Alex brought up the rear.

And as Jackie had predicted, no fairies occupied the tunnel, and no magical portal to the fairy palace had opened.

"Do you think we need Lämmy to show us the way?" asked Alex.

"What? Is he some kind of spirit guide?" laughed Mattie.

"Don't mock," warned Jeff. "We don't want to upset them."

"They won't come out with everyone here, I just know it," said Jackie.

"Well, I'm open to suggestions," said Mattie.

"Jackie, what do you think we should do?" asked Jeff.

"We should go sit under the Tree and wait for them to contact us," answered Jackie.

"Okay, Alex, back up," said Mattie. "Alex? . . . Alex? . . . She's gone!"

Jeff and Jackie turned quickly.

"She was right here," said Mattie. "She was right next to me."

On the tunnel floor, the pale blue light of Alex's phone added little to the illumination of the area. Jeff picked it up. A surprised and confused mouse scurried away into the darkness.

"Oh, no, not again," said Jackie.

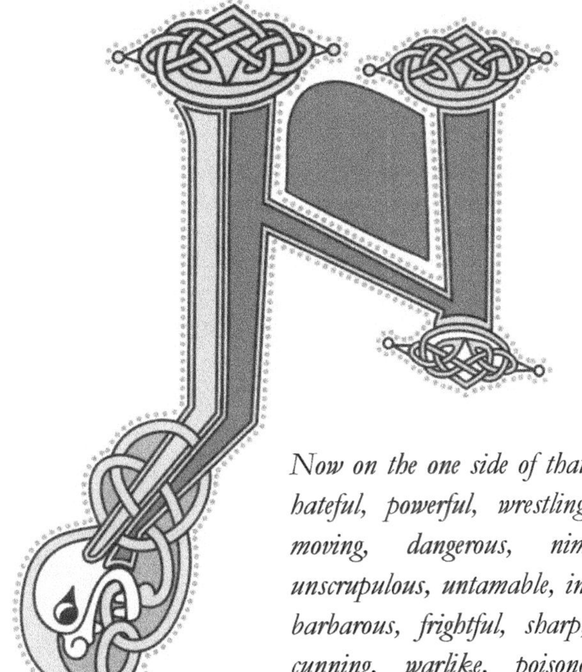

Vikings

Now on the one side of that battle were the shouting, hateful, powerful, wrestling, valiant, active, fierce-moving, dangerous, nimble, violent, furious, unscrupulous, untamable, inexorable, unsteady, cruel, barbarous, frightful, sharp, ready, huge, prepared, cunning, warlike, poisonous, murderous, hostile Danars; bold, hard-hearted Danmarkians, surly, piratical foreigners, blue-green, pagan; without reverence, without veneration, without honour, without mercy, for God or for man.

Cogadh Gaedhel Re Gallaibh:
(The war of the Gaedhil with the Gaill)
Or
The Invasions of Ireland by the Danes and Other Norsemen

From *the Book of Leinster*, circa 1160,
English translation by J. H. Todd, 1867

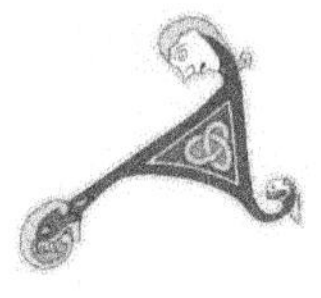 **A**lex could not survey her surroundings, the complete absence of light made that impossible, but she knew exactly where she was; she had returned to the cellar under the library of Kells Abbey. And this time she knew that it was not a dream.

Above her, beyond the stone ceiling and trap door, she expected to hear the cries of the monks and Vikings, and she braced herself for the horror to wash over her. But all remained chillingly silent and that was unbearably worse, as if nothing lingered above the cellar except death; as if hope lay in the agonized cries, even of the tormented, and all hope had perished.

She dared not move, afraid that any movement would result in contact with the unknown. She dared not take a breath, afraid that the sound of even the smallest activity would call the Vikings to her. She wondered if those buried alive felt this way.

Then she heard the grating of the trap door as someone pulled it open, and a shaft of light hurt her eyes. A man with long blond hair and an equally long blond beard, parted in the middle, thrust his head into the opening.

"The princess is here," cried the man. "We've found her."

He leaned forward. Alex saw red splashes of blood on his face and beard. He offered her his hand to pull her from the cellar. She tried to shrink back to the darkness, but only found the damp wall of the cellar.

"Be calm, Princess," said the man. "You are safe now." He called again. "She's here; tell Prince Oleif that we've found her. She's alive."

"No need for a messenger, Snorri," said Prince Oleif, as he entered the library. "I would think my father back in Dublin heard you." He peered into the cellar at Alex. "But he is correct, Princess, you are safe. Please come out of that hole."

Alex shook her head. Prince Oleif frowned then nodded to Snorri, who quickly dropped into the cellar and returned with the belligerent Alex draped over his shoulder.

"See what else the monks have hidden down there," ordered Prince Oleif.

A third Viking dropped to the cellar floor. The flicker of his torch showed an empty room.

"Nothing," said the third Viking. "Not even a jug of water. The princess would have starved to death down here had we not found her."

"Come on up then," said Prince Oleif. "Snorri, you can put the princess down now."

"Glad to," replied Snorri. "For a girl, her fists break as strong and sharp as the waves over the dragon's head when the longship strives against the tide." He pulled Alex from his shoulder and planted her feet back on the ground. "There, Princess, no harm done."

Alex glowered.

"Don't mind Snorri," said Prince Oleif. "He has an affinity for words. He fancies himself a poet. How is the saga coming?"

"I have 30,000 words so far," replied Snorri. "It would be done now if it wasn't for these constant interruptions. I can never find the time to write."

"He's writing an epic tale of worthy adventure and noble deeds," explained Prince Oleif to Alex. "What's it called again?"

"*The Saga of the Voyages of Skidbladnir and the Sons of Ivaldii from Asgard to the Edge of the World* . . . that's just a working title, of course - Snorri Sturluson at your service, Princess." He bowed to Alex.

Alex glowered still.

"I don't think she likes writers," laughed Prince Oleif. "Anyway, we must get you to Dublin, Princess."

"Stop calling me, Princess," objected Alex.

"I don't know if we can make it back before night fall," objected Snorri.

Prince Oleif ignored Alex to consider Snorri's objection. "Well, I don't fancy spending the night here. We'll have to fight the Irish every step of the way back to Dublin if word gets out that we're so far from home with such a meager show of arms."

"And we'll get hacked to pieces if we try to move in the dark. The Irish will just sit in the treetops and pick us off one by one. We won't be able to strike back if we can't see them. The princess will be safer if we wait until dawn."

"I'm not a princess," objected Alex.

"Of course you're a princess," argued Prince Oleif. He looked at Alex, still dressed in the jeans and sweatshirt which she wore when she stood next to Mattie in the tunnel. "But what are you wearing? Those are not the robes of a Viking princess. Why do you wear trousers?"

"I told you I'm not a princess," objected Alex. "You've obviously mistaken me for someone else."

"Even dressed as a boy, who else could you possibly be but Princess Estrid, daughter of Sweyn Forkbeard, King of Norway?"

"As I said, you're mistaken."

The prince tried to disarm Alex with his best smile, a tilt of his head and a raised eye brow. As his clothes and body still carried the blood stains of his victims, it didn't have the effect he sought.

"Come now; longships reach Dublin with news that the ship of Princess Estrid, daughter of Sweyn Forkbeard, became separated from their company during a storm and has landed to the North," explained the prince. "I am dispatched to find her and provide an escort to Dublin. I am told that she is beautiful; and even by Viking standards, you are beautiful. She has long golden locks; you have long golden locks."

"Coincidence."

"And the clasp on your waist? The insignia of the Royal House of Gorm, is that a coincidence?"

"What clasp?" Alex looked down. "You mean my belt buckle? No, that's . . . that's just a belt buckle; I got it in Fethard."

"You stole it?"

"Of course not."

"Princess, I understand. You've had a long voyage from Norway. And then to be attacked by these savages and thrown into a pit without food or water. You are tired and confu . . ."

"Why does everyone think I'm tired and confused?"

"And perhaps you received . . ."

"A knock on the head? No!"

"Be that as it may, Snorri is correct; we should not risk moving you tonight. We shall camp here at the Abbey and move with the rising sun." He turned to Snorri. "How many of the monks are dead?"

"Too many for the sake of commerce," replied Snorri. "I told you not to bring the Berserkers; they're more trouble than they're worth. Stark raving mad; they even killed a couple of our own men. We should save the Berserkers for when we have a real battle, not this harvesting."

"Father would insist. And how many escaped?"

"More than half; they scurried away faster than rats; and the place is more holes than walls. A few are trapped in the round tower. We need a ladder to reach the door, but we'll prize them out eventually. Do you fear a counterattack?"

Prince Oleif shook his head. "The monks won't come back until after we leave, but they will alert the Irish. Still, can't be helped. Wash down the Berserkers, make sure we have plenty of hostages, and double the watch. But I don't think that the Irish will try an assault on the Abbey; that's not their style. Hopefully, we can be out of here and halfway back to Dublin before they've had a chance to organize. In the meantime, Princess, we shall make you comfortable."

Prince Oleif took Alex's hand and escorted her from the library to the square. For the first time she attached images to the sounds she had heard while in the cellar; and the images did not allay her fears. Around the square lay dead and dying monks. In the center of the square before the chapel, the monks who remained alive, and had not managed to escape, sat on the grass, their hands bound and their bodies linked by strong rope, so that they could only move as a single unit. Vikings, fifteen or so, stood watch over them, axes at the ready, just in case. Some of the outer buildings smoldered with red embers. Whatever sensations Alex felt at that moment, comfortable was not amongst them.

"Put those fires out," ordered Prince Oleif. "The smoke can be seen from miles away."

"Let them see and thus live in dread of the Viking firestorm," said Snorri.

"Oh, that's good, Snorri. You should put that in your book."

Alex's eye searched the living and the dead for Brother Oswald. As all the monks appeared alike, to spot him proved no easy matter and she feared for his safety; but eventually she saw him, bound, and roped with the other prisoners, but alive.

The sacristy, which the prince had requisitioned for his own purposes, blazed with the light of a thousand candles, which the prince believed made the room a little more cozy and romantic.

A table lay festooned with the remnants of a meal, large enough to feed a party of twenty. It had served only for the prince and Alex. And Alex had refused to eat.

The prince tried to make small talk.

"I am sorry, Princess, that you did not see me at my best earlier, but as you see, a scrub of the face and a comb through the beard works wonders. And I am sorry we could find nothing suitable for you to wear."

"I'll survive," said Alex.

"I have sent scouts to find the longship which brought you to Ireland, but without any guidance from you as to where you landed, they don't have much to go on. Are you sure you can't remember?"

"Positive."

"And your entourage and baggage, likewise no sign of them. How you came to be separated from them is a mystery."

"Complete mystery," agreed Alex.

"And I notice that you have no appetite, Princess. Does the food not agree with you?"

"I'm not hungry."

"We can provide better when we get to Dublin. When did you last eat?"

"Jeff made some game hens last night . . ."

"Last night? Who is Jeff?"

"He's . . . my cook."

"Your cook? So, you do remember something; that is good. Your full memory will return, I am sure. Your mind is still troubled by your ordeal. I know for myself that battle can be quite stressful.

My comrades get a little boisterous after a battle; drinking and womanizing, but I always like to relax after a good fight. Say what you like about the monks, the bath house here is first class. There's nothing like a good, hot bath after a workout, don't you agree?"

"Is that what you call it?" scowled Alex.

"Estrid – may I call you Estrid? War is a dirty business; as the daughter of Sweyn Forkbeard, you of all people should know that; but that doesn't mean we can't be civilized about it."

"I don't think it's civilized to slaughter defenseless monks."

"Oh, hardly slaughter; just enough to win the day and not a single monk more. They're worth more to us alive than dead, believe me, with the prices that slaves are fetching today. Some of them lost a limb or an eye, and that will have an adverse effect on their resale value, but our medics will make sure they don't die. It's amazing what can be done with a bit of hot iron."

"Hot iron?"

"To cauterize the wounds."

"Uggh.!"

"Oh, don't say that! Uggh is such an ugly word to fall from such beautiful lips. I must confess before I saw you, I did fear the worst."

"What do you mean, *fear the worst?*"

"Well, you know what it's like with these arranged marriages; it's easy to get stuck with a pig-in-a-poke – Oh, I hope you don't think I'm a pig-in-a-poke?"

"What do you mean, '*arranged marriages?*'"

"You really have lost your memory, haven't you? It's as if you're from a different world altogether."

"Yes, perhaps you can enlighten me?"

"Your father, Sweyn Forkbeard, King of Norway, and my father, Sigtrygg Silkbeard, King of Dublin and York, arranged our marriage, to strengthen the alliance between the two royal houses. You have been sent here as my bride. When we get back to Dublin, we shall be married. You cannot remember any of this?"

Alex shook her head in shock.

"It is upsetting that you cannot remember. If ever I catch the bandits who did this to you; they took your memory; they took your baggage and servants; they even took your engagement ring."

"Engagement ring?"

"The one which our ambassador carried to Norway; you should have worn it on your finger. It's a shame; I worked with the jewelers myself to design it. Oh, wait though, I've just thought of something. Here."

Prince Oleif took a ring from one of his own fingers, took Alex's left hand and placed the ring on her third finger.

"This is the Ring of Thor; it is quite precious, and its history is long and full. Snorri has a chapter devoted to it in one of his sagas. Oh, I know it's too big for such a delicate hand, but . . ."

"It's stuck," cried Alex, as she tried desperately to pull the ring from her finger.

"You cannot remove it?"

"It's stuck," repeated Alex.

"Then it is meant to be."

"Oh, God!" moaned Alex. "Oh, God, oh, God, oh, God!"

"You are moved? I am touched also. Praise Thor."

"Oh, God!"

"You are overwhelmed. It's been a long day for all of us, and we have an early start in the morning. I suggest that you get some rest, and you'll feel better in the morning. I know the quarters we found for you are unsatisfactory for one of your position, but it's just for one night."

"I'll manage."

"That's the spirit. I'm sorry that your handmaidens cannot attend."

"Oh . . . wait a minute . . . my . . . handmaidens . . . yes . . . I forgot about those. On second thoughts I can't manage. I need an attendant."

"Estrid, that is not work fit for a Viking. I don't think any of my men would . . ."

"No, that's okay. Just some light work, fetching water, that kind of thing. Definitely not work for a Viking. A monk will do."

"I shall have one sent to you."

"No, let me pick. I always choose my own servants."

"Of course. Care for a stroll?"

Alex and Prince Oleif left the sacristy and walked to the square where the monks sat and shivered in the cold night air.

"Pick as many servants as you need," encouraged the prince.

"Oh, I only need one," said Alex. "Er, let me see . . . him, that one there."

"Bring that man to us," ordered the prince.

A Viking guard walked among the monks, who shrank away as far as their bonds would allow. The Viking wielded his axe and severed the rope which linked the chosen man to the others.

"On your feet," growled the Viking.

The monk obeyed.

"Come here, man," said the prince. "Is this the one, Princess? Is he suitable?"

"What's your name," asked Alex.

"Brother Oswald," replied Brother Oswald.

"He's not much to look at," said Alex. "But he'll do. Come with me, Brother Oswald. Goodnight, Oleif."

"Goodnight, Estrid," said the prince. "Sweet dreams."

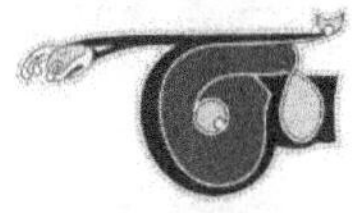

In the hut which the Vikings had selected for Alex to spend the night, she spoke to Brother Oswald.

"Are you hurt?" she asked.

Brother Oswald did not answer.

"Look, this is no time to become a trapeze artist or whatever it is those monks are called who have a vow of silence. I'm trying to save your life."

"I am not hurt, Lady Estrid."

"My name is Alex."

"But the Vikings called you . . ."

"Forget what the Vikings called me."

"As you wish, My Lady."

"Don't go all medieval on me; it's not my fault the Vikings have attacked the Abbey."

"On the contrary, My Lady, the Vikings came here in search of you."

"Call me Alex, please."

"Yes, Lady Alex."

"I'm not one of them, honestly. I'm not a Viking, no matter what they say."

"No, Lady Alex."

"Can't you drop the Lady and just call me Alex."

"I don't think that would be proper, Lady Alex."

"Oh, never mind. What makes you say they came here looking for me?"

"I have spoken with my fellow monks. They say that the Ua Ruairc came to the gate and questioned Father Abbot about you, whether you had been sighted or befriended by any of our order."

"Oh."

"Father Abbot did not reveal your presence to them. The Ua Ruairc are not friends of the Abbey, and not to be trusted, as we learned today to our cost. They demanded to search the Abbey. Father Abbot refused and ordered the gate barred to them. Alas, the Ua Ruairc merely acted as the agents of the Vikings. When Father Abbot refused their demands, they signaled for the Vikings to attack. I don't know how they could have arrived at the Abbey unseen, but we were not prepared."

"Why would the Vikings be looking for me? That doesn't make sense."

"Prince Oleif called you Lady Estrid."

"Yes, he thinks I'm a princess from Norway. He was sent to greet my ship and escort me to Dublin."

"Then it does seem logical that you are indeed Lady Estrid. Who else could you be? You're memory . . ."

"Please, don't start that again. There is nothing wrong with my memory."

"No, Lady Alex, but it is logical to conclude that the Vikings were at least searching for the Princess Estrid and believed her to be here. Someone must have informed them of your presence."

"I wonder who . . . I bet the fairies did it."

"Fairies, My Lady?"

"What do you think they're up to?"

"The Vikings?"

"No, the fairies, it has to be them. Who else could it be?"

"I could not say."

"Listen, I don't know how much time I have."

"I heard the guards say we must be ready to move an hour before sunrise. They want to reach Dublin . . ."

"No, not Dublin."

"Not Dublin?"

"No, I'm not going to Dublin; I'm going home."

"To Norway?"

"To Fethard."

"I am most confused."

"Just shut up and listen. You're as bad as Jackie. Any minute now, I'll probably be gone. I'm only supposed to be here while it's night."

"But this morning . . ."

"No, not night here - night in Fethard, so Jackie can get some sleep."

"Sleep, yes."

"So, when it's not night in Fethard, I'll be gone from here. But as we don't know what time it is there, I don't know how much time I have here. Understand?"

"Yes . . . no."

"Doesn't matter. What matters is how much you can tell me before I go. Jackie was supposed to talk to the fairies, but they're up to something, I just know it. Mattie said the fairies were cunning and we'll just have to be cunninger . . . is that a word? . . . never mind. Start talking"

"On what should we converse?"

Alex paused.

"No, first things first; if I just disappear, the Vikings will blame you and that's bad. They can't find you all alone. Is there a way out of here, outside the Abbey?"

"The Vikings said they would hold reprisals for any attempts to escape. I fear for my brethren."

"No, they won't do that; monks are worth more alive than dead, trust me. How do we get out?"

"The Abbey walls are manned with sentries; I do not imagine we could scale them undetected . . . If we could go unseen to the library, in the cellar . . ."

"No, that's no good, I've been down there. You'll be trapped and they'll find you."

"In the cellar is a secret door which leads to a tunnel, which in turn leads beyond the Abbey walls to the edge of the forest."

"What is it with the Irish and secret tunnels? No, that's good, the library is good."

"When I saw you earlier, when the Vikings found you, you did not possess the Book of St. Columkille. Neither did the Vikings have it. I watched the library all day. Is it still in the cellar?"

"Er, yes, I suppose it must be."

"Did the Vikings not search the cellar?"

"They must have missed it."

"That would be odd; it is a large book to miss. But still we should go that way; the Book must be preserved at all costs. But how to get there unseen?"

"You forget, I'm Princess Estrid. I can go where I please. And what I'd like now is to curl up with a good book before bedtime. You can show me to your library and help me select something." Alex moved to the door of the hut. "Come, Brother Oswald, obey your princess."

Alex strolled across the square as if she owned it. Brother Oswald trailed behind at a respectable distance. She turned the heads of a few Vikings, but none challenged her or her servant, and in a matter of moments they had entered the library. So far so good, but Alex had failed to consider the possibility that the library may have occupants.

"Princess, I thought you had retired for the night," said Snorri Sturluson. "It is late."

"Ah, yes, er . . . Snorri . . . what are you doing here?"

"It's a library; a scholar such as I seldom gets a chance to see one, what with all the pillaging. What brings Your Highness to the library?"

"I couldn't sleep. Brother Oswald was going to pick out a book for me."

"To read?"

"Yes."

"In the dark of your quarters?"

"Yes."

"By candlelight?"

"Yes. Do you have a problem with that?" She tried to sound royal and intimidating, but she felt Snorri could read her like a book.

"No, Your Highness. Prince Oleif asked me to examine the books, to see if any are valuable enough to remove to Dublin, but I'm sure he would want you to choose first."

"And are any valuable enough?"

"If we had more time, we would take them all, but it's imperative that we travel quickly and therefore lightly, with Bóruma on the march against us. Still, I had expected to find one, the Book of Columkille."

"Never heard of it."

"In Dublin, it is called the Book of Kells."

"Doesn't ring a bell."

"Perhaps your manservant knows of its location?"

"Brother Oswald, do you know what Snorri is talking about?"

"The Book of St. Columkille is usually kept in the sacristy, Princess," Brother Oswald said truthfully, as befit his vocation.

"It isn't there," said Snorri. "I already searched there. So where is it now?"

"Perhaps one of the brothers took it . . ."

"Obviously."

". . . to the library for repair."

"I've searched the library. It's not here either."

"Then . . . then . . ."

"Yes."

"Then . . . I cannot recall."

"I could jog your memory," said Snorri. He glared at Brother Oswald and stroked the handle of the axe lodged in his belt.

"Snorri, you will not harm my servant," objected Alex. "Good staff are so hard to find."

"Your Highness," Snorri answered, but his gaze remained fixed on Brother Oswald.

"Well, we shouldn't keep you, Snorri. I know you are busy looking for books and everything. Have you searched down by the pigsty?"

"Would Your Highness like me to help in the selection of your book? These monks know nothing about Viking tastes."

"No, I think we can manage, thank you. Good night, Snorri."

Snorri finally tore his gaze away from Brother Oswald and towards Alex. His hostile glare turned instantly to a friendly, but insincere, smile.

"Good night, Your Highness." He bowed and departed.

"Thought he'd never leave," said Alex. "Now, just make sure there's no one else lurking in the library."

A quick inspection showed they were alone. The entrance to the cellar remained open; the stone cover still to one side.

"It's dark down there," said Alex, stating the obvious.

"There are some candles already in the cellar, unless the Vikings have removed them," said Brother Oswald. He picked up a lit candle from a desk. "I shall go down first and light them, and then you can follow."

Brother Oswald dropped to the cellar floor, found, and lit the candles. They did not provide nearly enough light, but at least they allowed Alex to see the monk and thus avoid falling on him.

"Come on down, Lady Alex," he whispered.

Alex dropped into the cellar.

"I cannot find the Book," said Brother Oswald. "It is not here, it's not here," he panicked.

A voice came from the library.

"Your Highness?"

"Oh, God, Snorri is back," whispered Alex. "Quick, where's this passage?"

"But the Book?"

"Forget about the Book."

"But the Book?"

"Your Highness, where are you?"

"Forget about the damned Book. Where is the tunnel?"

"This way," said Brother Oswald, hurt and confused by such language coming from the mouth of a lady.

He fumbled against the west wall of the cellar and pressed stones until one clicked and a door swung open. In seconds, Alex and the monk entered the tunnel and the door to the cellar swung back in place to hinder any pursuant Vikings.

The tunnel ran about 500 yards before it emerged from the ground by a cluster of rocks and trees.

Brother Oswald extinguished the candles and peered out to the darkness. Behind him, he could see the evening lights of the Abbey. Ahead of him lay the black of the night-time forest. "All is clear, Lady Alex," he whispered.

"Watch the rabbit holes," said a voice, and a man, sword in hand, stepped from behind a tree. "Isn't that what I's said now, lads?"

"You was right, Fergal." A second man stepped out, also sword drawn. "You said they'd come this way."

Four more men appeared. They did not all have swords; two had wooden clubs with ugly, rusty nails, which protruded from the business end. The fourth man held two ropes which danced wildly, and he fought to maintain his balance; for the other ends of the ropes attached to two excited, slobbering Irish wolfhounds, both as large as the man who held them.

"Come on out, monk. Come on, don't be shy," said the man called Fergal. He flashed a smile so big it almost reflected off the steel of his sword and bounced around the trees. "Come out, little rabbit, before we's send in the pups to play with you's. Come and say hello to Fergal and the brothers Ua Ruairc."

The Rock of Cashel

Make a valiant resolution,
O handsome, active heroes,
Which way you will go to the south
Into the country of Munster of the great forts.

Caithreim Cellachain Caisil,
(The Victorious Career of Cellachan of Cashel)
Or
The wars between the Irishmen and the Norsemen
in the middle of the 10th Century

From the *Book of Lismore*, circa 1480,
English translation by Alexander Bugge, 1905

 **"S**he was right next to me," repeated Mattie.

"Well, she's not here now," grumbled Jeff.

"But she was right . . ."

"Okay, don't go on about it. Maybe Alex went back to the kitchen. Let's get back there."

They returned to the pantry stairs and ascended.

Jackie felt that they would not find Alex in the kitchen or anywhere else on the premises, and a brief search, conducted in stealth and hushed whispers so as not to disturb the adults, proved her right.

"She's not in our bedroom," said Jackie. "No pigs either, but the Book of Kells is still there."

"That doesn't sound good," said Mattie. "What shall we do now?"

"Let's go sit under the Tree," said Jackie. "But I don't think it will do any good. The fairies won't come out with you two there. You should go to bed."

"We're not leaving you alone down here," objected Jeff.

"Okay, I warned you. Prepare for a long, boring night."

After Jackie ordered them to turn out the kitchen lights, they went to the bar and sat down under the Tree. In whispered tones, they discussed their quandary, but still had no positive ideas to deal with it other than to wait and see. And once again, events confirmed Jackie's words. Nothing happened.

Mattie drifted in and out of slumber. His eyes insisted on closing and no amount of rubbing could compel them otherwise. His work rate at the soccer match had drained him and his body needed rest. Jeff, although no less tired than his brother, fought the urge to sleep and he tried heroically, through small talk, to prevent Jackie from dwelling on the fate of her sister.

But Jackie remained wide awake and listened to every sound: Jeff's voice, Mattie's heavy, regular breaths and occasional snort, the wind on the street outside, the patter of rain against the windows. But mostly she strained to hear the fairy song. It drifted in waves, as if she walked through a fog of variable density. But she could hear it and she felt the fog under her, a cloud of fairies as they moved through the tunnels below the Gatehouse, to and from the fairy palace. In ones and twos and then in groups, she felt the fairies gather beneath her, their song grew louder and stronger; and it permeated up through the Tree, from its roots to its leaves, and then floated down over her and Jeff.

"I think we should . . .," began Jeff.

Jeff did not finish his sentence. Instead, he joined his brother in the land of Nod, finally overcome by his need to rest; a desire encouraged and, Jackie suspected, facilitated by some fairy magic. She held up a hand.

"Hold that thought one second," she whispered. "I'll be right back."

She rose to her feet, walked through the kitchen to the pantry and peered down the steps to the tunnel, which now emitted a fairy glow.

"Hello, Lämmy," she said to the fairy horse. "About time you showed up. Why did you make me wait so long?"

The fairy horse turned away from her and disappeared into the tunnel. Jackie followed. The underground passages appeared as they had on the previous night, fully ablaze with fairy lights and the tiny, winged creatures which moved along them. Soon Jackie stood once more before Queen Eeviin, who again bade Jackie to sit at the foot of her throne.

"You tricked me," said Jackie.

"Who dares to feel anger at the Tuatha Dé Danann," sang Queen Eeviin in reply.

"Jackie of the Ua Ruairc," sang the fairies.

"Jackie of the Ua Ruairc is an ungracious guest," sang Queen Eeviin.

"But you tricked me," said Jackie.

"The Tuatha Dé Danann play no tricks on their guests. Our hospitality is renowned."

"Did you or did you not send Alex back 1,000 years in time to Kells Abbey?"

"Is this not what you requested of us?"

"No; I asked for a good night's sleep, that's all."

"And did you sleep well, Jackie of the Ua Ruairc?"

"That's not the point."

"We have offended you; and you have offended us with your accusation. Perhaps it would be better that you receive your honor and depart from our company. How should we honor you?"

"Oh, no, I'm not falling for that. I'm not going to ask for my wish until Alex is safe."

"Is your sister in danger?"

"You tell me - you sent her back in time."

"Only when we sing you our lullaby; as you requested and as we promised. She shall return when you are rested, as she returned earlier."

"Well, you can unpromise. I don't want Alex going back in time every night."

"The Tuatha Dé Danann cannot break an oath. To do so would cause our song to end. Would you break your oath to us?"

"What does that mean?"

"Until you claim your honor, through the hours of the darkest night, we shall sing you a lullaby and you shall wake refreshed. We had agreed. When you claim your honor, our promise will be fulfilled, and your rest will once again be your own."

"You can't just stop doing it?"

"We cannot stop our song."

"Can I use my wish to stop it? And I'm just asking here, not wishing."

"We cannot honor you in that way; to take back what was freely given is not honorable."

"Can't I just give it back to you?"

"To return a gift from the Tuatha Dé Danann is not honorable."

"Then what shall I do?"

"Request your honor as the Child of the Charm and your sister shall be returned to you."

"No, not yet . . . And another thing; why Kells Abbey? Why did you send her there?"

"One place is as good as another to you humans."

"No, it isn't. Why Kells Abbey and why 1,000 years ago?"

"A thousand years is a moment in time to the Tuatha Dé Danann."

"But not to us humans. You call me Jackie of the Ua Ruairc. Why do you call me that?"

"It is a familiar enough name."

"But there are Ua Ruairc at Kells Abbey."

"Is that so?"

"Yes, as I think you already know. Are the Ua Ruairc at Kells our ancestors?"

"If that is so, your sister should have much to discuss with them."

"Such as?"

"We cannot tell. The discourse of humans is of no concern to us."

Jackie knew that in spite of the queen's evasive answers, nothing which had happened could be called random or coincidence. Jackie guessed that the fairies searched for something; and that something must have a connection to Kells Abbey; and that the fairies had enrolled her and Alex to help find it. She pressed on with her questions.

"What if the discourse is not of humans? What if the subject under discussion is Tuatha Dé Danann?"

"Why would the Ua Ruairc talk of the Tuatha Dé Danann?"

"You tell me?"

"Humans sing of the Tuatha Dé Danann. Once they worshiped us. Still they fear us. But they sing as children. They do not comprehend us. They cannot know the Tuatha Dé Danann."

"But there are many legends about the Tuatha Dé Danann; are they not true?"

"Truth and falsehood intertwined."

"If humans did understand you, what would they sing?"

"They would sing of our glory and our fall."

"As you did yesterday."

"They would sing of our treasures, found and lost."

"Lost? Have you lost something?"

"They would sing of our battles."

"Did you lose something in battle?"

"They would sing of our betrayal."

"Truth and falsehood intertwined," chorused the fairies.

"Falsehood, betrayal, something lost, is that it?" demanded Jackie. "Something stolen from you? What was stolen? What's it got to do with Kells Abbey? And the Book; is it to do with that?"

"They would restore the honor of Prince Nuada of the Tuatha Dé Danann," sang Queen Eeviin.

"So, it has nothing to do with the Book?"

"They would sing to the Queen of Slievenamon."

"How about a straight answer? I can help if you let me. Trust me."

"Jackie of the Ua Ruairc wants our trust, yet she does not trust us," sang the fairies.

"Yes, I do!"

"There is no trust in the Ua Ruairc."

"Jackie, are you down there?"

This last voice came from the pantry, and it belonged to Jeff. In the time it took Jackie to raise her head to answer, all traces of the fairies had vanished, and she stood alone in a pitch black tunnel. Jeff flicked the switch to turn on the electric bulb and the sudden brightness hurt Jackie's eyes. Jeff and Mattie came down the stairs.

"Are you all right?" they asked her.

"Like all boys," answered Jackie. "Your sense of timing is terrible."

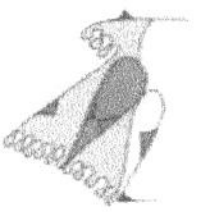

In the kitchen, Jackie found her cousins and, much to her relief, Alex, freshly returned from the 11th century just as Fergal Ua Ruairc threatened to release the hounds.

"I hope your night was better than mine," said Jackie.

"Only if your night included an axe murderer and some wolves about to bite your head off," replied Alex.

"So, you're saying your night wasn't better than mine?"

"That's what I'm saying. Still, it could be even worse, I suppose."

"How?"

"If the wolves kill me, I won't have to marry Prince Oleif." Alex held up her hand to display the Ring of Thor, still stuck on her finger.

"Who's Prince Oleif?"

"He's a Viking."

"Oh."

"Is there any soda bread left? I'm hungry."

"I'll make you both some breakfast," said Jeff. "Sounds like you need it. Then we can talk."

"But not for long," said Mattie. "Mam has a trip to Cashel planned for us, and Jeff and me need to be back in time for soccer practice."

"There's no time for soccer practice," said Alex. "Unless you can tell me everything is fixed with the fairies."

"There's always time for soccer practice."

"And is everything fixed?"

"Not exactly," said Jackie.

"What do you mean, not exactly? Did you meet with the fairies?"

"Oh, yes, been there, done that."

"And?"

"And . . . er."

"Did you tell them to stop sending me back in time?"

"Oh, yes, did that."

"And?"

"And they said they couldn't break a promise."

"But you made them, right?"

"Not exactly."

"Look, I'm not going back again; I can't. You don't know what it's like. It's horrible. I just can't go back again."

"I'm working on it, okay. Don't nag."

"Don't nag? You do realize that if I go back, there is a good chance the wolves will eat me? You do realize that, don't you?"

Jackie did not reply.

"What exactly did happen with the fairies?" asked Alex.

"Yes," said Mattie. "Tell us everything. Jeff, hurry up with those eggs."

"The fairies said they couldn't break a promise, but the spell on you would be broken once I had made my wish; at least, that's what I think they said. It's difficult; they sing in riddles."

"Then you've got to make that wish," said Alex. "I can't go back again. The fairies can't make me do that."

"Hang on a minute," said Jeff. He returned with a breakfast plate which he placed in front of Alex. "Don't be too hasty with the fairies."

"That's what I thought," said Jackie.

"But she's got to make that wish," said Alex, and she tore the corner from the piece of soda bread with her teeth.

"I think they want something," said Jackie. "I would have found it out too, except these two idiots came blundering down into the tunnel and scared them away."

"No breakfast for you," said Jeff. "If that's how you feel."

"No, sorry, it's just that I thought I was on to something when you shouted out."

"What exactly?"

"Nothing is exactly with her," sneered Alex.

"The fairies want something," said Jackie, ignoring her sister. "I think it has to do with Kells and that is why they've sent Alex there; to get it for them."

"Why me? Why don't they send you? You're their friend."

"Is it the Book? You didn't tell them we have it did you?" said Mattie. "We can't just hand over the Book of Kells to them; that would be worse than handing it over to the Gardaí."

"I asked that, but I don't think that's what they want. If they were after the Book, there would have been no reason for them to send Alex back a second time, 'cause the Book's here now, not there."

"Then what do they want?"

"I don't know. They said something about restoring the honor of Prince Nuada. Does that mean anything to you?"

"Nuada, as you already know, was a king of the Tuatha Dé Danann," said Jeff. "One of the four treasures is called the Sword of Nuada."

"Could it be they've lost it?" asked Mattie.

"They're not likely to misplace their greatest treasure, now are they? Not the sort of thing you just leave unattended."

"They sang about betrayal," said Jackie. "Maybe it was stolen from them?"

"Alex, did you happen to see a sword at Kells?" asked Mattie.

"Let me think . . . one or two, yes," said Alex between bites of breakfast. "or hundreds, mostly with blood on them. Swords, axes, daggers, spears, hammers, spiked clubs, some other things that I don't know the names of, but I know would hurt a lot."

"It all makes sense now," said Jackie.

"It does?" asked the others in unison.

"The Sword of Nuada has been stolen from the Tuatha Dé Danann. They want it back."

"What about the Book?" asked Mattie.

"Their greatest treasure has been taken from them." said Jeff. "So, they've taken ours. They want a trade. Jackie, you're a genius."

"And you're not an idiot after all," said Jackie.

"What about me?" asked Mattie.

"The jury's still out."

"But we've got the Book, not them," said Alex. "What's to stop us from just returning it to Trinity?"

"Because it wasn't taken from Trinity. It was taken from Kells a thousand years ago, by you. You have to return it to Kells."

"Read my lips, I'm not going back."

"You must."

"Plan B: You make your wish, I don't go back in time anymore, and we get rid of the Book under a bush somewhere."

"That won't work."

"Why not?"

"If you don't take the Book back, Ireland will lose its greatest treasure."

"It's upstairs in my case."

"No, it isn't. The Book in your case is not a thousand years old. The ink is still wet on the pages. It's not the same as the one in Trinity . . . well, it is the same, but it's different. It's not complete without its history. If we just handed it in, it would be dismissed as a fake."

"Not my problem. Any more bacon?"

"Alex, you have to do this."

"Okay, genius, let's talk it through, shall we? What does the Sword of Nuada look like?"

"I don't know?"

"Are you even sure that the fairies have lost the Sword?"

"No, but . . ."

"If I found the Sword, how do I get it back?"

"Er."

"And then how do I get the Book back to Kells?"

"You don't have to be so difficult, you know."

"To sum up: you want me to go back in time, where Snorri the Viking is waiting to put an axe through my head and put the episode in his latest poem, if the wolves don't eat me first. Second, if I avoid certain death, I have to find a sword, not just any sword but the one and only Sword of Nuada and bring it back, a sword which seems to have eluded the fairies for a thousand years but should be no problem for a girl from California, even if she doesn't know what it looks like. Then I must return the Book of Kells. And I have to do it all while shopping for a wedding dress for my marriage to Prince Oleif."

"Exactly."

"Why *exactly* do you say this makes sense to you?"

"Because I'm beginning to understand the fairies. I think I can tell what they are singing."

"Is that based on anything more than just a hunch?"

"No."

"I prefer my plan."

"But think of Ireland's heritage."

"Ireland has other treasures; it'll survive; which is more than I can say for me if I go back. No! Meet with your fairies, make your wish, and get me out of this mess."

"Okay, Ollie, except for the obvious."

"And what's that?"

"We've been set up; the fairies must have planned this all along. They won't just let it drop. We have to be smarter than them. This is like Luxembourg all over again."

"What happened in Luxembourg?" asked the boys.

"Don't ask," answered Alex. "Old history."

"It was just last week," objected Mattie.

"Still, let's just concentrate on now, shall we?" said Alex.

"At any rate," said Jeff. "If the fairies sent you back in time to get the Sword, that can't have been a coincidence, they did it on purpose. And it can't have been because of anything Jackie said."

"Ha, acquitted!" cried Jackie. "Oh, and another thing, can you take us to Slievenamon?"

"Not today, Mam has other plans. Why do you want to go there?"

"The fairies sang about someone called the Queen of Slievenamon. I think we should talk to her."

"You definitely don't want to talk to the Queen of Slievenamon," said Mattie.

"Why not?"

"The Queen of Slievenamon is a Banshee," answered Jeff.

Aunt Róisín entered the kitchen.

"Still eating?" she asked. "Come on, hurry up. We can't come back from Cashel until we get there."

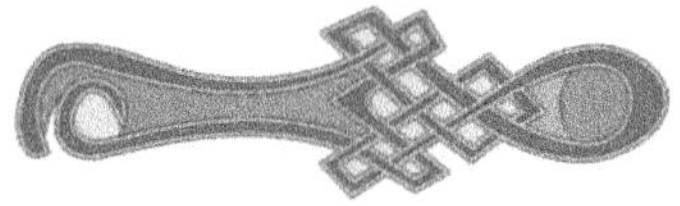

The Devil's Bit Mountain in Northern Tipperary is so called because according to legend, Satan took a bite out of it. In doing so, Satan broke a tooth, which caused him to spit out the fragment. That fragment, which came to rest 20 miles south of the mountain, is known today as *Carraig Phádraig* or the Rock of Cashel.

For crows in search of directions, Cashel is 9 miles north-east of Fethard, and a few extra yards if the crows travel by car along the R692 and through the Golden Vale, the route taken by the O'Rourkes.

And rising up from the town and the fertile plain of the Golden Vale, abruptly, dramatically and in isolation from its surroundings, stands the Rock of stratified limestone originally called *Sid-Druim*, the Fairy Hill, but over time came to be known as *Cais-il*, the tribute stone, as the tribes gathered there to pay tribute to their kings.

They parked the car, but did not immediately head towards the Rock, for Jeff insisted on a detour to Main Street so that he could purchase some items for his planned dinner. He entered a small shop and reappeared carrying a small bag, which contained a wheel of cheese.

"Cashel Blue," he explained to Alex and Jackie. "Quite possibly the finest cheese in all of Ireland. Not as sharp as a Stilton, but plenty of character and creamy. We'll have a nice watercress, pear and Blue salad this evening."

"And it's made here in Cashel?" asked Jackie.

"Ha, that's the funny thing," said Mattie. "It's made in Fethard."

"At the Beechmount Farm," said Jeff. "They also produce a very tasty cheese from sheep's milk called Crozier Blue."

"Where's Crozier?" asked Jackie.

"Not *where*, *what*. A crozier is a bishop's staff; you know like the shepherd's crook. The Crozier Blue is named for St. Patrick."

"And it's made from sheep's milk," said Mattie. "Bishop's crozier, shepherd's crook, get it?"

"Mattie, I suggest that you leave the puns to Jackie," said Alex. "She's worse at it than you."

Having filled Jeff's shopping list, they headed towards the Rock, paid the entrance fees, and entered the grounds, through the graveyard of High Crosses, to view the buildings, mostly 12th and 13th century, and once a prominent symbol of the power and dominance of the kings and Church. And even now, as its buildings lay in gothic and romantic ruin, the Rock's dominance over the landscape was unquestioned, its ability to extract tribute from its visitors undiminished.

"Centuries before the Vikings came to Ireland, the Rock of Cashel, also known as St Patrick's Rock, was the traditional seat of the kings of Munster, with Óengus mac Nad Froích converted to Christianity by St Patrick himself," summarized Aunt Róisín from the tourist guide. "St Patrick baptized him in blood by driving his crozier through the king's foot."

"Ouch!" said Jackie.

"In 1101, King Muirchertach Ua Briain donated his fortress on the Rock to the Church. It was a political move to consolidate power as much as a religious one: an alliance with the church gave him a big advantage over his rivals. They added the cathedral and chapel."

"Ua Briain? That would mean *of Brian*, right? Like Ua Ruairc is of Ruairc?"

"Technically, Ua means grandson or more liberally, descendent. Today, O'Brian and O'Rourke."

"Would that be Brian Bóruma mac Cennétig?" asked Alex.

"Brian Boru, yes. I'm surprised you know his full name. Where did you learn that?"

"So, the kings were descended from Brian Boru?" asked Alex, ignoring the question.

"No, there were Munster kings before him, but in 964, Brian's older brother, Mathgamain, seized control by capturing the Rock of Cashel. Brian became king of Cashel in 976, when his brother was murdered. Brian went on to be High King of a unified Ireland and freed the land from Viking control."

"When was that?" Alex sounded suddenly anxious.

"It didn't happen over night, but the last great battle against the Vikings was the Battle of Clontarf."

"23rd of April, 1014," added Jeff. "Good Friday."

"Where is Clontarf?"

"It's now part of Dublin, north of the Liffey, I believe. Brian Boru was killed during the battle."

"Allegedly aged 88," laughed Mattie. "When I'm 88, I'll probably be in a nursing home. Can't see me charging around a muddy field, engaged in hand-to-hand combat."

"Ironically," read Aunt Róisín. "In 1647, the town and Rock were sacked by English troops, under the command of Boru's descendent, Murrough O'Brien. It was quite a massacre. The rock was set ablaze. Depending on whom you believe, between one and three thousand were killed. No one was spared. They even smoked the priests and monks out of their hidey-holes in the chapel and executed them."

As patience was never Jackie's strong point, she did not stay to listen to her aunt. She broke away from the others. She skipped to the High Cross of St Patrick and saw the man himself, crozier in hand. She danced through the cathedral and looked up to see a canopy of clouds instead of a ceiling. She ran to Cormac's Chapel and made faces at the carved heads in the archway. She stopped at the sarcophagus, which perhaps still held the body of King Cormac. Then to Jackie's surprise, for Alex usually never made an effort to keep up with her, she found her sister at her side.

"Immense, eh, Alex?" she asked. "I bet it has a secret tunnel."

But Alex did not reply. Her face turned quite pale. Her movements slowed. Her pulse quickened. Her breath became shallow. Her eyes welled. These changes, quite small and undemonstrative, would have gone unnoticed by the others, but Jackie noticed and instinctively felt that this was more than a conventional display of Alex' dourness.

"Alex, are you okay?" asked Jackie.

Amongst the ruins on the Rock of Cashel, Alex could see the ghosts. Not real ghosts, of course, for she had met real ghosts, and they possessed more substance than those before her now. These ghosts, she knew, had no substance other than that which she gave them; they were mere shadows. They were the ghosts of dead Irish and Vikings, dead a thousand years. But it didn't matter that they died a thousand years ago, for Alex had talked to them just last night, when they had been very much alive. Was the gap between life and death really so slender? And the tightrope between the two worlds on which she now balanced, how thin was that? What if she should fall? Which way would she fall? How far would she fall?

"Alex, are you okay?" repeated Jackie.

And amongst the ghosts stood a small girl with bright red hair.

"War is coming," whispered Alex.

Somewhere in Between

The Fairies, William Allingham, 1850

"**W**hat shall we do?" Alex sighed and put down her phone. She hadn't felt in the mood to text anyone, so she had used her time to surf the internet.

"I think we're going to need a big, strong hero to rescue us," said Jackie.

"We both know that's not going to happen."

"Then it's up to us girls, as usual."

Upon their return from Cashel, the sisters rested in their bedroom at the Gatehouse. They had declined the invitation from Mattie and Jeff to watch them at soccer practice, and they had declined the invitation from Uncle Bob to sit in the bar with the locals.

Alex lay on her bed, gazed at the ceiling, and sighed again.

"This isn't one of your usual, miserable moods, is it?" asked Jackie.

"I can't go back there."

"You keep saying that."

"But I can't."

"Then tonight, we'll go with Plan B: I'll ask the fairies for my wish and stop it."

"You can't do that either."

"Why not?"

"What about the Book of Kells?"

"But this morning . . ."

"I know what I said this morning, but I've had time to think about it. And then there is this." Alex held up her hand with the ring finger.

"I don't understand?"

"I've been there twice. The first time I returned with the Book of Kells. The second time I returned with this ring. I can't get the ring off my finger. I'm stuck with it. If I don't go back, they don't go back."

"And?"

"I have these images in my head all the time of the monks getting killed; I can't get rid of them. There was one monk. He was trying to escape, and he was running straight at me. I was afraid he would lead them to me. I prayed he would go away and take the Vikings with him . . . and he did . . . and the Vikings caught him."

"That wasn't your fault."

"I prayed it would be him instead of me and they killed him."

"It wasn't your fault."

"And that's the hardest image of all to live with, but it's stuck inside my head, and I can't get rid of it."

"All this happened a long time ago. It was just a coincidence that you were there. You couldn't have changed anything."

"They were looking for me."

"Just coincidence."

"And I'm worried that in exchange for the Book and the ring and the images, I've left something behind in their place."

"What?"

"Me."

"You?"

"Jackie, I'm scared. I don't feel like I'm all here; like some part of me is back there or I'm somewhere in between. If I go back, I'll leave even more of me there. If I keep going back, eventually all of me will be there and none of me will be here."

"So, I'll make my wish."

"You can't, not yet."

"Why not?"

"Whatever piece of me is there has to come home first, otherwise I'll forever be just a shadow, like those at Cashel."

"Now you're being a drama queen."

"No, I'm serious. The Book and the ring don't belong here; and I don't belong there. We have to get it all straightened out before you make your wish. I have to give the ring back to Prince Oleif."

"You're breaking off the engagement?" laughed Jackie. "It'll break his heart. Mom has ordered the invitations."

Alex laughed too. "He's not so bad really, for a Viking. And he's actually quite good looking underneath the mud and blood."

"So, you're not breaking off the engagement? Mother can send the invitations after all."

"Stop that! Don't even joke about it. And the Book, I have to take that back. And I have to get me back."

"How do we do that?"

"I'm hoping your little talks with the fairies will give us the answer."

"At Cashel, you said war is coming. What war?"

"The Viking, Snorri, said that Brian Boru was on the march, and they were in a bit of a hurry to get back to Dublin."

"I'm sure that the Irish and the Vikings were fighting all the time."

"No, this is different. It is Eastertide in the twelfth year of the reign of the High King, Brian Bóruma mac Cennétig."

"So?"

"It's April, 1014. Any day now, the Vikings and the Irish are destined to meet at the Battle of Clontarf, the last great battle. Clontarf is in Dublin. If I go back, the Vikings will take me to Dublin. I'll end up right in the middle of that battle."

"You escaped from the Vikings."

"Only to fall into the hands of the Ua Ruairc, and they work for the Vikings."

"You can't be sure of that."

"If they don't, then they work for Brian Boru. Either way, I'm on my way to Dublin just in time to get slaughtered. I just googled the battle; many of people died that day, a lot of people."

"But you're protected by the fairies. You'll be safe."

"I'm not so sure. Back there, everyone thinks I'm Princess Estrid, daughter of the King of Norway. I googled her too. She went to Ireland and married Prince Oleif. I don't think it was a happy marriage."

"Why do you say that?"

"Because Prince Oleif died on the 23rd of April, 1014, at the Battle of Clontarf. We don't know what happened to Estrid after that. Some say she died at the prince's side during the battle."

"OMG! You can't go back."

"I have to. But the fairies don't care about me. I'm not counting on them for protection."

"Then we'd better make sure that they do care."

"What do you mean?"

"I have a wish and if we can find out what exactly they are trying to do by sending you back, then we should be able to use that to our advantage."

"Well, whatever we do, we'd better hurry, because I don't think I've got more than a day or two before all hell breaks loose."

"I think I hear voices downstairs; the boys must be back from playing with their friends. Come on, let's go down. Maybe Jeff's cooking can cheer us up."

"You shouldn't wind him up like that," argued Mattie.

"He deserved it," argued Jeff.

"But he's the boss. What if he drops you from the team?"

"He won't do that, will he? That's the whole point."

Mattie and Jeff argued about soccer. Uncle Bob and Aunt Róisín argued about a customer. And on the TV, a Gardaí spokesperson announced that their investigation had uncovered several promising leads in the case of the missing Book of Kells, and that arrests were imminent. The girls almost decided to turn around and head back to their bedroom, but they didn't.

"Hello," said Jackie. "Is this meeting open to the public?"

"Oh, hello, dear," said Aunt Róisín. "Pay no attention to us. Robert, get back in the bar and deal with it."

Uncle Bob turned to the girls. "She always calls me Robert when she's angry with me; never Bob." He smiled and left the kitchen. Aunt Róisín followed him.

"What's going on?" asked Jackie.

"Oh, nothing, just part of the usual day-to-day activities in a pub," said Mattie. "One of Dad's old friends thinks he can sponge a free drink or two."

"What about you two? Why are you arguing?"

"It's nothing," said Jeff.

"Jeff had an argument with Fennelly about Tommy Powers," said Mattie.

"Tommy? That's the one who's no good at soccer?"

"Yes, that's him."

"Why were you arguing about him?"

"It's nothing," repeated Jeff.

"We're playing the semi-final, tomorrow; got drawn at home against Limerick. Now we're in the semi, were guaranteed a medal of some sort, even if we don't win the cup."

"So?"

"So, everyone who's played in the tournament gets a medal. Everyone in the squad has played at some point, even if it was just to come on as a sub near the end - everyone except Tommy. Jeff told Fennelly that he thought Tommy should play in the semi, so he can get his medal."

"That sounds fair."

"Fair doesn't count with Fennelly; he wants to win. Can't say I disagree with him. To be honest, having Tommy on the pitch is worse than playing with 10 men."

"Winning isn't everything."

"No, it isn't," agreed Jeff.

"The thing is, it just may be everything. If we win the semi, we go to Dublin for the Final. Fennelly says there are rumors that some scouts from England are coming to watch."

"Scouts?"

"Rumors are Manchester United and Liverpool are sending scouts to watch the final. If we impress them, who knows what the future holds. Fennelly doesn't want to jeopardize that just so Tommy can hang a plastic medal around his neck. Can't say I blame him; it could mean a coaching job for him too, if we win."

"I'll make dinner," said Jeff and he moved to the pantry.

"Jeff is a bit of a musketeer," whispered Mattie. "All for one and one for all. Thing is, it's him who stands to gain or lose the most."

"How?"

"He's not only our captain; he's the best player on the team by far, perhaps the best player in Tipperary. If the scouts come, it's him they've come to watch."

"So, he should be ecstatic."

"He should be; it's the chance of a lifetime. But he wants to do right by Tommy as well."

"So, you win the semi, Tommy plays for the last minute, he gets his medal, you all go to Dublin and Jeff signs on the dotted line for Manchester United. Everybody wins, except Manchester United, of course."

"Now why didn't we think of that? Except Fennelly won't risk putting in Tommy unless we're winning by 10 goals."

"So, score 10 goals; it can't be that difficult if you have the best player in Tipperary."

"Limerick won't be an easy team to beat: they're big and physical, and they like to make things tough for their opponents. It's like playing against 11 Andy Brennans. But I like your optimism."

"It's my middle name."

Jeff returned from the pantry. "Can you believe I forgot to buy the walnuts?" he said.

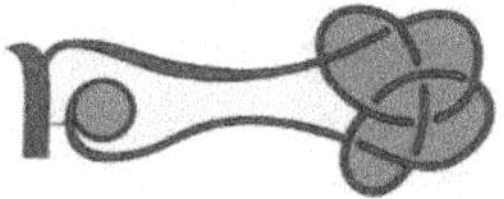

Despite the absence of walnuts, Jeff's dinner did not disappoint, but it still failed to raise their spirits. Talk around the kitchen table was muted and insipid. Aunt Róisín put this down to fatigue from a hectic touring schedule and trepidation regarding the upcoming semi-final. After dinner, the cousins sought out the companionship of the locals in the bar.

Outside the Gatehouse, the wind howled, and the rain came down in a deluge, formed miniature lakes on the road and bent umbrellas to its will. It pounded on the Gatehouse in the manner of a goon squad which demanded the expulsion of those who had taken sanctuary inside.

Even the few locals who had braved the elements and now supped ale in the bar behaved themselves more than usual; Banter was scarce, and a somber, fog-like mood lay over the Gatehouse. Uncle Bob shook his head: no one liked a quiet pub, especially not the owners.

On the TV, a government spokesperson continued to assure the public that the Book of Kells would be found at any minute, and that the Gardaí had started to conduct door-to-door enquiries. On cue, a particularly strong gust of wind knocked at the windows and made everyone jump.

"A good night for a ghost story," said Seán Murphy.

"None of that," said Uncle Bob. "The place needs cheering up."

But Jackie interjected. "Mister Murphy, what do you know of the Queen of Slievenamon?"

"The queen? Your uncle's right, best not to talk of banshees," said Seán Murphy. "On a night like this, many a fool would mistake the wind for the queen's howl . . ."

Everyone paused to listen to the wind.

". . . But it's just the wind."

Everyone felt foolish, then relaxed.

". . . Or is it?" Seán Murphy winked at Jackie and laughed. He took his pint of Irish Red, walked over to the cousins, and sat down next to Jackie.

"What's all this about the Queen of Slievenamon?" he asked. "You're here for a holiday, not a wake."

"Mister Murphy . . ." began Jackie.

"And what's with this Mister nonsense? Only the magistrates call me Mister. It's Seán to my friends."

"Seán . . . who is the Queen of Slievenamon?"

Seán Murphy sipped on his beer. "Are you sure you want to know? Wouldn't want you to have trouble sleeping."

"Don't worry about me sleeping. That's not a problem."

"Some say she's a beautiful young girl, about your age I imagine, with long flowing locks of scarlet hair. And she spends all her time, when she's not announcing death's arrival, combing her hair with a brush made from ivory and gold."

"And she lives on Slievenamon?"

"She's not a vindictive spirit, but very shy and easily startled. If you walk on Slievenamon, you may come across her. You should quietly turn around and walk away. If you surprise her, if you startle her, that's when she cries."

"Have you ever seen her?"

"Not I, but before I was a youngster . . . What's that thing you do in America? That school dance every year?"

"You mean Prom Night?"

"Yes, that's it. The tradition around here, our version of Prom Night, is that on the last day of school, the kids all climb to the top of Slievenamon for a party. There was a boy at school, a few years before my time I admit, so this is just hearsay, but there was a boy named Kevin Grogan. One year, he climbed to the top of Slievenamon with the other children. At the top, when everyone's having a good time, and Kevin and the other boys are passing 'round a bottle of illicitly gained cider, Kevin claims he can hear singing. The others don't hear it, but Kevin does. So, he leaves them and goes off to investigate. He sees a girl sat under a tree. She is gently humming a soft tune as she combs her hair. She's about his age, but he doesn't recognize her as one of the girls from town. But he's never seen anyone so lovely in all his life and he feels it only polite to say hello."

Seán Murphy took a long, steady drink from his pint and savored it.

"You just paused for dramatic effect," said Jackie.

Seán Murphy nodded. "They say the howl was heard from Fethard to Castletown. All the other children came running to find out what had caused the scream. And under the tree they found poor Kevin, dead as can be."

"Did you hear the scream?"

"As I said, before my time. Some around here says they've heard. Then again, some folks hear banshees every time the wind gets up. You hear singing, you say?"

Jackie nodded.

"It's not always wise to go in search of the song. Sometimes, it's best to walk away. The Queen of Slievenamon only cries when she is startled. Best not disturb her."

As the storm raged, the locals were reluctant to leave the warmth and safety of the Gatehouse, and Uncle Bob was reluctant to throw them out, but rules were rules, so out they went. Seán Murphy was the last to depart.

"Goodnight, Seán," said Uncle Bob. "Hurry on home now."

"Hurry I shall, Bob," Seán Murphy replied and peered out to the street. "A proper night to keep to your bed and let the storm pass. Goodnight, Mattie, Jeff. Goodnight, Young Misses. Goodnight, all."

He pulled the collar of his coat around his ears and stepped into the street. After a few paces, the sideways rain enveloped him and obscured him from view. Uncle Bob closed and bolted the front door.

"What terrible weather," said Aunt Róisín. "How about a nightcap before bed?"

Jeff went to the kitchen. He returned some minutes later carrying a tray which held six mugs of hot, steamy liquid. He put the tray down and handed two of the mugs to Alex and Jackie.

"What's this?" asked Alex.

"Hot toddy," replied Jeff.

"What's in it?"

"Tea, honey, lemon, some other ingredients."

"What other ingredients?"

"Best not ask." Jeff smiled. "Old secret family recipe."

Aunt Róisín also smiled. "I think I'll take mine to bed and curl up with a good book. Thank you, Jeff. Bob, are you coming up?"

"Be right there," said Uncle Bob. "Boys, make sure everything is locked up and switched off."

"We will," they said.

"Goodnight then."

"Goodnight," echoed the cousins.

They waited for the noise from above to subside before anyone spoke.

"Now what?" asked Mattie.

"Now we wait," said Jackie.

"Again? That didn't get us very far last night."

"Aagghh! Shut up" snapped Alex. "You don't have to wait; you can always go to bed."

"Sorry. I wasn't criticizing; I was just saying."

"Sorry. I wasn't criticizing either. I'm just anxious. Good hot toddy, Jeff, whatever's in it."

"Thanks. I'll just go and make sure everything is locked out back. Mattie, come and help."

"I'll . . ." began Mattie.

"Come and help," Jeff insisted. He nodded sideways at the girls.

"I'll come and help," said Mattie.

"We'll be in the kitchen if you need anything," Jeff said to the girls.

The sisters nodded in silence and sipped their drinks. When they were alone, Jackie spoke.

"If you don't want to go back, I can make my wish. You might have to go back for a little while, just until the fairies appear, but I can make the wish real quick and get you back."

"What will you wish for?"

"I've decided on a pony."

"Let's go sit under the Tree."

They took their drinks with them to the Tree and sat down on the floor. Alex held her drink in her right hand. Jackie held her drink in her left hand. With their other hands they held each other.

"Please don't wish for a pony."

"I was just kidding . . . What do you think Jeff put in the toddy?"

"Don't know, but it's good."

"Sort of makes you warm inside. That'll help."

"Help what?"

"On a night like this."

"What do you mean?"

"When it's cold and wet on the outside, it'll keep me warm on the inside."

Alex suddenly realized what her sister meant.

"Jackie, no!"

"I have to. The Tuatha Dé Danann said I had to sing to the Queen of Slievenamon."

"Jackie, no, you heard Seán Murphy."

"But I have to, it's obvious."

"Jackie, don't . . ."

As Alex began to object, Jackie felt her sister's hand slip away. Not that she loosened her grip, if anything she tightened it. But it didn't help. Alex dissolved to nothingness.

And as Alex faded away to the 11th century, something in return faded into the 21st. Jackie felt the hand in hers, growing firmer and persistent. Except, she realized as the horror grew in her, it was no longer a hand she held. It resembled a hand, but the fingernails felt in desperate need of a trim, and the whole seemed covered in thick hair. Not hair but fur! She held, she confirmed with a glance, a paw. And attached to the paw was a dog: a great, big, huge, enormous, angry, snarling, slobbering, sharp-fanged Irish wolfhound.

"Aaahhh!" Jackie screamed and dropped both the paw and the hot toddy. The hound's jaws snapped.

Ua Ruairc

*Every time a child says, "I don't believe in fairies,"
there is a fairy somewhere that falls down dead.*

Peter Pan, J. M. Barrie, 1904

 **M**ean, petty, brutal, vindictive, dangerous, short-tempered, greedy, dishonest, back-stabbing, two-timing, obnoxious, and ugly comprised some of the many adjectives used to describe Fergal Ua Ruairc. And these came from the list used by his friends, when he had friends, which was seldom. What his enemies called him contained many worse attributes which we cannot reprint here. Fergal Ua Ruairc had many enemies. Consider him a medieval version of Andy Brennan, but without the charm, and armed to the hilt (*literally, look it up*).

Even more than collecting enemies, Fergal liked to make money. So, the capture of a runaway monk brought a smile to his scarred and weathered face, for he could make a nice, tidy profit on the monk. Technically, the Vikings had already paid him for the monk, for his assistance in the sack of Kells Abbey, but Fergal reasoned that his prevention of the monk's escape exceeded the terms of his agreement with the Vikings, and that additional reward should follow.

A runaway princess? Now that was an entirely different matter. The Vikings would pay a considerable price for her return. Had cash-registers been invented by the 11th century, the one in his head would have gone kerching, kerching.

"You's found that hound yet?" Fergal bellowed at his brother, Art, who had just reappeared at the campsite.

"Dog's run away," replied Art, drearily.

"Of course it's run away; you's let go of the rope. Why'd you's let go of the rope?"

"I thought you said to let them down the rabbit hole."

"Forget what I's said; just go and find him. Sorry, Princess," he turned to Alex as Art lumbered away into the dark forest. "Art's not what you's call the sharpest arrow in the quiver." He turned again. "Go with him, Donnchad," he ordered a second brother. "Make sure he's doesn't lose his self as well. And find that dog; it's worth more than the two of you's put together."

Donnchad frowned but obeyed, which left the four remaining Ua Ruairc brothers, and the one remaining Irish wolfhound, to guard Alex and Brother Oswald.

"Where's my's manners?" said Fergal. "This is Tighernán, Niall and Aedh. Boys, say hello to the Princess Estrid."

"How'd you know she's the Princess Estrid?" asked the brother called Tighernán.

"Well, who else would it be, you's cudgel? I's swear our's dad gave me's all the brains, and the rest of you's got eggs. Say hello to the princess."

"Hello, Princess," they said.

"And what's the dog's name?" asked Alex, with a show of bravado and sarcasm.

"Who him? Why he's named . . . Dog, I's suppose. What do you's mean, what's his name?" said Fergal, baffled by the question.

"Then what's the other dog called?"

"He's called Dog as well."

"Isn't that confusing?"

"Er . . . no, they're dogs. Hoy, why you's so interested in my's dogs?"

"I like to know the names of the animals trying to kill me."

"No, you's got it all wrong. These dogs wouldn't harm you's, they's just a bit playful."

"Didn't seem that way when they were trying to bite me."

"No, Art let go of the rope, accidental like; they's just playing with you's. Why'd you's think they's have names?"

"No reason; I'm just trying to make conversation."

"Never you's mind conversation. Why don't you's tell Fergal what you's was doing in the rabbit hole with this here monk?"

"It seemed like a nice night for a walk."

"In a dark tunnel?"

"Yes, why not?"

"Well, if you's don't want to share you's secrets with you's friends . . . Niall, stick a pin in the monk; see if he's more in the mood for a chat."

Niall pulled a dagger from his tunic.

"You'll do no such thing!" yelled Alex. "Leave my servant alone."

"Servant is it? Not assailant or kidnapper? We's thought we's was rescuing you's."

"Well, you're not. And if you harm my servant, it'll be your head on that pin. You're dealing with a princess, don't you forget." Alex wondered how far she could take the bravado before she pushed them over the edge.

"Sorry, Princess. No need to argue with poor Fergal," said Fergal. "It's just some larking between friends. Honestly, you's think you's be happy for a bit of company, walking through these woods at night, what with all manner of miscreant hiding in the trees."

"Just don't touch my servant."

"Upon my's word." Fergal held his hand to his heart. His brothers sniggered.

"Yes, well, don't."

"Still, good job we's found you's; we's can take you's back to the Abbey."

"I don't want to go back to the Abbey."

"Oh, but you's must, Princess."

"I'm a daughter of a king, I don't have to must anything; I shall do as I please. Now if you and your brothers would please step aside, you've already taken up far too much of my time."

"Princess, as much as I's like to oblige, it's more than my's life's worth to let you's go a roaming."

"I don't care much about your life."

"We's got a job to do. Round up the runaways said Prince Oleif."

"You know Prince Oleif?"

"Got the orders from the man his self. Round them's up, Fergal, he said, round them's up and brings them's back. I's can't let the prince down; me's and he's good mates."

"I'm not a runaway."

"Well, I's suppose I's can let you's be on you's way, but not the monk; he's comes with us to the Abbey."

"I need my servant."

"Sorry, Princess, orders is orders. If it's company you's need, I's suppose I's can spare one of the brothers to look after you's. Of course, with fewer men to guard the prisoners, I's can't says I's can vouch for the monk's safety; there's all manner of miscreant between here and the Abbey."

"I don't see any prisoners."

"Ah, but looks can deceive. And my's good friend, the prince, won't take too kindly if I's just let you's go and fall into danger; no, he's won't take kindly to that at all . . ."

Alex scowled.

". . . I's sees we're getting nowhere. Why don't we's all go to the Abbey and get it sorted? Tighernán, go find Art and Donnchad. Those two would get lost in a barrel. And be quick about it, I's sure the prince is worried about his princess."

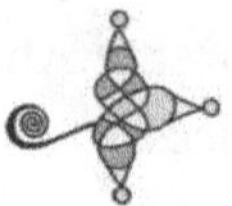

Alex acquiesced. She felt it didn't matter much, one way or the other, what she did. She was not supposed to be here. She was lost, and whether she hid in the woods or went to Dublin with the Vikings, it was all the same to her. But the more she thought about it, the more she realized that her escape may depend on what she could learn in the meantime. She didn't think she could learn much by hiding in the woods, so back to the Abbey she went.

However, she did care about Fergal's mistreatment of Brother Oswald. In spite of his boast about prisoners, she saw only two, herself and the monk. On the walk back to the Abbey, Fergal constantly threatened the poor man, and whipped the back of the monk's legs to drive him along, as if taking cattle to market. His Ua Ruairc brothers fared no better. Tighernán had returned with Art and Donnchad, but not the valuable wolfhound, and Fergal lashed out at them with crude oaths and angry threats.

He would then turn to Alex and smile and wink, as if he considered her his friend and co-conspirator in a secret, little game. Alex did not hide her disgust and contempt. She knew his type. He bullied those he believed were powerless and fawned at the feet of those he believed could raise him up. He was a social climber in a society which tolerated his methods . . . until he bullied the wrong person, whom he eventually would, and society would then show just how intolerant it could be. Alex shuddered to think that this hideous man could be her ancestor.

"Estrid, my love," cried Prince Oleif when Alex appeared before him in the sacristy. "We were all so worried about you, weren't we, Snorri."

Snorri grunted.

"Found her's down by the west wood, My's Lord," said Fergal. "All alone, she's was. Thought it best to offer my's protection."

"I am in your debt."

"Didn't do it for reward, My's Lord. My's Lady seemed lost and in need of help. You's knows Fergal, always does what's right, does Fergal. No, no reward necessary, My's Lord."

"Reward, yes, of course you shall have a reward."

"Of course, it's a pity that the runaways missed our snares, but that can't be helped. The safety of the princess must come first, that's what I's says. Pity that; lost a pretty penny on the day, but at least the princess is safe."

"And of course, you shall get your compensation for the monks. I wouldn't want to deprive you of your contract."

"My Lord, the Ua Ruairc have already been compensated for the monks." Snorri objected.

"Not now, Snorri, not now. Fergal is right: the safety of Princess Estrid is above the petty considerations of property. But Estrid, what were you doing outside the Abbey walls? Why did you run from Snorri?"

Alex had planned her reply. "I didn't run."

"You didn't? Did the monk abduct you? Snorri, the monk must be punished."

"No, the monk didn't abduct me. He's a loyal servant and I don't want him harmed."

"Then can you explain how you came into the company of the Ua Ruairc?"

"I was in the library, looking for something to read – Snorri was there, he can tell you."

Snorri grunted again.

"As a poet, you need to expand your vocabulary," Alex teased. "Anyway, it was dark in the library, and I didn't see that the trap door to the cellar was still open – someone had forgotten to close it," she accused. "I fell in, and Brother Oswald came to my aid. While I was down there, I found the secret passage to the west woods – honestly, I have to say that your men did a poor job of searching the cellar."

"Yes," agreed Prince Oleif. "A very poor job. Snorri, we have to do better."

Grunt!

"As a good Viking, I understand the value of a slave, so I decided to see where the passage went, to see if any of the runaways had gone that way."

"That was very brave of you, my love. You could have met with danger."

"I laugh at danger."

"Ha, spoken like a true Viking."

"At the other end of the passage, I met the Ua Ruairc."

"That she's did, My's Lord," agreed Fergal. "That's where we's found her's."

"Well, that's that all cleared up," smiled Prince Oleif. "But I'm so glad you are safe."

"And, My's Lord, she's not the only thing we's found."

"Oh!"

"We's have a surprise for you's."

"Oh, I do love a surprise. What is it?"

"Aedh, give me's that sword."

Aedh complied with Fergal's order, pulled a rag-covered object from his belt, and handed it to his brother. Fergal removed the rags to reveal a sword and scabbard. The scabbard, made of white gold and precious jewels with an intricate, inlayed design of ornate calligraphy, glittered magnificently in the dim room. Fergal handed the scabbard to Prince Oleif.

"What is this?" said the prince. He examined the scabbard. "I have never seen such exquisite workmanship." He drew the sword from the scabbard and held it high. The sword's blade and hilt were fashioned from a single piece of steel which resembled a complex, Celtic knot of intertwining trees, animals, and mythical creatures, and which culminated at the hilt with a pair of lions with rubies for eyes, and who held diamonds in their mouths. As Oleif turned the sword, it reflected and magnified the candlelight until the room glowed brightly and hurt their eyes. "It's so light, almost as if I held a vision. Where did you get it?"

"Found it," Fergal lied.

"No one loses a sword such as this. Where did you find it?"

"On the road to Kells. There it was, just laying there in the middle of the road. Hello, says I's, what a marvel is this. Bet Prince Oleif would appreciate that."

"You're so thoughtful. Just look at the jewels, they alone must be worth a king's ransom. What do you want for it?"

"Think of it as a gift, My's Lord."

"A gift? Surely not?"

"A gift from me's to you's for your marriage to the Lady Estrid. A wedding gift fit for a prince and princess."

"That is most generous, Fergal Ua Ruairc."

"What's a trinket or two between friends?"

"When we get back to Dublin, I shall shower you with trinkets."

Grunt!

"So, I'll just go back to my hut now," said Alex, sickened by this display of friendship.

"Actually, there's been a slight change of plan." Prince Oleif sheathed the sword.

"Change of plan?"

"Yes, our scouts have reported that the vanguard of Brian Bóruma is closer than we had thought. We can no longer wait for daybreak. We must make all haste to Dublin."

"I'll just go freshen up."

"No, there isn't time. Fergal is correct, your safety is paramount. The Irish are a nuisance, but I wouldn't want to face the wrath of Sweyn Forkbeard should any harm befall his lovely daughter. We must break camp, but that will take some time. You must depart now. We shall follow."

"Now?"

"Yes, I cannot guarantee your path to Dublin if you should hesitate."

"I'm not walking all the way to Dublin."

"No, certainly not, you are a princess. We have saddled a horse for you."

"I can't ride a horse. And weren't you concerned about me wandering around the countryside on my own? Didn't we have that conversation just a minute ago?"

Prince Oleif turned to Fergal.

"Can I impose on the Ua Ruairc for one more charge? You will be amply rewarded."

"We's don't seek reward, you's knows us, My's Lord," said Fergal.

"I want you to escort Princess Estrid to Dublin. Keep her safe until we can join you."

"My's honor, My's Lord."

"I'm not going to Dublin with the Ua Ruairc," objected Alex.

"Quite right," said Prince Oleif. "I don't think six men are enough to protect you. Snorri, you shall go with them. Take as many men as can travel swift and light. Leave the packing to us. Go quickly, my love, before I decide I can't bear to be parted from you again and change my mind. When you arrive, tell my father to prepare for our wedding."

Grunt!

In the best of conditions, the journey from Kells to Dublin was a tough, two-day march. Snorri demanded that they complete it in one and pushed them harder than even Fergal would have dared.

Alex sat side-saddle on a large, shaggy shire horse; Brother Oswald had instructed her in the correct manner for a lady to mount and ride. She had never ridden a horse before, so she had no benchmark for comparison, but she determined that nothing could feel more uncomfortable.

The Vikings wondered when they had last seen such an incompetent and uneducated woman. Even by princess standards, she seemed hopeless - an insult to Viking womanhood. But as the daughter of Sweyn Forkbeard, the slightest criticism could prove fatal, and they therefore kept their opinions to themselves. The kindest amongst them agreed that Princess Estrid had twisted her brains, poor child, and required the full-time care of a nurse. Others speculated that a seið-kona[#2] had turned the evil eye on her, in which case someone else needed to have their eyes plucked out to compensate, probably the monk.

The horse ambled on in complete indifference to Alex's suffering. The rest of the party trotted on foot to keep up with the horse, Brother Oswald, and Fergal at the horse's head. Fergal insisted on holding the reins of the horse to guide it.

"Wouldn't want you's to fall, should the horse step in a hole," he said. "Prince Oleif wouldn't like that."

"You seem to care a great deal about what Prince Oleif likes and dislikes," said Alex.

"Me's and the prince are good friends."

"So, I saw. That sword was an extravagant gift."

#2, Seið-kona: in Norse mythology, a seið-kona was a practitioner of dark magic. Seið magic affects the mind by illusion, madness, forgetfulness, hypnosis etc. The spell could be broken by blinding the seið-kona.

"Think of it as my's wedding present to you's."

"You are very generous. Where did you get it?"

"Like I's said, found it."

A low growl came from behind them.

"I don't think Snorri believes you," said Alex.

"He's can believe what he's likes."

"Anyway, it's quite a sword. I can't imagine it would have been made by anyone from around here."

"No, not these peasants; too smart for them's."

"So, who do you think made it?"

"Don't know."

"The writing on the scabbard; and the way that it shone in the candlelight; it seemed almost magical, wouldn't you say."

"Don't know nothing about magical."

"And you found it."

"That's what I's said."

"Lucky you."

"I's always been lucky."

"And you're always finding things, I bet."

"I's come across my's share from time to time."

"Still, it's a precious thing to lose. I would imagine its owner is quite upset."

"Former owner; finder's keepers."

"Former owner. I bet they're looking high and low for it. It can't have been carelessly lost, not something so valuable. It must have been stolen."

"Can't say."

"And then the thief lost it so that you could find it. I bet the owner – former owner – must be quite angry. Whoever it was must be rich and powerful to have such a treasure. I wonder what they'd do to the thief if they caught him. Something nasty I expect."

"Not my's business."

Alex wanted to say, 'But it is my business, you lying, two-faced weasel. You made it my business. I'm in all this trouble because you took something that didn't belong to you. I may never get home because of you. And if ever they catch you, I hope the pain will be much worse than sitting on a horse.' That's what she wanted to say, but instead she remained silent.

"Keep up the pace," snarled Snorri from behind them.

Somewhere in the overcast, murky sky, the sun rose from the east sea and floated towards the Aran Islands and midday, but it didn't manage to penetrate through the drizzle. The group pressed on for hours at breakneck speed, without rest, drink, or nourishment, until Alex decided that she could no longer sit on the horse and keep her sanity.

"We have to stop," she shouted. "Just five minutes, please, we have to stop. I'm a princess, I need a time-out."

Snorri grunted but raised his hand to signal a halt.

"Ten minutes, Princess," he offered. "I would suggest that you eat something. When we resume the march, we won't stop again until we've crossed the Liffey."

"Snorri, what would I do without you?" asked Alex. "Always concerned about my welfare."

"Just following orders. I'll see you safe in Dublin, even if the march kills the rest of us."

"Between you and your friends, the Ua Ruairc, I can't imagine anything horrible happening to me, unless of course, one of you do it."

"The Ua Ruairc are no friends of mine."

"I hear that a lot. But Prince Oleif seems to like them?"

"Prince Oleif likes everyone."

"Not you though? You're a bit more cautious?"

"I just follow orders."

"And write sagas."

"Yes, and write sagas."

"Will you write a saga about us?"

"No, one can only write sagas about the heroic deeds of our ancestors. There's nothing heroic about us."

"I don't know; you could die in a great big battle against the Irish. Wouldn't that be heroic?"

"Then I wouldn't have lived to write the saga."

"I suppose you've got a point. Do you want to die in battle?"

"Any Viking worth his salt wants to die in battle."

"And go to Valhalla?"

"Yes, it's every man's ambition."

Under the roof of the Golden Shields,
With the Valkyrie, to sing,
At Odin's table, to dine,
In Asgard's greatest hall, to drink
With the heroes of the Golden Shields.

"That's poetic; did you write that?"

"A meager effort for great deeds."

"How about Prince Oleif? Does he want to die in battle? He seems to have a sensitive side. He doesn't appear much like a Viking to me, not compared to the rest of you - no offense."

"Do not concern yourself about the prince's courage. He would not command my axe had he not proved his worth. The prince has the daring of a hundred Vikings."

"So, he's looking forward to Valhalla as well?"

"For all his . . . affectations, the prince is the best Viking amongst us. Should battle come, he will lead us, even to Valhalla."

"Yes, I know he will."

"Princess, we must continue."

"I need to powder my nose, first."

"What is wrong with your nose?"

"Nothing, it's just an expression. I need a little privacy."

"We cannot allow you out of our sight."

"Just a minute, that's all. I won't wander far."

"I shall post men."

Snorri set four men in a perimeter, faced outward to give Alex the privacy she needed. But Alex thought she saw a fifth face staring at her from the trees, the face of a woman, gaunt and haunting. She hurried back to Snorri.

"I think we're being watched," she said.

"We must hurry," said Snorri.

The sun began its descent and the march resumed. Snorri estimated that they could not reach Dublin before nightfall, but he demanded that they redouble their efforts, regardless. Alex and the horse continued their uneasy relationship. Alex's bones burned, but she knew that she travelled in comfort, compared to those on foot. Brother Oswald said nothing, but she could tell that the exertion taxed him to the limit.

Alex wondered when she would return to the 21st century; and if she would still be on the horse when it happened. And if it did happen while she was on the horse, the Vikings and the Ua Ruairc would certainly notice. Well, Alex concluded, if they couldn't respect her privacy, it would just serve them right.

Twilight passed and now, so close to their goal, came the most dangerous part of their journey. Snorri ordered close ranks and no undue conversation. He estimated that if they encountered any Irish, the reputation of the Viking as merciless maniacs would hold most at bay, but they had no real defense against arrows launched at them through the darkness. With so few men at his command, Snorri mostly feared an encounter with a force from Brian Bóruma's army; against that he would have no defense at all. All they could do then would be to ask Valhalla to uncork a few extra kegs of wine. It almost made him wish that he had chosen a Berserker or two to travel with them.

"Don't you's worry, Princess," whispered Fergal, in defiance of the ban against talk. "If there's any trouble, I's won't let them's take you's alive."

"You're too kind, Fergal," said Alex.

"Not at all. I's shudder to think what they's do to you's. They's evil barbarians. They's don't often see such beauty. For jealousy, they's scalp you's head of its golden locks. They's put you's feet to the fire. They's turn you's innards . . . no, don't bear thinking about. Put it out of you's mind, My's Lady, don't give it another thought. Best not dwell on their evil, grizzly, barbaric, torturous ways."

"You're such a comfort, Fergal."

Brother Oswald stumbled.

"Here, monk, keep up," snarled Fergal. "If you's delay us and the princess is captured, I's be doing some torturing of my's own, understand?"

Brother Oswald climbed to his feet and struggled to return to his place at Alex's side. She could see that he was near to collapse. If they did not rest soon, there would be nothing left of the monk for Fergal to torture.

"How could you do it, Fergal? Why do you do it?"

"Do what, Princess?"

"You worked for the Vikings at Kells Abbey. You sold the monks into slavery."

"A good day's business, if you's asks me's."

"If the Irish attack, will you fight with the Vikings against them?"

"Naturally, what kind of question is that? The Ua Ruairc ain't afraid of a fight."

"But to take sides against the Irish. How could you do that? How could you betray your own people?"

"My's own people? What you's taking about?"

"Your people, the Irish."

"Pah, don't make me's laugh."

"You're not Irish?"

"Not the Ua Ruairc. We's Vikings of long standing, descended from the old Norse, the Hrothekr and the kings of Breifne. I's got noble blood running through my's veins, I's have. Why you's and me's are practically cousins. Fergal Ua Ruairc comes from fame and fortune, and he's'll be famous his self one day, even after death comes for him. He's'll be famous, mark my's words."

"I look forward to that."

"Torchlight ahead," whispered Tighernán.

Snorri came forward to inspect. "It's the Ford of Áth Cliath," he said. "A few more minutes, if low tide allows, and we'll be across the Liffey and into Dublin."

The tide co-operated and they crossed the ford, made of wattle, and floated raft-like across the mud flats. Viking guards and brothers came out to greet and escort them. As Alex reached the safety of the Dublin side of the river, she turned back to survey the path they had just taken, as if she expected to see fiery eyes peer at her from the darkness. She saw nothing and turned back. And there at her side stood a woman and a girl. She knew the woman to be the same one she had encountered in the woods. The woman's features were half hidden under a hood and obscured by shadow, but Alex felt certain it was the same woman. And the girl with the shocking, waist-length, red hair was the same one she had seen at the Rock of Cashel. Alex could not help but stare at them, but the exchange unsettled her, for she stared into expressionless faces: their eyes black as night and their stares vacant. As her horse continued forward and the women remained stationary, Alex finally found the strength to turn away and the encounter faded.

The Queen of Slievenamon

It was not the grace of her queenly air,
Nor her cheek of the rose's glow,
Nor her soft black eyes, not her flowing hair,
Nor was it her lily white brow;
'Twas the soul of truth, and of melting ruth,
And the smile like a summer dawn,
That sold my heart away one mild May day,
In the valley of Slievenamon.

Home Longings
(also known as *The Maid of Slievenamon* or the *Tipperary Anthem*),
Charles J. Kickham, 1849

“Aaahhh! Nice doggy, good doggy,” screamed Jackie as she ran from the bar to the kitchen, passed her cousins and entered the pantry, the wolfhound in hot pursuit.

“What the hell was that?” asked Mattie.

In the pantry and out of sight, Jackie’s screams continued for a while, accompanied by the sound of growls, snarls and tin cans as they bounced off the stone walls and floor. Then all went silent.

Jeff and Mattie leapt to their feet, but before they could reach the pantry, Jackie reappeared.

“Hello, boys,” she said. “What’s new?” She tried to look calm and collected, but her flushed face and shortness of breath betrayed her.

“What the hell was that?” repeated Mattie.

“What?” asked Jackie innocently.

“The dog.”

“Oh, that, er, yes, I, er, think we have a wolf in the house.”

“That wasn’t a wolf, it’s an Irish wolfhound,” said Jeff.

“Is it really?” asked Jackie. “Is that what it is? Well, fancy that. I didn’t have time to notice, but it did seem to have a lot of, er, teeth, fangs, I suppose, yes, definitely fangs. Is there any of that hot toddy left?"

"Where is it? What have you done with it?" asked Mattie.

"It's okay; I took care of it."

"What did you do?"

"I locked it in the tunnel. I don't think it can get out."

"What's going on down here?" Aunt Róisín appeared at the kitchen door. She had her dressing gown pulled tight around her, as if she would burst at the slightest touch.

"Oh, er, nothing, Mam," said Mattie. "Jackie spilled her hot toddy."

"Yes, sorry, Aunt Róisín," agreed Jackie. "It startled me. Sorry, I cried out."

Aunt Róisín briefly inspected Jackie for corroborative evidence of their story. Jackie did appear drenched in hot toddy. "I thought I could hear a dog?" she pressed.

"A dog? No, no dog," said Mattie. "Oh, wait, that was the television. Jeff was channel surfing. When Jackie spilled her drink and screamed, Jeff accidently pressed the volume control by mistake, didn't you, Jeff."

"Er, yes, that's right," sulked Jeff.

"Where's Alex?" asked Aunt Róisín.

"She went to bed," said Jackie.

"And that's where the rest of you should be," scolded Aunt Róisín. "It's early enough when we rise, without having our sleep disturbed."

"Sorry, Mam," said Jeff. "We're just going up."

"We'll just clean up the spill first," said Mattie.

"Well, see that you do, and be quiet about it. Goodnight," said Aunt Róisín, and she turned and left the kitchen.

"Goodnight," said the cousins sheepishly.

"That was a close one," said Mattie.

"Cheer up, Jeff, we're still alive and kicking," said Jackie.

"I just don't like lies, that's all . . . I take it that Alex is gone again?" asked Jeff.

"And we got the wolf in return. I think I preferred the pig."

"Any sign of the fairies?"

"No, nothing . . . oh, hang on a minute." Jackie could see a familiar light radiating from the bar. "Wait here."

She went to the bar. The fairy horse hovered in the branches of the Tree.

"Hello, Lämmy."

"And if the child so dares to see,
And I will follow who follows me."

Sang the horse.

"That might be a bit awkward just now, Lämmy; there's a great big wolf in the way. Can you put it to sleep or something?"

The fairy horse floated across the bar, but instead of going to the kitchen, it went to the window.

"Is there another way to the Palace?"

The fairy horse floated through the window and out across the street. The lashing rain soon made it invisible.

"You don't want to take me to the palace, do you?"

The horse song floated in from afar.

"And I will follow who follows me."

"Where are we going?" But Jackie had already guessed the answer. She looked out of the window. "It's a bit wet out there; I'll need my coat."

She returned to the kitchen.

"I need to go to Slievenamon. Who's going with me?"

"What, now?" asked Mattie.

"Yes, of course now."

"You can't go now," said Jeff.

"Why not?"

"Have you seen the weather?"

"It's just a bit of rain."

"It's a gale."

"Sorry, impossible."

"If you don't want to go, I'll go on my own."

"What about the fairies?"

"I don't want to see them, tonight. I have to see the Queen of Slievenamon. You can talk to the fairies if you like."

"I'm not going down in the tunnel, there's a great, big, mental wolfhound down there," said Mattie.

"Yes, there is that as well," agreed Jackie, as she put on her coat. "So, you may as well come with me to Slievenamon."

"Still impossible," said Jeff.

"Fine, I'll go alone." She left the kitchen and then returned. "Can I borrow an umbrella?"

"There's one by the bar door," said Mattie.

"Fine." She left and once again returned. "How do I get to Slievenamon? Does anyone have a map?"

"Jackie, sit down," said Jeff.

"The sooner I go, the sooner I can be back."

"It's five miles to Slievenamon. In the dark, in this weather, it would take you hours to get there. Wait for morning."

"Can one of you drive me there?"

"We're not stealing Dad's car."

"Can I get a taxi?"

"Not at this time of night. What would you tell the taxi driver? A mad woman wandering around Slievenamon in a storm, looking for a Banshee. They'd lock you up for sure. Then the Gardaí would come knock on the door. We don't want that with the Book of Kells upstairs."

Jackie sat down. "This is impossible," she huffed.

"That's what I told you."

"But what shall we do? I must speak to the Queen of Slievenamon."

"Just sit tight for now. In the morning, we'll get Mam or Dad to drive us to Slievenamon. If that story Seán Murphy told us about the Banshee is true, it'll appear in the daylight just as easily as the nighttime."

"But we're wasting time. What about Alex?"

"If we wait for morning, Alex will be back. Perhaps she'll have some news. Best we get some rest and start fresh tomorrow."

"There might not be a tomorrow for Alex."

"What do you mean?"

"Nothing, I'm just worried."

"Let's get some sleep."

"What about the wolfhound?" reminded Mattie.

"He's safe enough in the tunnel," reasoned Jeff. "When Alex returns, I guess the dog will go back to its own time."

In the morning, Uncle Bob agreed to take the cousins to Slievenamon.

"I have business in Waterford, so I can't stay with you, but I can drop you off and pick you up on my way back; is that okay?"

"That's perfect," they agreed.

Alex had returned and with the absence of growls from the tunnel, they decided that they were ahead of the game.

"What did you find out last night?" asked Alex.

"Not a great deal," replied Jackie. "But I did have a wolf chasing me."

"Did you meet an axe murderer?"

"No."

"Then I still had a worse night than you. What did you learn from the fairies?"

"Er, we didn't have a chance to speak to the fairies."

Alex bowed her head. "I don't believe this. I'm going mad."

"But at Slievenamon, we can speak to the Banshee."

"And just how is that going to help? I told you last night not to go near her."

"But Lämmy wants to take me to her, and the fairies said I should talk to her. I think it's really important."

"She's dangerous. What if you make her cry?"

"We'll just have to chance it. How was Kells?"

"I'm not in Kells anymore. I'm in Dublin now. I guess I've got one more day until my wedding and two more days until my husband dies."

"So, picked out a nice dress yet?"

"Not yet; there are not many shops in 11th century Dublin."

"No Louis Vuitton?"

"Haven't found one. But I think I've seen that Sword everyone is so excited about."

"The Sword of Nuada?"

"Yes, Prince Oleif has it. Fergal Ua Ruairc gave it to him as our wedding present."

"You've met the Ua Ruairc?"

"And I wish I hadn't. Fergal is a hideous man, and his brothers aren't much better. I can't believe we're descended from them. Before you ask, I think Fergal stole the Sword from the fairies. He denies it, but I know it was him."

"That would make sense. That must be why the fairies are using us. An O'Rourke stole their Sword, and an O'Rourke must return it. You've got to get that Sword."

"I'll work on it next time I'm there, sometime between the wedding and the funeral."

"You made more progress than we did."

"Oh, and I found these in my pocket this morning." Alex pulled out two small metal disks with an intricate Celtic design and colored engravings.

"You brought these back with you?"

"Brother Oswald gave them to me as a wedding present. As my slave, he can't afford a real present, so he made them for me. Wasn't that sweet? He's a nice man, I shall miss him."

"They're beautiful. What are they?"

"They are letters, like in the Book of Kells. They're the letter *A*. See, *A* for Alex. I'll get them made into earrings."

Uncle Bob stopped the car at the foot of Slievenamon. Jackie and the boys climbed out.

"I'll think I'll stay with Uncle Bob, if that's okay?" said Alex.

"But you'll miss what's up there," pleaded Jackie.

"I don't want to see what's up there," snapped Alex.

"Okay, okay, you don't have to go."

"That's fine by me," said Uncle Bob. "Alex is the only sensible one here. The rest of you must be mad wanting to climb Slievenamon in this weather."

Although the rain had subsided somewhat, it still poured down heavily, and the grey-black clouds which hovered over the mountain still looked ominous.

"I'll stay with Alex," volunteered Jeff.

"No, it's not necessary," said Alex.

"I insist." Jeff climbed back in the car.

"Are you sure you don't want to do this another day, when the weather is better?" asked Uncle Bob.

"No," said Jackie. "It has to be today, else we won't have time."

"We'll pick you up here in about four hours."

"Okay, see you then."

Uncle Bob reversed the car down the narrow lane before he turned and drove away.

"Now which way to the Banshee?" asked Jackie.

"Up," said Mattie. "If the Banshee is anywhere, she'll be at the Rock."

"The Rock?"

"It's a cairn, up at the summit. It's a mound of stones, said to cover a grave and a secret passage."

"You don't say? Secret passage, who would have expected that?"

As they climbed the mountain, the weather once again closed around them. By the time they reached the Rock, the rain resembled that usually found only in novels such as Wuthering Heights. Umbrellas were useless. Coats were useless. They reached the Rock soaked to the skin.

They inspected the Rock.

"I don't see an opening," cried Jackie, struggling to be heard above the rain.

"I think the Irish would have found it by now had there been one," cried Mattie. "This is getting a bit uncomfortable; maybe we should go back down?"

"Not yet."

"But we'll die out here in this weather."

"Not yet. Let's walk around the Rock. You go that way; I'll go the other."

Jackie began a clockwise inspection of the Rock. As Mattie vanished from sight behind her, Lämmy came into view.

"There you are," said Jackie. "Sorry I'm late."

The fairy horse turned and passed through the stone of the cairn, as if it brushed aside a door made of cobwebs.

"Wait, how did you do that?"

Jackie climbed to the rocks and pressed her hand against them. They offered no resistance; they were an illusion. Jackie followed, but unsure of her footing on the imaginary stone, she tumbled forward and fell into the cairn. When she had recovered her equilibrium, she saw a mirror. The mirror sat on a table. Before the table stood a stiff-backed chair. And on the chair, the Banshee sat and passed a brush over her long, red hair. Then the Banshee turned to face Jackie and her mouth opened.

"Please don't scream," pleaded Jackie.

"Why would I scream?" asked the Banshee. "I was expecting you."

"You were expecting me?"

The Banshee nodded towards Lämmy, who moved towards her and floated at her shoulder. "I sent for you."

"Lämmy is your horse?"

"Lämmy, as you call him, is a Púca. He belongs to no one. He is a free spirit. But he is also my friend. I asked him to call on you. I would have come myself, but my presence tends to . . . unsettle people."

"You are the Queen of Slievenamon who the fairies said I should talk to?"

"I am she. Welcome, Jackie of the Ua Ruairc."

"Thank you. Er, I don't suppose I could fetch Mattie? He's getting soaked out there."

"It would make no difference. There is no passage of time inside the cairn. No matter how long you remain, to your cousin on the outside it is less than a moment."

"Oh, all right."

"You come in search of answers."

"You can help me. You know about what the fairies did to Alex?"

"I know."

"Can you help?"

"Not in the way you expect. I can only help you prepare."

"Prepare for what?"

"Your sister is not with you?"

"No, she didn't want to climb the mountain."

"That is understandable, but it is your sister who must prepare. Your sister did not climb the mountain, because she did not wish to see me. She is afraid of the Banshee's kiss."

"Why should she be afraid of you?"

"Because your sister is my sister, or at least that is her destiny."

"What is her destiny?"

"To join the Sisterhood of the Banshee."

"You're joking, right?"

"Worse than the Banshee's cry is the Banshee's kiss. Your sister has had death stolen from her."

"I don't understand."

"Her time is broken, she is not of this time or that, and thus cannot be of any time. Unless she is returned to her time, your sister will soon become my sister."

"You mean she'll turn into a Banshee, like you?"

"She will weep for the death of others, but none can weep for her. The Sisterhood of the Banshee will care for her."

"Does Alex know what's happening to her?"

"She suspects. She has caught glimpses of my sisters. They are gathering around her to welcome her. Eventually, she must come to us. When we embrace her, the journey will be complete."

"I can't let that happen. The fairies said that when I make my wish, Alex will stop going back in time."

"It is too late. The faerie would return less than they took. Her time is broken."

"Can it be mended?"

"That is why I sent for you. What would you give, Jackie of the Ua Ruairc, to mend your sister?"

"Everything."

"Then listen."

"I'm all ears."

"Your sister need not fear me, we are kindred spirits."

"How so?"

"I am the Queen of Slievenamon. As with your sister, I was once human, before my time was broken. Do you know why the Banshee cries?"

"To forecast the death of someone."

"There are worse things than death. I cry because of the images in my head. The banshee's scream is one of pain. But we do not cry for the dead. We cry for the living. We cry to absorb their pain at the loss of their loved ones. We take that pain to ourselves. We take those images from their heads. We live with that pain forever, and forever with each death, it grows."

"That must be tough."

"That is but a part of it."

"There's worse?"

"We cry in witness at what we cannot experience. Our time is broken. We cannot die. To die is human. We cry to be human again."

"And that's what will happen to Alex if I don't stop it? You said you and she are kindred spirits?"

"I am the Red Queen of Slievenamon, but once I had golden hair. I was once human too, a thousand years ago, and destined to be a queen amongst men. My name is Estrid."

"OMG, you're Princess Estrid?"

"I was on a journey to meet my betrothed when my time was broken. There is a price to be paid for everything, even magic, especially magic. When the Tuatha Dé Danann sent your sister back in time, I was the price paid. And the first man for whom I cried was my own betrothed."

"Alex said Prince Oleif died at the Battle of Clontarf."

"Thousands died that day, and the weeping of the Banshee was boundless. The faerie do not consider the fate of humans to be of consequence, but they are wrong, all fates are entwined."

"I'm so sorry, it's all my fault."

"Not so, the Tuatha Dé Danann' plans were long years in the making."

"All this for a stupid sword? Why didn't they just take it back?"

"Once stolen, the Sword of Nuada Airgetlám was hidden by Norse magic. They could not take it back. Their magic failed them. You and your sister were chosen because you can go where the Tuatha Dé Danann cannot; they told you as much."

"The Otherworld?"

"The Banshee walks the Otherworld. The Sword is watched over by guardians of the Otherworld."

"But Alex says she's seen it."

"That was a thousand years ago."

"I don't care about that. I don't care about the Sword. I don't care about the Vikings. I don't care about the fairies. I just want my sister back. How do I do that?"

"Return that which was taken."

"How do I do that? How do I mend my sister?"

"Magic can only be undone by magic. And there is a price to pay. Are you prepared to pay that price?"

"Yes."

"Do not be hasty; you do not know what that price may be; I do not know."

"I'm prepared."

"Then attend closely. In my thousand years of walking this land, I have searched for a magic to undo the spell upon me. I have found such magic, but I cannot wield it, and neither can you."

"Then what good is it?"

"This much I have learned. The magic cast by the faerie must be uncast by the faerie. It must be bargained for with the faerie. There is a spell and there is a charm, and as I have warned, there is a price to pay."

"What's the spell?"

The purple of the Wolf
To the hair of the Banshee,

The edge of the Sword
Replaced by the Word,
To the hair of the Banshee,
The song of the Faerie.
Replaced by the Word,
Restored by the Sword,
Returned by the Heart.

"Can you write that down?"

"You must remember."

"Okay, okay." Jackie repeated the verse a few times in her head. "What's the charm?"

"You must determine that for yourself."

"Would a straight answer be too much to ask? Could you possibly be of any less help? How are the spell and the charm used?"

"You must look to Matthew."

"Mattie? What does it have to do with him?"

"Use everything which has been given to you."

"That's not really much, considering. The hair of the Banshee? Where can I get Banshee hair? Oh, Can I use some of your hair?"

"I am not the Banshee of the spell."

"Oh, goody. Let me guess who is. Can I have a clue?"

"One more thing - Alex must embrace the Sisterhood."

"No, you said that's bad. That's not what she should do."

"She must embrace the Sisterhood and give them what I shall now give to you."

The Banshee moved to the table and opened the wooden box which was on it. From the box she retrieved an object about 12 inches long, a Viking drinking horn. It was carved with the image of a longship and around the rim were Norse runes.

"What is it?"

"It is a drinking horn. Once the fairy spell is broken, your sister will no longer be under their compulsion to return to the past. But return she must."

"Why? Once we're done, she won't want to go back."

"But she must once more return, and it will be her desire. The horn will help her to fulfill her desire."

"What does it say?"

Unharmed go forth,
Unharmed return,
Unharmed back home.

"It is a blessing from the Goddess, Frigga, wife of Odin. Drink three times from the horn and recite the lines. On the first line, whoever drank from the horn will be transported to the time of the horn. On the second, whoever drank shall be returned to their own time. At the third line, the horn shall return to its own time."

"Alex has to give this horn to the Sisterhood? Where will she get it?"

"It is in the possession of Prince Oleif."

"What should be drunk from it?"

"That is not important, but it can only be used once while it is out of its time. And it can only be out of its time if Alex gives it to the Sisterhood to take to the Otherworld. That is why she must go to them. If she fails then the horn in your hands will crumble to nothingness."

"I knew it was just like *Back to the Future* . . . Never mind. Alex still won't want to meet your Sisterhood. Can't she just bring it back with her, next time?"

"If you succeed in breaking the faerie magic, she will no longer be able to return with objects not of her time."

"And if I don't succeed? No, don't answer that."

Mattie walked anti-clockwise around the Rock. He saw Jackie come the other way.

"I told you this was a waste of time, there's no way in – what have you got there?" he said on seeing the horn.

"I might have the answer, but I'm not sure. Let's go down," replied Jackie.

"You've given up on finding the Banshee?"

"No, she gave me this."

"What? She couldn't have done; you were only out of my sight for a couple of seconds."

"It just seems that way because you were having so much fun. Come on, let's go down before we get any wetter."

"I think that's impossible."

At the foot of Slievenamon, Uncle Bob, Jeff, and Alex were waiting.

"Good timing," said Uncle Bob. "We just got back ourselves. You idiots look like two drowned rats. I told you not to go. I don't know what Róisín will say when she sees you, but I'll get the blame, no doubt."

"Oh, no," said Jackie. "It wasn't that bad, was it Mattie?"

"I think it's let up a little, probably even stop now," agreed Mattie. "Good job too, otherwise our match tonight might get cancelled."

"They won't cancel the match," said Jeff. "Not even if you were a drowned rat. They have a schedule to keep."

"And so do we," said Uncle Bob. "Come on; let's get you back to the Gatehouse."

Jackie and Mattie climbed in the back seat with Alex.

"Watch out," cried Alex. "You'll get me all wet."

"Sorry," said Jackie. "Here, hold this," she whispered.

"What is it?" whispered Alex.

"The answer."

"You've figured it out? You know what you're doing?"

"Yes . . . well, maybe . . . I'm not entirely sure . . . but I think we're close."

"You're not instilling me with a great deal of confidence. Do you know what you are doing or not?"

"Yes, trust me."

"Oh, God, we really are in trouble, aren't we?"

"Trust me."

"Oh, God."

Mattie's opinion of the weather proved correct. In fact, the farther away they got from Slievenamon, the drier it became, until by the time they had reached Fethard, the rain had stopped, and the sky was merely overcast.

"Told you," said Mattie. "Though I expect the pitch is going to be waterlogged tonight."

"We'll go ahead with the game anyway," said Jeff.

"Yes, we will," said Jackie.

"Oh, God," said Alex. "Why do I get the feeling you're up to something?"

Jackie has a Plan

Little Sister, whom the Fay
Hides away within his doon,
Deep below yon seeding fern,
Oh, list and learn my magic tune.

Mor of Cloyne, Alfred Perceval Graves, 1909

 **"I** have a plan," announced Jackie.

"Is it a cunning plan?" asked Mattie.

"All my plans are cunning."

The cousins walked back to the Gatehouse from the just concluded semi-final against Limerick, which the Fethard boys had won one-nil, in a hard-fought, no quarter-given match played more on mud than grass. Mattie was ecstatic to have reached the final. Jeff showed no similar excitement.

"Why so glum, Cous'?" asked Jackie.

"We should have let Tommy Powers play," grumbled Jeff.

"Fennelly was never going to allow that," argued Mattie. "Not with the score so close. Limerick almost pinched one at the end."

"It's just not right; Tommy should have at least had a moment on the pitch."

"Don't worry, there's still the final. Tommy still has a chance to get a medal," said Jackie.

"What if we'd lost instead of won?"

"But you didn't. Good grief, I have a plan. Who wants to hear it? Alex, do you want to hear it?"

"War is coming," grumbled Alex.

"What is wrong with everybody? You just won your match. You're going to play the final in Dublin, where Liverpool United will see you and sign you for millions of dollars."

"Manchester," corrected Mattie.

"Where Manchester United will see you and sign you for millions of dollars. And I have a plan. Everybody should be ecstatic."

"I'm ecstatic," said Mattie.

"Jeff, what delights are you cooking for us tonight?" asked Jackie.

"Don't feel like cooking," answered Jeff. "Let's just get a pizza or something."

"Is your brother always like this when he's won a soccer match?" Jackie asked Mattie.

"Only if I played better than he did," answered Mattie.

"So, let's get that pizza and sit down, and I can cheer everyone up with my plan."

"Your cunning plan?"

At the kitchen table, the cousins munched on the pizza, while Jackie told of her meeting with the Queen of Slievenamon, recited the spell and showed the Viking drinking horn.

"We have a place in San Diego, José's Pizza, where we all hang out," said Jackie. "But their pizza tastes different from this somehow, even when it's the same toppings."

"It's the local variations in ingredients, growing conditions, oven temperatures, that kind of thing," explained Jeff, who had started to cheer up a little.

Only Alex remained completely glum and silent. She sat by the table and tapped away at the screen of her phone. The others didn't feel inclined to challenge her on it.

"So, let's hear this plan of yours."

"First, according to the spell, we need a couple of things: the hair of the Banshee and the purple of the wolf, what do you think that is?"

"No, idea," said Mattie.

"Wolfsbane," said Jeff.

"Wolfsbane?"

"Wolfsbane' petals are purple."

"But wolfsbane is poisonous, isn't it?" asked Jackie.

"Yes."

"It figures. Where can we get wolfsbane?"

"We can't."

"Of course we can; we need it for the spell."

"There was some at Blarney Castle," said Mattie.

"And we're a long way from there. If Jackie needs the wolfsbane tonight, we'll have to find some closer to home."

"You haven't got any you keep handy to put in the stew, when Mattie annoys you?" asked Jackie.

"Wish I did."

"Well, let's leave that for a minute. What about the hair of the Banshee?"

"Good luck with that."

"No seriously, that one is easy."

"Did you get some on Slievenamon?" asked Mattie.

"No, the queen said her hair wouldn't do."

"Then whose?"

Jackie glanced sideways at her sister.

"She means me," said Alex.

"You're not a Banshee," objected Mattie.

"Yes, I am, I can predict deaths."

"No, you can't."

"I predicted the death of Prince Oleif."

"You read that on Wikipedia. Anyone can be a Banshee if that's all it takes. Alex, you are not a Banshee."

"Not yet, but there's still time." Alex tapped away.

"What I mean is the spell is to reverse the curse on Alex," said Jackie. "So, she must be the Banshee referred to by the spell, and her hair must be the Banshee hair. It makes sense."

"I'm starting to think you never make sense," said Mattie.

"So, we have to take wolfsbane' petals, which we don't have and wrap them around Alex's hair, which may or may not be Banshee hair. What next?" asked Jeff.

"Then we have to cut the petals with the Sword of Nuada."

"Which we also don't have."

"Which Alex will get from Prince Oleif."

"What's this *replaced by the Word*?" asked Mattie.

"Er, I'm not sure; I was hoping you could tell me?"

"Me, why me?"

"The Banshee said I should look to Mattie. Use everything we've been given and look to Mattie."

"Then it's no good looking to me, I don't know a thing."

"What have we been given?"

"The Book of Kells."

"The Ring of Thor that's on Alex's finger."

"A drinking horn."

"Alex's earrings. Anything else?"

"The Book of Kells," cried Jeff.

"We already listed that," said Jackie.

"No, don't you see, the Book of Kells is the Book of the four Gospels: John, Luke, Mark and . . ."

"Matthew," cried Jackie and Mattie together.

"Look to Matthew must be connected with the Book of Kells."

"Quick, Mattie, get the Book out of Alex's suitcase," said Jackie.

"What if Mam or Dad see it?"

"We'll just have to chance it."

Mattie ran upstairs and returned moments later with the Book. He pushed aside the pizza box and placed the Book on the table.

"It's all in Latin. Where do we start?" he said.

"Look to Matthew," offered Jeff.

"Which one's Matthew? Alex, which one's Matthew?"

"How should I know?" grumbled Alex without looking up from her phone.

"It's your book."

"I don't know Latin."

"It must have something to do with the word we need to find. There must be a word that is part of the spell."

"That narrows it down."

"Mattie, start looking for a word."

"You're joking, right? There are millions of words in here. It's impossible."

"*I come not to bring peace, but to bring a sword,*" quoted Alex.

"Alex, did you just speak gibberish?"

"It's from the Gospel of Matthew: Chapter 10, Verse 34."

"How do you know that?"

"It's here on Wikipedia; anyone should know that, if that's all it takes." She held up her phone.

"So, it has to do with the Sword of Nuada? We were right about that."

"No, what was the line from the spell?"

"*Replaced by the Word.*"

"I think the sword has to be replaced by something else."

"Why do you think that?"

"Because, also according to Wikipedia, when the monks wrote the Book of Kells, they made mistakes, and one mistake they made was in Matthew 10:34. They misspelled *sword.* I don't think it was a mistake, I think they did it on purpose."

"So, we have to find which word they put instead of sword. Mattie, quick, turn to the page with Matthew 10:34."

"It's in Latin."

"Yes, we know that."

"So, what does Matthew 10:34 look like in Latin? This is hopeless."

"Alex, can you get an English to Latin translation?"

"Won't do us any good; we're not looking for the translation of Matthew 10:34. They changed it, remember."

"So how do we find it?"

"The Banshee said use everything we've got, what else do we have?"

"The Ring of Thor, Alex's earrings and the horn."

"The Ring has writing on it, but it's in Norse, it can't be that. Same with the horn."

"But the earrings are . . . taken from images from the Book of Kells. Alex, where are the earrings?"

"Upstairs by my bed."

"Mattie."

"Yes, I know, go fetch them."

Mattie departed and returned with the earrings.

"Okay, Mattie, your mission, should you decide to accept it, is to find these images in the Book of Kells."

"And what will the rest of you be doing?"

"We have to find some wolfsbane."

"Where are we going to get wolfsbane? You can't just order it from the pizza shop, you know."

"Er, apparently you can, look."

Purple petals protruded from the pizza box.

"Don't touch them," ordered Jeff. "If that really is wolfsbane, they're deadly."

"Oh, God, we haven't eaten any of them, have we?" shuddered Jackie.

"I don't remember ordering wolfsbane as a topping."

"I ordered them," said Alex. "And no, we haven't eaten any. I just did it."

"You? How?"

"You reminded me that we'd seen wolfsbane at Blarney Castle. That also reminded me of something else from Blarney Castle. Remember the Wishing Steps near the Witch's Kitchen. I walked down them backwards and you said I was entitled to a wish."

"I remember."

"I just made my wish. I didn't make one then. I thought I'd save it until I needed it."

"You said you'd save it for a rainy day."

"It certainly rained a lot today."

"You had a wish, and you didn't tell me about it?" fumed Jackie.

"I didn't know it would work; it could have been superstitious nonsense."

"I was worried about you all this time and you had a wish."

"Don't get upset. It got you the wolfsbane, didn't it?"

"Yes, but we could have used it to get you home."

"Don't you think I tried that? It didn't work in the 11th century, as hard as I wished, I didn't come home."

"Oh, that's all right then."

"Can we just get on with it?" interrupted Jeff.

"Where are we so far?" asked Jackie.

"Mattie, any luck with the Book of Kells?"

"No, nothing . . . oh, hang on . . . here's the first image . . . and here's the second, they're both on the same page."

"Do you think that's the page with the word on it?"

"I've no idea. It would help if somebody could read Latin."

"Alex, look up that quote anyway."

"*Non veni pacem mittere sed gladium*," recited Alex.

"Anything look like that on the page? It won't be exactly the same."

"God, this is hard to read . . . *veni pacem mittere sed gladium* . . . it's here, I've found it, but it's the same . . . no wait, that isn't gladium; it says *gaudium* I think."

"Alex, what does gladium mean?" asked Jackie.

"Sword."

"Good, we're getting somewhere. What does gaudium mean?"

"Joy."

"Joy? What is that supposed to mean?" asked Mattie.

"I come not to bring peace, but to bring joy?" said Jeff.

"What brings joy?" asked Jackie.

Alex tapped away. "Manfred Mann's Earth Band."

"Who?"

"Manfred Mann . . . a British rock band from the 70's."

"It can't be that. What else."

"Gustav Holst."

"Who again?"

"Holst . . . classical composer, wrote something called *The Planets*. That has a song called *Jupiter, bringer of Joy*."

"This is absolutely not helping."

"Jupiter, fifth planet from the sun . . . Roman god . . . town in Florida."

"Wait, go back. Roman god."

"Jupiter, Roman god of thunder."

"Now, that can't be a coincidence."

"What can't?"

"Who's the Viking god of thunder?"

"Thor."

"And whose ring is Alex wearing?"

"The Ring of Thor!"

"Can you cross-check Thor and Jupiter?"

"Says they are the Viking and Roman versions of the same god."

"So, if we read the spell correctly," summarized Jackie. "We must take some of Alex's hair, touch it with the wolfsbane petals, then touch it with the Ring."

"Does the Ring touch the hair or the petals?" asked Mattie.

"The, er, hair, let's go with the hair. Then the Fairies have to sing something."

"What?"

"Er . . . it mentions the hair and the Ring again. The fairies must have to sing about them and that will bring Alex back."

"What about the Sword?"

"Forget the Sword; it's replaced by the Word."

"So, we do all that and Alex is saved?"

"*Returned by the Heart* . . . It must mean that. What else could it mean?"

"It could mean many things. If we get it wrong, who knows what will happen."

"What about the drinking horn?" asked Jeff.

"Oh, that's not part of the spell. That's for something else."

"What something else?" asked Alex with concern.

"I'll explain in a minute. Does anyone have a bag or a box to put the wolfsbane in?"

"It's already in a box," said Mattie.

"I can hardly take the pizza box to the fairy palace, can I? I'll look like an idiot. We need something smaller."

Jeff went to a drawer and returned with a small zip-lock storage bag. "Will this do?"

"Perfect."

"Don't touch the petals with your bare hands," warned Jeff. "I've got some kitchen gloves here, put those on for protection."

Jackie put on the gloves, tentatively picked up the petals and placed them in the bag. "Now we need some of Alex's hair. Where are the scissors?"

"You're not cutting my hair," complained Alex.

"Just a lock, that's all. Do you want to get home or not?"

"I'll get the scissors," said Mattie. He opened a second drawer and took out a large pair of shears.

"Good God, watch you don't cut my head off with those things. Watch you don't cut more than a small piece, either."

Mattie walked behind Alex and with a quick snip the deed was done.

"Mattie, rub the hair against the Ring."

"This is so stupid," said Alex. "Are you sure you know what you're doing?"

"Do you have a better idea?"

Mattie took Alex's hand and brushed the Ring against the lock of hair.

"Now in the bag," ordered Jackie.

Mattie complied and Jackie ran the zip to close the bag.

"There, all done," she removed the gloves. "Now, I'll give the bag to the fairies, they'll sing a few words, and everything will be back to normal – well, as normal as it's ever going to get."

"What about the charm?" asked Alex.

"What charm?"

"You said the Banshee said there was a spell and a charm. What about the charm?"

"Oh, I'd forgotten about that. Don't worry it's all under control."

"You know what the charm is?"

"Think so."

"Care to share it with the rest of us."

"Best not, in case I'm wrong."

Alex groaned. "And this is your plan, is it?"

"Jackie's most excellent and cunning plan," said Mattie.

"Wait a minute," frowned Jackie. "This is nothing at all like my plan."

"Absolutely no way, José," said Alex.

"But you've got to, otherwise the plan won't work," argued Jackie.

"I am not going anywhere near those people."

"Those people are the Sisterhood of the Banshee; they're your friends."

"They might be your friends, but I'm not messing with them."

"The Queen of Slievenamon said that you had to get the drinking horn from Prince Oleif and give it to the Sisterhood."

"And the second I do that, I turn into one of them. I don't think so."

"You have to give them the horn."

"Look, I've had enough of this. If your so-called plan works, then I'll be home and everything will be back where it should be. At that point, I've no intention of visiting 11th century Ireland ever again."

"The Queen of Slievenamon said you will want to go back. You won't be able if you don't get the horn."

"The Queen of Slievenamon seems to know an awful lot about what I want. I won't do it, it's too dangerous. End of discussion."

"I think Mattie is right."

"Mattie is right about what."

"You're not a Banshee."

"And I intend to keep it that way."

"But if you're not a Banshee, then what's in the bag is ordinary Alex hair and not Banshee hair, and therefore the spell won't work."

"It's too late to think about that."

"No, it's a major problem. I don't know what will happen if the hair is not genuine Banshee hair."

"But we know it isn't because I'm not a Banshee."

"You would be if you just went to the Sisterhood."

"Are you serious?"

"Yes, it's the only way – before the spell is cast, we have to be certain that the hair is Banshee hair, and we can only do that if . . ."

"How does me going to the Sisterhood help? You already have the hair. It's either good enough now or it isn't."

"I thought . . ."

"You thought what?"

"I thought I could give you enough time in the 11th century to get the drinking horn and reach the Sisterhood before we tried the spell."

"Just how will that work? You want me to text you from the 11th century – Jackie, I'm all set, cast the spell?"

"Something like that."

"You're an idiot."

"I'm the only idiot you've got."

"If it all goes wrong, I'm stuck as a Banshee for eternity. I won't come back."

"If it all goes to plan, you'll be a Banshee just long enough for the spell to work. The queen says you're going to turn into one eventually anyway. My wish can't stop that. This is the only way."

Night drew near, and with it Alex's trepidation about her unavoidable destiny. The sisters sat under the Tree. Uncle Bob and Aunt Róisín retired for the night. Mattie and Jeff were banished to the kitchen.

"Promise me you'll think about it," pleaded Jackie.

"If I get the horn, and if I get it to the Sisterhood, how will you know?"

"I'll have to guess. If I leave it until the last minute before sun rise, that'll give you the most time."

"But time works differently there, it doesn't pass in the same way. A few hours here for you might be a few days for me. In which case, everyone will be dead or fighting to avoid death or even worse . . . married."

"Get the horn as soon as you can, give it to the Sisterhood and go hide somewhere."

"And the Sword of Nuada?"

"We don't need it; and if the spell works, you couldn't bring it back anyway. Drop the Sword."

"The fairies will be disappointed."

"They'll just have to wait another thousand years."

"I suppose I'll be going then . . ."

They embraced.

"Wish me luck."

"Good luck. Wish me the same."

"You should get out of here."

"Why?"

"In case whatever comes back in my place is worse than the wolf."

"No, I'll stay right here."

"Whatever happens, don't let them talk you into making that wish, not even to bring me back. If the spell doesn't work, I don't think I want to come back."

"The spell will work, I guarantee it."

They hugged again, and Jackie felt her sister fade away. She braced herself for whatever might appear in return, but nothing did; at least nothing she could see.

"Oh, Alex, this doesn't look good," Jackie confided to the nothingness.

She returned to the kitchen and Mattie and Jeff.

"Okay boys, here's the plan," she said.

"Not again," groaned Mattie.

"I'm going down into the tunnel."

"You're not waiting for your Lämmy friend?"

"No, not this time. You see before you the take-charge, pro-active Jackie."

"Okay, what do we do?"

"Wait here."

"What? All night?"

"If you want to. Or you could go get some sleep; it's a big day tomorrow, what with us all going to Dublin and you getting ready for your soccer match."

"We'll come with you."

"No, thanks, you seem to frighten the fairies. Best if I go down alone."

"We'll wait here for you," said Jeff. "Shout us if you need anything."

"I do need one thing. Can I have the photo album? Something to look at while I'm waiting for the fairies to appear."

Jeff retrieved the family album.

"Take the Book of Kells, it's smaller," joked Mattie.

"No, I want to look at the family," Jackie smiled. "Okay, that's about it, thanks. I'll be going now. Don't wait up." She turned and walked to the pantry.

"We should go with her," grumbled Mattie.

"I know, but she's right," said Jeff. "For whatever reason, this is strictly between Alex and Jackie and the fairies."

Jackie sat in the tunnel and flipped through the pages of the family album. No fairies had appeared, but she knew it was only a matter of time; and eventually the fairy lights twinkled into view, and the wall between the tunnel and the fairy palace vanished.

But Jackie did not rise. She continued to flip back and forth amongst the pages of the album, as if engrossed. The fairy song washed over her. She ignored it. The fairies swarmed around her, curious and angry at her indifference to them. Jackie ignored them. Queen Eeviin sang to her. Jackie flipped a page. The queen materialized beside her.

"What is so engrossing, Jackie of the Ua Ruairc, that you forget your manners in the company of the Queen of the Grey Rock?" asked the queen.

Jackie looked up. "Oh, hi, sorry, I didn't see you. I was looking at some pictures."

"Pictures?"

"Yes, photographs of my family. A lot of old ones. Most of the family in these pictures are all gone now. Here's one of Great Grandfather Aedan O'Rourke, standing next to the Tree. Do you want to see?"

"We have no need to see," sang the queen. "We can recall all who we've met in perfect image."

"The Tuatha Dé Danann don't have picture albums?"

"Do not the pictures fade with time?"

"I suppose so. I suppose everything fades with time."

"How may we honor you, Jackie of the Ua Ruairc?"

"I'm not quite sure I'm ready to say, just yet."

"Do you not wish for your sister's return?"

"Who, Alex? Oh look, here's one of Alex as a baby with Aunt Róisín and Uncle Bob. This must have been taken at my Christening. So, you don't have any pictures of the great Tuatha heroes? No paintings either? Nothing etched onto glass or silver? Little doodles in a scrapbook?"

"We have no need of such."

"I think that's sad."

"You are sad? How may we comfort you?"

"Would you like to hear about my family? After all, you told me about the history of the Tuatha Dé Danann."

"The history of a simple, human family cannot compare to the legend of the Tuatha Dé Danann, rulers of Ireland."

"I suppose you're right. The O'Rourkes are nothing special compared to that. Still, I hear one of my ancestors did something that the Tuatha Dé Danann still sing about in legend."

"I would doubt it."

"Of course, he wasn't named O'Rourke back then, you probably know him better as Fergal of the Ua Ruairc."

"We would not stain our song with that name."

"No, but he is the one, isn't he? The one who stole the Sword of Nuada. How did he do that? How did a stupid human get the better of the mighty Tuatha Dé Danann?"

"He tricked us with sacred oaths which he then broke."

"What oaths?"

"He came as ambassador of the Vikings to swear allegiance to the Tuatha Dé Danann. He swore on the Sword, but it was a subterfuge to allow the Vikings to attack us and steal the Sword."

"According to Alex, he used a similar trick at Kells Abbey. That's the trouble with family. There's always one or two black sheep. Why does the Tree grow in our pub?"

"Trees grow where they will, unless chopped down by humans."

"Awe, there's Mattie and Jeff in little soccer outfits. They can't have been more than five or six when this picture was taken. Don't they look cute? You never got the Sword back, did you? Do you want to know why?"

"Speak."

"It's protected by the magic of the Ua Ruairc."

"You are human, you have no magic."

"The Ua Ruairc are also Viking, and the protection of the Viking gods was placed around the Sword. Would you like your Sword back?"

"You know where it is?"

"No, but I know what magic protects it, and with your help I can remove that magic. Then it should be a piece of cake for the great Tuatha Dé Danann to get it back."

"Why would the Ua Ruairc help us?"

"Awe this one is nice." Jackie had turned a page of the family album. "Aunt Róisín and Uncle Bob at their wedding, with my mom and dad standing next to them. Did you know Alex is getting married? But she doesn't want to, so that's a problem."

"Problems can be solved."

"That's what I think. And with your help, we can kill two birds with one stone. I feel like the family owes it to you."

"You must not harm the birds; they are of nature."

"It's just a figure of speech. The trouble with family is if one has a problem then the whole family has a problem. This is a family album, but there's people in this book who aren't even family. But that's okay because they're friends. Sometimes friends can be so close they become family, and they deserve to be put in the book. Alex and I have lots of friends and family. We met some of them here in Ireland this week. They brought us presents. They didn't even know us, but they went out of their way to come and say hello and bring us presents; and not because we're some powerful kings or magicians, but because we're family. You can keep your legends and kings. You can keep your magic. I'd rather have family. We're not all like Fergal. Some of us are quite pleasant, once you get to know us."

"How may we honor you, Jackie of the Ua Ruairc?"

"Why are you so quick to honor a descendent of the ones who stole your Sword?"

"You are the Child of the Charm."

"I am, aren't I? I'm special. More special to you than most humans. Maybe more special than you realize. Other O'Rourkes have kissed the Blarney Stone, but it didn't make them special, did it? Why not Uncle Bob, or Mattie or Jeff?"

"Once we have honored you, the spell on your sister will be broken and she shall return to you."

"Except we all know that she won't, not all of her anyway. Maybe not even half of her. I know we've had our differences, but she is still my sister and, in this case, half an Alex is definitely not better than none. Before I make my wish, you have to help me bring Alex home the proper way. Alex in exchange for the Sword. What do you say?"

"You do not know the location of the Sword. Your offer is a poor one."

"It's the best offer you've had in a thousand years. Come to think of it, it's you who made the offer. You've been planning this all along. Why did you send me to the Queen of Slievenamon? No, don't tell me. I already know. And I already know why the Tree grows in the bar. It would have been nice if you'd just come out and told me up front, it would have saved a lot of trouble, but you didn't trust me. *'Jackie of the Ua Ruairc wants our trust, yet she does not trust us,'* that's what you sang to me. I suppose I don't blame you after the way Fergal behaved, but to get my sister back, I've no choice but to trust you, and you have no choice but to trust me if you want your Sword. Only if we work together can we do the right thing. What do you say? Yes or No?"

"What sing you, oh Noble Host?" sang Queen Eeviin. "Should we help the human child?"

"Majestic and Terrible Queen," sang the Tuatha Dé Danann. "The Sword of Nuada Airgetlám has been too long out of our sight. It is time for us to act."

"I'll take that as a yes," said Jackie. She slammed shut the family album and pulled out the zip-lock bag. "Good. Now, pay close attention, 'cause I'm only going to say this once."

Frigga's Day

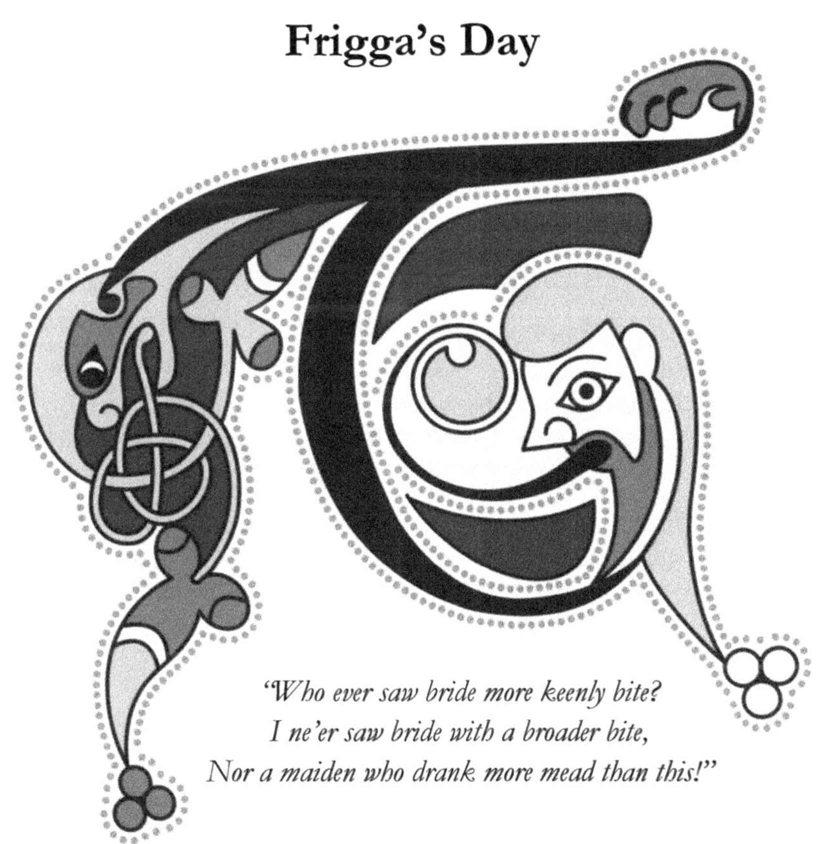

The Poetic Edda, 1000 to 1300 C.E,
from the English translation by
Henry Adams Bellows, 1923

Alex woke in the bedroom assigned to her on her arrival in Dublin. She felt refreshed, as if she had slept for a week. Had she fallen asleep? She wondered if sleep was even possible between the centuries. Then she panicked at the idea that a week really had passed. What if time stretched? Her first trip had lasted an hour or two. Her last visit had seen her trapped in this world for a whole day. How long would she have to spend this time, before the sun finally returned to Fethard?

The bed, at least, was a welcome improvement over the saddle of the horse. But the bedroom as a whole disappointed; Alex had visited Disney World and seen real princess's accommodation. The king's palace bore no resemblance. In reality, it was nothing more than a wattle and daub hut, the largest in the city no doubt, and augmented with apartments which branched out from the central, great hall, but wattle and daub nonetheless. Instead of carpets, straw covered the earth floor. Instead of tapestries, dried mud adorned the walls. She felt that her status as royalty entitled her to better.

The bedroom had no door, just a curtain, which was now pushed aside by a woman, a handmaiden, thought Alex, and most likely a slave. "My Lady, the king desires that you breakfast with him," said the woman.

"I'll be right there," answered Alex.

"Do you require assistance in your dress?"

"No, tell the king I'll be right there."

The woman took up a position outside the bedroom and Alex threw back the bed covers. She still wore the clothes from the previous night in Fethard. Alex reached the curtain and peered into a great chamber, the mead hall. At the center of the hall, smoke from a fire pit rose up and out of a hole in the ceiling. Rain dripped back into the hall in exchange. Around the hall stood wooden benches, where Vikings and visitors would sit during the day, and where the slaves would sleep at night.

Next to the fire pit, stood a large wooden table loaded with bowls of meat, fish, cheese, bread, fruit and jars of wine. At the table sat the burly figure of King Silkbeard. He dined alone. Occasionally, he gruffly ordered a servant to fill his drinking horn.

Alex took a deep breath and stepped into the hall. "Morning," she called with as much enthusiasm as she could muster.

"By Oden's beard, get dressed, Girl!" roared the king in reply, and he spat out the crushed bones of a chicken leg.

Alex retreated to the bedroom, although the force of the king's command made no other choice possible. A cursory glance around the bedroom showed nothing in the way of a wardrobe except for a solitary chest with some clothes on top of it. She returned to the curtain and whispered to the maid.

"Er, a little help here," she asked.

The maid entered.

"Yes, My Lady."

"Er, is that it for clothing?" Alex asked pointing to the chest.

"Yes, My Lady. We were warned that you had arrived without baggage. The dressmaker has been summoned, but in the meantime, a lady of similar size to you has provided you with the kirtle and hangerock."

"Oh, thanks, er, kirtle?"

"We were also warned that My Lady is not well, that her memory . . ."

"Don't say it, just help me get dressed."

"If My Lady would remove her . . ."

"No, I'll keep these on, thank you very much. Just show me what goes over the top."

"As you wish, My Lady. First the kirtle."

The maid retrieved the white woolen under dress with long sleeves, a single piece which hung from the neck to the ankles. It had no buttons, zippers, or laces to tie. With the maid's help, Alex pulled the kirtle over her head.

"Now the hangerock, My Lady."

The blue hangerock (or apron) was almost as large as the kirtle, made of two pieces of linen, braided together to form a tube with shoulder straps. Alex and the maid repeated the tug of war. With her 21st century clothes underneath, the combination made a stuffy and cumbersome ensemble.

The maid completed the effect by pinning two oval broaches to the hangerock. "There, My Lady. I know you are used to better, but the dressmaker has been summoned."

"So you said. Am I fit to breakfast with the king now?"

"I shall announce you, My Lady."

"Then see if you can find out what's happened to my servant, Brother Oswald, and bring him to me."

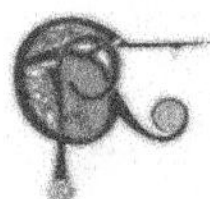

If Alex had expressed surprise at Prince Oleif's dearth of Viking stereotypes, then the prince's father, King Sigtrygg Silkbeard, made

up for it in abundance. He appeared a Viking from head to toe, from inside to out, from his broad-shouldered exterior, hidden to some extent by his big bushy beard, to his gruff demeanor.

"Your father got the better bargain with this marriage," said the king. He picked up a wedge of goat cheese and bit into it.

Alex wondered how the words could come out of the king's mouth at the same time he shoveled food in it. The king took a gulp of wine; it flowed out of his mouth and down his beard and took remnants of cheese with it.

"Come on, Girl, eat."

The combination of the king's eating habits and the sounds and smells, which emanated from what she guessed was a stable at the north end of the hall, worked to suppress Alex's appetite. She picked at the corner of a piece of bread.

"And now your dowry is lost with your gowns."

"I'm sure my . . . father will make up the loss," said Alex.

"The alliance is the . . . burp . . . important thing. Dublin may be an outpost of the empire, but it sits on the trade routes. Can't . . . belch . . . be bettered for trade; you remind your father of that."

"Next time I see him, I promise."

"What word from my son? Why did he not escort you?"

"Prince Oleif? Oh, he was sort of busy packing. I'm sure he'll be along at any minute."

"He'd better hurry or he'll miss the . . . burp . . . wedding."

"Yes, that would be a shame."

"And the battle, I need him here for that."

"He wouldn't want to miss that for the world."

"I sent for the dressmaker."

"Yes, my, er . . . I was told that."

"Can't have you wed in sackcloth. That dress isn't fit for a slave, let alone a . . . belch . . . princess. I don't know if we'll be ready in time. Tomorrow will be busy. First the wedding and then the battle."

"Tomorrow?"

"Of course, tomorrow."

"But isn't that too soon for a wedding?"

"It's Frigga's Day. All marriages are on Frigga's day. And it was negotiated with your father. It's in the contract. If you don't wed tomorrow, you'll have to wait a whole week."

"I can wait. What's a week after all? Then Oleif and I will be together for ever."

"We can't wait a week; we have to get you wed before the battle."

"Why?"

"If my son gets killed in battle, there will be no marriage, no dowry, and no alliance with your father. No, you wed tomorrow, assuming my son has returned by then . . . belch."

"Can't you postpone the battle?"

"Postpone the battle?" The king ejected a mangled combination of meat, bread, cheese, and wine from his mouth. "By Oden's beard, what kind of talk is that?"

"It sounds like there's an awful lot on your plate." *Not to mention your beard and clothes* Alex added silently.

"Once we start the wedding, I don't want the Irish to spoil the feast. And they won't want to sit in the field a whole month while you sup honey. Tomorrow, the Irish celebrate their festival of Good Friday. The last thing Bóruma will expect from us is to attack on such a sacred day. We'll have the advantage of surprise. It must be tomorrow. Then we can return to your wedding festival, a month of feasting to celebrate the victory over the Irish, and the merger of the families of Silkbeard and Forkbeard. What an alliance that will make."

"If you say so."

"It is too bad that none of your entourage survived the journey from Norway to be with you on your joyous day, but your friend, Fergal Ua Ruairc, has agreed to act as your kinsmen."

"How kind. That Fergal just can't do enough for me, it seems."

"And there is yet more good news from Norway: your brother, Prince Anwud, should be here by morning. With any luck, you will have blood relatives at your wedding after all. Anwud will act for your father."

Alex tried not to show her consternation at this news. If the brother of the real Princess Estrid turned up, then she would be exposed as an imposter.

"He's also bringing a few good men to the fight; kill two birds with one arrow. Thor's thunder, where's that dressmaker?" the king bellowed. "If she's not before me in the next minute, I'll make a dress of her skin and use her hair for boot laces."

The maid returned with a second woman and Brother Oswald.

"The dressmaker is here, My Lord," said the maid.

"About time. And who's the . . . burp . . . holy man?"

"Brother Oswald is my servant," said Alex.

"Christian monk?"

Brother Oswald nodded.

"Can you read the Latin, monk?"

Brother Oswald nodded again.

"And write?"

Brother Oswald nodded a third time.

"Don't say much do you? Good! I have need of a scribe with knowledge of the Christian ways. I'm thinking of an alliance with your king in Rome, or whatever you call him. In the meantime, if you can work a needle and stitch, you can help the dressmaker; otherwise keep to your mistress's side until I call for you . . ."

Snorri entered the hall.

"Snorri, you have reports for me?"

Snorri nodded.

"What, have you all lost your tongues? Are all the men mute who come from Kells?"

Snorri opened his mouth, "My Lord . . ."

"Never mind," roared the king. He stood up. Food scattered and wine spilled. "Breakfast over. Dressmaker, make a dress. Snorri, with me to the Thingmote.[#3]" Belch, burp, fart. He stormed out, leaving a cloud of scraps in his wake.

Prince Oleif and the party from Kells arrived just before sunset. Alex did not see him immediately because he insisted on taking a hot bath first to remove the dust of the journey. Then he went to the mead hall, where the king had assembled his advisors for a war council.

The king declared the meeting off-limits to women and he had Alex confined to her room, where the maid and dressmaker worked on her wedding dress. For decorum, Brother Oswald waited outside the curtain. Although the king had banned Alex from the meeting, she could still hear every word spoken between the consumption of vast quantities of alcohol.

"What do you know of Bóruma's strength?" the king asked his son.

"Their main camp lies about a mile north of the Liffey," replied Prince Oleif. "They are about ten thousand men, but they are disorganized, poorly armed and bicker amongst themselves. Their tribal leaders don't trust each other. I wouldn't be at all surprised if they are thousands fewer by morning."

"How do you know this?" asked Snorri.

#3 Thingmote: Had Alex bothered to ask, she would have found that the Thingmote was a circular mound, about 40 foot high and 240 foot in circumference. It was a kind of Viking parliament, where laws and speeches were made. The Thingmote in Dublin stood where Dublin Castle stands today. Of course, Alex couldn't be bothered to ask, so we may never know.

"Because, dear Snorri, they gave us a guided tour. We ran into them on the Kells road."

"And they let you pass?"

"Yes, they invited us in for a few drinks. We had a bit of a chat and then we said we had to get back to Dublin before nightfall. So, they escorted us to the ford and waved goodbye."

"They didn't take you for ransom or slaves? None killed?"

"No, they said the honorable thing would be to meet us on the field of battle. Rather sporting of them, I thought. Bóruma shook my hand and asked that I pass on his compliments to the king."

Burp!

"Speaking of depleting the ranks," continued Prince Oleif. "As we crossed the ford, we saw longships sail out to sea. There had to be at least 60 of them. What's that all about?"

"That is our allies, Sigard of Orkney and Brodir of Man."

"Are our allies, or were? Why are they sailing away from Dublin with six thousand Vikings on the eve of battle? How many men do we have left to defend the city?"

"See what happens when you miss the Thingmote. Don't worry, we still have a thousand armed men to defend Dublin."

"Ten to one odds. I know we're Viking and they are rabble, but still."

"Not ten to one. Sigard and Brodir have deserted us . . . or so it will seem to Bóruma, but it is a clever ruse, invented by Snorri at the Thingmote. The ships have merely sailed over the horizon. They will return before morning to the north of the Irish, and we'll have them surrounded."

"We also arranged for a slave to escape," said Snorri. "He'll make it to Bóruma's camp with the news that the Viking lords have quarreled and that Brodir and Sigard have betrayed us, and that they seek an alliance with Bóruma in exchange for Sigtrygg Silkbeard's throne and property. The Irish won't know what hit them."

"Snorri, you are a tactical genius as well as a scholar," beamed Prince Oleif.

"We'll get you wed early morning," said the king. "Then we'll join our brothers in the field."

"Tomorrow? Frigga's Day?"

"Yes, of course, tomorrow. Why do you and your bride seem shocked that you'll be married on Frigga's Day?"

"No, it's not that. Of course, we'll be married. It's just that doing battle with the Irish tomorrow, it's a holy day for them, they won't be prepared for a fight."

"And that will make our surprise all the more effective."

"But is that fair?"

"Sometimes I worry about you. Are you sure you're my son?"

"Of course, it's an excellent plan."

"The only thing that remains is to decide who will carry the Ravens into battle."

"Are the Ravens necessary," asked Snorri. "The victory is already assured."

"Nothing is assured. Do you think I really trust that Sigard and Brodir will return? What if they flounder on the sea? The Raven Standard will guarantee our victory, either way. Thrall, bring it here."

The slave commanded by Silkbeard came to the center of the mead hall. He carried a banner. On the banner were the images of two Ravens: Huginn and Muninn, the messengers of Odin. Legend had it that the army which marched behind the Raven Standard was invincible.

"But prophecy has it," said Snorri. "That whoever carries the Raven Standard will be the first slain on the field."

"With the Ravens before us, we cannot lose. And our victory will be even sweeter when the Norse gods defeat the Irish gods on their holy day. Who will carry the Ravens into battle?"

"I will," said Prince Oleif.

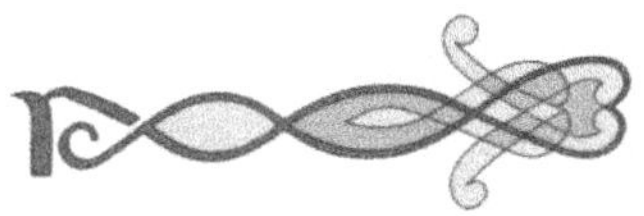

With the council concluded, Alex joined Prince Oleif for dinner in the mead hall. They were not alone. The king felt in a mood to celebrate his upcoming victory over the Irish, so Alex and the prince had to settle for a not-so-quiet corner away from the fire pit. Alex ordered Brother Oswald to stay close at hand.

"I overheard Snorri say it's bad luck to carry the Raven Standard," said Alex.

"Snorri worries too much and overdoes the superstitions. It's just a flag," replied Prince Oleif.

"But it will still make you a target for the Irish."

"That's my job, I have to lead my men to battle."

"You could get killed."

"Then Valhalla, here I come."

"I think Snorri has your safety at heart."

"He is a good man."

"We're getting married in the morning. I don't think it's fair to make me a bride and widow on the same day."

"Now you're worrying too much. I've seen the Irish, there's not a real warrior amongst them apart from Bóruma, and he's an old man who can no longer wield a sword. No, Snorri was also right when he said that the Ravens were not needed. One look at the berserkers and the Irish will flee. We shall wed in the morning, and then I'll go hunting for some new Irish slaves. I'll be home for dinner."

"Oleif . . ."

"Yes, my love?"

". . . About this wedding . . . I'm not sure I can go through with it. I'm not sure I'm ready to get married."

"Marriage is a big step, I agree. But our fathers have drawn up the contract. We don't have much choice in the matter. I, for one, am pleased with my father's choice for me. You are beautiful and so different from any other girl I've ever met."

"More different than you could imagine."

"Vikings are not supposed to have feelings of a romantic nature. I asked Snorri if he would compose a love poem for me to read to you, but he refused. He said that such a poem carries witchcraft in its words to entrap us."

"He's very wise."

"The skalds of Sweden have such poetry. It is forbidden by death, but I have read some."

> *Well considered, the woman's worth the whole of Iceland,*
> *Heavy though my heart of Hunland, and of Denmark;*
> *Not for all of England's earth and kingdoms would I*
> *Forego the golden-braided girl, ay, nor for Ireland.*[4]

"That is beautiful, how can it be forbidden?"

"We are Vikings, we must only think of honor and duty. Fortunately for me, duty, honor, and love will all come together tomorrow. It will be the best day of my life."

"And a good day to die?"

"I could think of no better."

"But I'm still not ready. I don't know what to do."

"Of course, your illness has not yet abated. Don't worry, the ceremony is simple. All the important things have already been done, although Father is still angry about the dowry. All we have to do is show up."

#4. Skalds (Maiden-Song) really were outlawed on pain of death for the skald who wrote them. The verse quoted here is taken from 'The Skalds: A Selection of their Poems with Introduction and Notes' by Lee M. Hollander, University of Michigan Press, 1945.

"There's got to be more to it than that?"

"It's easy, Father will mumble some words about gods and sacrifices, and you just copy me."

"I'll mess it up."

"Look, let me explain. In the morning, your old clothes will be stripped away and burned, and then your maids will bathe you and dress you in your bridal gown."

"My old clothes?"

"Yes, to signify the end of your old life and the start of your new. We'll hold the marriage here in the hall. Father will conduct the ceremony. First, I will present you with your morning gift. Then Father will sacrifice a goat. Then we will exchange swords."

"I don't have a sword."

"Oh, that's a problem." The prince mulled it over for a few seconds. "Tell you what, why don't you use the one that Fergal Ua Ruairc gave to me . . ."

Although too far away to have heard the mention of his name, Fergal, who sat by the fire pit, at the right hand of the king, turned to Alex and Prince Oleif and raised his mug of wine, as if to toast the happy couple.

". . . It is a beautiful weapon, worthy of your marriage." The prince signaled to Brother Oswald and gave orders. "Monk, in my quarters, you'll find a sword in a white scabbard, you know the one. Take it to your mistress's room."

Brother Oswald obeyed.

"Then Father will say a few more words," continued Prince Oleif. "And last, we share a drink of honey-mead from the marriage horn. Well, mostly honey-mead, with a little bit of the goat's blood sprinkled in it."

"Marriage horn?"

"Yes, we have a particularly fine drinking horn. It's been used in family weddings for generations." He called for a slave. "Bring the marriage horn so my bride may see it."

The slave obeyed and handed the horn to Alex. She recognized it instantly.

"See the runes around the rim," said Prince Oleif. "And the finely engraved longship."

"Our drinking from the horn will signify our wedding is complete and that the honeymoon has begun. It's party time. We'll have the goat for dinner. Of course, we'll have to go and slaughter the Irish before we can get too carried away with the feasting, that can't be helped; consider it another wedding gift."

"This is all happening so fast. Tomorrow . . ."

"Today."

"Today?"

"Yes, we have talked the night away. It is midnight. It is now Frigga's Day, our wedding day."

Around the fire pit, the clatter of drunken Vikings continued. In her conversation with Prince Oleif, Alex had almost blotted it out, so that it became mere background noise. And so, she did not notice another Viking enter the mead hall. He had an announcement to make. To gain the attention of the king and his entourage, he pulled out an axe and banged the handle three times hard against his shield. The noise subsided a little.

"My Lord," shouted the Viking. "I bring greetings from Prince Anwud of Norway. He is at the door and seeks admittance."

"This is welcome news, my love," said Prince Oleif. "Your brother made it in time for your wedding."

"Er, Oleif, will you excuse me a minute?" said Alex. She quickly stood and tried to disguise her sprint across the hall to her room as a casual, elegant glide.

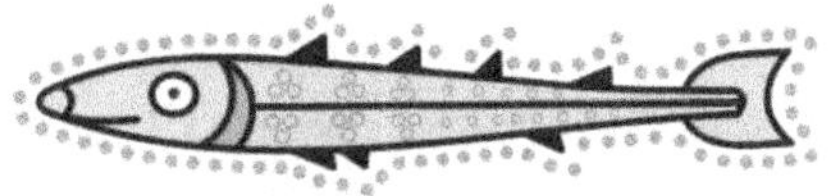

"Oswald, we have to go, and we have to go now!"

"My Lady?"

"Don't bother to pack, we must hurry . . ."

The confused monk started towards the curtain.

". . . Not that way, is there another way out?"

"No, My Lady; that is the only exit."

Alex looked around the room for an opening which would contradict him. She saw none. Then as she looked back to Brother Oswald, she saw that he held the Sword. She pulled the Sword from its scabbard and raised it. She had expected that it would take all her strength, but the Sword proved remarkably easy to wield. Alex swung the Sword and struck the wattle wall. The Sword passed through the wall as if it passed through air. The wall splintered, a gap appeared and Alex, braced for resistance but finding none, fell through it. Before the dust had settled, she stuck her head back through the wall and beckoned to the monk.

"Not anymore. Come on."

Brother Oswald followed Alex through the hole in the wall.

"Which way?"

"It doesn't matter, just as long as it's away from here . . ."

"*Estrid?*" Alex heard the prince call.

". . . Er, this way."

Alex dragged Brother Oswald west, by rows of neat little cottages and vegetable gardens, connected with wattle walkways. Nighttime had fallen and not even the moonlight could penetrate the cloud-filled, dark sky, the only lights came from fire pits inside the cottages and the occasional beacon of the watch. This proved both good and bad: in the dark, pursuit would be harder, but it also made obstacles difficult to see and avoid.

Beneath their feet, the walkways ended, and muddy earth began, but they continued west until they came to the city wall. Below the wall, they spied a campfire. Its light outlined those gathered around it as unidentifiable silhouettes, but Alex heard one speak.

"Well, I say it was rude to invite Fergal to the wedding and not us," said a voice which Alex recognized as belonging to Tighernán Ua Ruairc.

"Damn," thought Alex. "It's Fergal's brothers."

"And I say it was wrong of Fergal to give away that sword to the prince," added Niall Ua Ruairc. "Worth a fortune, that sword."

"He only did it after he tried to prize out its jewels," said Tighernán. "Tried and failed, broke three knives, and cut himself in the trying. Couldn't sell it as is and couldn't break it and sell the jewels separately. If Fergal has his way, the prince will end up paying for it in installments."

Alex tried to shoo Brother Oswald away from the camp, but the Ua Ruairc wolfhound detected the presence of strangers and began to bark. Alex tugged at Brother Oswald, and they turned north, away from the camp. The sound of the barking dog and Tighernán's subsequent curses receded to the south. But Alex had no time to celebrate their escape, for soon another obstacle presented itself. The Liffey blocked their path.

"Which way, Oswald, which way?" she implored.

"Where does My Lady wish to go?"

"Home, that's all . . ."

The increase in barks and curses signified that the Ua Ruairc had now also decided to explore to the north and closed in on them.

". . . We just need a place to hide until morning - This way."

Alex started to run east, back towards the cottages. Brother Oswald chased after her. As they approached the first of the cottages, its door opened and a strong light from the interior exposed the fugitives as if caught in a search light. A woman and young girl with blazing red hair appeared in the doorway. Alex recognized them as members of the Sisterhood of the Banshee. The sound of the Ua Ruairc to the west combined with that of the Vikings to the east. She heard Prince Oleif lead the search for her.

"Estrid? Estrid?" he called.

She only had moments until they found her. She looked at her hands and realized that she still carried the Sword and drinking horn. And she realized the futility of escape. Alex then raised her eyes toward the Banshees.

"I have something for you," she cried.

The Banshees nodded.

"Promise me that Oswald will be safe?" she begged.

The Banshees nodded again.

In the distance, but now closer, Alex could hear the increasingly anxious cries of Prince Oleif and she knew the time had come.

"Oswald, I have to say goodbye now. These . . . women will hide you. There's a big battle coming later today, keep away from it. You'll be safe in the city until it's over, then you can make your way back to Kells as best you can."

"My Lady, you need protection," said Brother Oswald.

Alex smiled. "No, Oswald, I need to trust my sister. This way."

She led the monk along the wattle garden path and approached the Banshees.

"I don't want him to die. You must not cry for him. Is that understood?"

The Banshees nodded again and then stood aside to allow them to enter the cottage. Once Alex and Brother Oswald had entered, the Banshees closed the cottage door to the outside world. More Banshees stood against the walls, mere silhouettes in the shadows. Alex gave the drinking horn to the Banshee who stood before her and then considered the Sword.

"I think this belongs to the fairies." She handed over the Sword. "All right then," she asked the Banshees. "How does this embrace thing work?"

In Dublin's Fair City

Prose Edda, Snorri Sturluson, circa 1220,
translated by A.G.Brodeur, 1916

 **"I** have magic in this bag," said Jackie. "I have wolfsbane and the hair of a Banshee. All I need to complete the spell is the song of the Faerie."

"And what should we sing?" sang the Tuatha Dé Danann.

"I need you to sing something uplifting. Since I got here, you've done a lot of singing, but it's all been a bit sad. The spell refers to the Word and the Word, as far as I can tell, is *Joy*. I need you to sing the spell I am about to say, but you have to be glad to sing it. You need to think happy thoughts as you sing. The spell will only work if you mean it. For me, this spell will bring Alex back. For you, it means you will get your Sword; that should make you happy."

"The return of our Sword is a joyous prospect. Lead us in song, Jackie of the Ua Ruairc," sang Queen Eeviin.

Jackie began and the Tuatha Dé Danann followed.

The purple of the Wolf
To the hair of the Banshee,
The edge of the Sword
Replaced by the Word,

To the hair of the Banshee,
The song of the Faerie.
Replaced by the Word,

Jackie said the final two lines of the spell, but the Tuatha Dé Danann did not join her.

"What's wrong?" she asked, but the Tuatha Dé Danann remained silent. "What's wrong?" she pressed again.

"I think they are tongue-tied," said Alex, as she walked into the palace.

"Alex! Alex!" Jackie jumped up and ran to her sister. "It worked, you're back."

"Hello, Sis. Yes, I do believe I'm back. One second, I was in a cottage in Dublin, and then the Sisters showed me a secret passage. I stepped into the passage and next thing I know, I'm here."

"Is it you? Is it all of you?"

"I think so. I feel . . . whole again. Yes, I'm back."

"Oh, I'm so glad to see you."

"So am I. You cut it a little close."

Jackie stood back. "You're not married, are you?"

"No, I ran away before the ceremony began."

"You're not a Banshee, are you?"

"No, I've left the Banshee behind as well."

"Was it horrible?"

"The most horrible thing you can imagine. Banshees have to live with such sadness that . . . no, let's not talk about that, even talking about it is horrible. Lucky for me the feeling only lasted a moment before the spell set me free. I'm back. And you are the joy bringer."

"Me? It was nothing. I couldn't have done it without the fairies . . . I mean Tuatha Dé Danann." Jackie turned. "You all did great, give yourselves a high five."

But the Tuatha Dé Danann still kept silent.

"What's wrong with you? We did it. We got Alex back. Now you can get your Sword."

"Another of the Ua Ruairc has tricked us," said Queen Eeviin. "We are a Fay People."

"No, we did it together. I didn't trick . . . wait a minute . . ."

Jackie faltered, frozen instantly in fear at the implication of the queen's words. It was not what Queen Eeviin had said which affected her, it was that she had said it - spoken it and not sung it.

"Oh my God," whispered Jackie.

"What's wrong?" asked Alex.

"Queen Eeviin said I tricked them."

"Well, you didn't, so she's wrong."

"No, you don't understand - she said it."

"You're correct, I don't understand."

"She said it, she didn't sing it. The Tuatha Dé Danann don't speak, they sing. Something has gone horribly wrong. Queen Eeviin, I didn't trick you, honest."

"First the Ua Ruairc steal the Sword of Nuada," said the queen. "Now they steal our song."

"We haven't stolen it, it's just . . . misplaced. I'll help you find it," said Jackie.

"Without our song, we are a doomed people, condemned to live and die as humans."

"No, I'll fix it."

"And all will eventually die without our song. The rains will die. The land will die. Nature itself will die."

All around the sisters, the little balls of light which were the Tuatha Dé Danann began to fade.

"This is not happening," cried Jackie. "I won't let it happen. I'll make my wish now. I wish for Tuatha Dé Danann to have their song back."

"Without our song, we cannot honor you," said Queen Eeviin. "Our magic was in our song."

The Faerie lights went out, one by one.

"Don't go," cried Jackie. "We can work this out."

But the Faerie continued to disappear.

"Where are you going? Come back."

"We go to die, Daughter of the Ua Ruairc," said Queen Eeviin. "Out of sight of humans."

"No, I can help. Trust me."

"We shall trust no more. We shall sing no more."

With that, Queen Eeviin faded from view and the sisters found themselves alone in the palace, in almost complete darkness. Only the hint of light from the passage to the kitchen prevented an absolute blackout.

"Would you say that went well?" asked Alex.

"Oh, dear," said Jackie. "I don't think things went according to plan."

"Come on, Sis, you're the optimistic one, remember? Is that your friend, Lämmy, over there?"

From the passage, a new ball of light appeared.

"Lämmy, at least you are still here," said Jackie as the fairy horse entered the palace. "They've stopped singing. What shall I do?"

> *"The child of woman wishes for song,*
> *But cannot sing in harmony.*
> *The child of man wishes for dreams,*
> *But cannot cast the spell of sleep."*

"You said that when we first met. What does it mean?"

> *"And if the child so dares to see,*
> *And I will follow who follows me."*

"Where to now, Lämmy. Everything is still messed up, and I don't know what to do."

"In Dublin's fair city,
Where the girls are so pretty."

"Dublin? We have to go to Dublin? Then what?"

But Lämmy did not answer. The fairy horse turned and floated away.

"Why must they always answer everything with a riddle and then just disappear? It's very annoying."

"I guess we have to go to Dublin to find out," answered Alex. "Don't know if I want to go back so soon, but I promised Jeff we'd go and watch his soccer match."

"Oh, Alex, I think I really messed things up this time. I don't want to be responsible for the death of the fairies. What shall we do?"

Alex removed her Viking apron and kirtle and dropped them to the ground. "First, we shall go and pack."

"It just never ends," said Mattie. "Now I've heard everything. A fairy horse singing Molly Malone, *'Cockles and mussels, alive, alive, oh.'* What is happening to Ireland?"

"I'm officially depressed," said Jackie.

"Welcome to the club," said Alex.

"I don't see that we've accomplished much," said Jeff. "We still have the Book of Kells upstairs, Alex still has the Ring of Thor stuck on her finger, and the magic spell seems to have killed the fairies."

"At least Lämmy is still singing, that must mean something, and we got Alex back," said Mattie.

His comment was met by a gloomy silence.

"Oh, thanks for the warm welcome," complained Alex.

The four cousins slumped at the kitchen table, elbows down and chins on hands. Mugs of tea went undrunk. Alex pushed away a plate of soda bread. Depression lay over the kitchen in multiple layers, making movement slow and dull. And most depressing of all, the sun shone bold and bright in a clear blue sky.

"I don't see how I got it wrong," said Jackie. She turned the plastic bag of wolfsbane and Banshee hair over in her hands. "Alex, are you sure you were a Banshee at the time we cast the spell?"

"Positive," answered Alex. "Believe me; you would know the difference between human and Banshee. It's not pleasant."

"Then I give up," Jackie tossed the bag on the kitchen table. "The fairies must have had too little joy in their hearts when they sang."

Alex picked up the bag and looked at it. A puzzled expression appeared on her face. "Er, Jackie?" she said.

"What?"

"The hair of the Banshee part of the spell."

"What about it?"

"What if it wasn't?"

"What if it wasn't what?"

"What if it wasn't hair of the Banshee?"

"Well, we knew we were taking a risk when Mattie cut your hair before you actually were a Banshee, but it was the only chance we had."

"I think it was a bigger risk that you imagined."

"What do you mean?"

Alex held up the plastic bag. "Mattie didn't cut my hair."

"Of course he did, we all saw him."

"I, er, this is going to sound silly. Mattie didn't cut my hair. I was, er, wearing an extension. He cut off a bit of that. What you've got in the bag is hair extension of Banshee."

"OMG! no wonder things went wrong."

"What's hair extension?" asked Mattie.

"Never mind," said Alex.

"A wig?" exclaimed Jeff. "You wear a wig?"

"It's not a wig," rebuffed Alex. "It's a hair extension, to augment my natural beauty. Don't laugh; extensions are very popular in California just now."

"I am utterly devastated," said Jackie.

"Maybe if we went back to the Queen of Slievenamon she could help us?" said Mattie.

"Brother, I don't know if you remember, but we're going to Dublin today," said Jeff. "We have the soccer final tomorrow."

"Slievenamon won't do us any good," agreed Jackie. "Lämmy said Dublin was the next stop and that's where we should go. Off to Dublin."

"Not unless you get your bags packed," said Aunt Róisín, who had just entered the kitchen and caught Jackie's last words. "Come on, the lot of you. Seán Murphy is here to look after the pub while we're gone. We have to get to Thurles for the train. Come on, jump to it."

The cousins ran upstairs to their bedrooms. Alex opened her suitcase and looked at the Book of Kells.

"What shall we do about the Book?" asked Jackie.

"We'll take it with us to Dublin. It will be safer for everyone if we dump it there rather than in Fethard. We can drop it near Trinity College. Of course, no one will believe it's the real thing anyway."

The girls quickly packed, throwing everything into their cases rather than folding carefully. To make room for the Book of Kells and the drinking horn, Alex transferred much of the content of her case to that of her sister.

"Oh, I just forgot one thing," said Jackie. She retrieved a vanity case and selected a pair of scissors.

"You're not going to cut my hair, are you?" asked Alex.

"No, I'll be right back."

Jackie ran out of the bedroom and down the stone staircase to the kitchen. She returned a few moments later with a small green object in her hand.

"What have you got there?" asked Alex.

"It's a leaf," said Jackie. "From the Tree."

"You've cut a leaf from a fairy tree? Are you out of your mind? You've heard all the stories about how dangerous that is. What on earth were you thinking?"

Jackie returned the scissors and placed the leaf in the vanity case for safe keeping. "I'm thinking it was the right thing to do," she smiled.

And so off to Dublin went the O'Rourkes. Uncle Bob courteously offered to fetch the sisters' cases from their bedroom, but on straining his back, instantly regretted it and complained that the girls should have purchased lighter souvenirs.

As the car returned towards Thurles, Jackie waived goodbye to the castle, locals, pubs, horses, Fethard and Slievenamon. Her optimism had returned and, despite the absence of a new cunning plan, she had a good feeling about Dublin.

Alex, on the other hand, slumped into the seat and didn't look back. For Alex, this may have seemed normal behavior, but in spite of Alex's protestations that she was fine, Jackie could tell that her sister remained troubled by her adventures in the 11th century, and that her briefest of times as a Banshee had amplified her melancholy.

Once in Dublin, as evening approached, they settled in their hotel at the centre of the action: Temple Bar. And while Uncle Bob and Aunt Róisín proceeded to the hotel bar, where someone else would serve the drinks for a change, the cousins headed out to the cobble stone streets for some exploration before dinner.

Temple Bar buzzed with tourists and street performers. Vendors and café owners jostled for trade. On the corner of Crown Alley, a man in a Viking costume held a board which advertised a local fish shop. As wave after wave of energy hit her, Jackie felt a burst of sensory overload, in other words, Heaven. Alex cheered up considerably. Mattie joined in Jackie's exuberance. Jeff looked at the menus in restaurant windows and shook his head in disappointment at what he considered a wasted opportunity to showcase Irish cuisine to the rest of the world.

Other than the pending cup final, they would have two whole days to play tourist, so they walked out of Temple Bar towards College Green, where they loaded up on pamphlets from the Visitors Information Center, before they wandered farther and eventually found themselves on Grafton Street.

"Louis Vuitton," beamed Jackie, as she snapped a picture of the shop on her phone. Not that they ever purchased much from the famed fashion house, but the sisters had a mission to visit every store in the world. They competed with their friends in San Diego, and Dublin would put them in the lead.

"Molly Malone," cried Mattie, as they came across the statue dedicated to the famous Dubliner. "*Crying, 'Cockles and mussels.'*"

Above the noise of Grafton Street, Jackie heard a reply.

"Alive, alive, oh."

She looked at the others. No one else had heard it. She smiled.

Ardan Fennelly had placed Mattie and Jeff under strict orders to get a good night's sleep on the eve of their big game. Fennelly was already upset that the boys did not travel on the team bus with the rest of the squad, and was only placated when Uncle Bob assured him that he would enforce a strict curfew and get the boys to the stadium in time for the warm-up session before the game.

But curfew was a loosely defined and ambiguous term, for the O'Rourkes felt it compulsory to take the girls to the *Brazen Head*, Ireland's oldest pub, for a dinner of Irish stew and an evening of folklore, storytelling, and music. Johnny the Storyteller weaved stories from history with fairy tales and magic to a room full of tourists, mostly American and for some reason, Norwegian. The Storyteller's soft, dulcet tones captured and captivated all who heard him, as if he had the fairy song in his voice.

"If only you knew," thought Jackie.

"Alive, alive, oh."

The following morning at breakfast with Aunt Róisín, the girls pored over the tourist literature. Uncle Bob and the boys had already left to rendezvous with Fennelly.

"Where to first?" asked Aunt Róisín. "We have just enough time for one or two things before we have to join your uncle to watch the boys."

"Whatever," said Alex, who had fallen back into malaise, owing to a lack of sleep, and afraid that the 11th century might yet claim her. But she had remained in her bed all night, and for that she was grateful. "Let Jackie pick."

"Oooh, oooh, this one," cried Jackie and she held up a pamphlet.

"What it it?" asked Aunt Róisín.

"St. Michan's Church," said Jackie.

"A church?" groaned Alex. "I was wrong, don't let Jackie pick."

"No this is a good one. It has a crypt with mummies in it."

"That sounds even worse."

"According to legend, it was a visit to St. Michan's which inspired Bram Stoker to write Dracula."

"Jackie, haven't you had enough of vampires?"

"No, we have to go, it'll be fun."

"Whatever."

"St. Michan's Church it is then," said Aunt Róisín.

From Temple Bar, the church entailed a short walk in glorious sunshine. Aunt Róisín insisted that they first walk west, by the Cathedral of the Holy Trinity, better known as Christ Church Cathedral. It lay in the old Viking part of the city and was founded by King Sigtrygg Silkbeard after his pilgrimage to Rome in 1028.

Across from the Cathedral, and connected to it by an enclosed stone bridge, stood the building which housed the exhibit known as *Dublinia*, which in turn, promised to tell you everything you could possibly want to know about the Vikings in Dublin. Alex felt she already knew too much.

Then they looped north, stopped by the Brazen Head to snap some more pictures, and then crossed the Liffey by way of the Father Mathew Bridge, site of the first bridge across the river built in 1014, the *Bridge of Dubhghall*. They arrived at St. Michan's a few moments later.

As with the Cathedral, the Vikings were reputed to have built the church, although their original structure had long since gone and the current one only dated to 1686. The interior of the church contained an organ, circa 1724, on which a musician named Handel composed a little ditty called *Messiah*. But most (non-worshipping) visitors came to see the mummies. The O'Roukes joined several other tourists (again, Norway well represented) and a tour guide led them out of the church to the south side and some stone steps leading down to the crypt.

The tour guide stopped at a padlocked door and produced a key. "Just a precaution," he said. "The mummies are likely to be taking a stroll to the pub if we don't keep the doors locked." He descended the steps to the crypt and bade his guests follow. "We have several mummies," he intoned as he moved from chamber to chamber. "As well as some other famous residents, including the Sheares brothers, who were executed in the customary manner by the British following the Rising of 1798."

"What's the customary manner?" asked Jackie.

"Hung, drawn and quartered," answered the guide.

"Cool," said Jackie.

"And here we are," said the guide on arriving at the last chamber. "The famous mummies of St. Michan. The oldest, known as the Crusader, is more than 900 years old. That's him in the corner, at rest with his sword. We are not entirely sure why their bodies are so well preserved; some have speculated that our proximity to the Liffey plays a part. It is a tradition that visitors to St. Michan's pay their respects to the deceased by shaking hands with the Crusader."

"Cool," said Jackie.

"Gross," said Alex.

"It is also considered to bring good luck," added the guide. "For those who wish, please form in single file, and enter the Crusader's vault one at a time. I would also ask that you stroke the Crusader's hand with the lightest of touches; the Crusader is very old and brittle and needs to be treated gently."

"Come on," said Jackie, falling in line behind the Norwegians. "We need all the luck we can get."

"I think I'll pass," said Alex.

But others had already closed behind her and blocked her retreat. Alex's only option was to go forward to the vault. Ahead, Jackie touched the Crusader's hand and moved from the vault.

Alex's turn came. She wondered if she could fake it, just reach out, but not actually touch the mummy. As she lowered her hand and looked at the Crusader, horror overtook her.

"Oh, God," she cried and pushing by the others in line, ran from the crypt and back into the daylight. "Oh, God," she gasped again, and tears welled up in her eyes.

"The Crusader has that effect sometimes," joked the guide. "Especially on the young ladies."

Jackie caught up with her sister. "Alex, what is it? What's wrong?"

"That's not a crusader," stammered Alex. "That's a Viking - That's Prince Oleif!"

It took a while to calm Alex, and also to convince Aunt Róisín that Alex's outburst was merely a panic attack brought on by claustrophobia. Then the three jumped in a taxi and headed to Phoenix Park, the site of the soccer final, where they found Uncle Bob on the sideline with Fennelly and the perennial wallflower, Tommy Powers.

"Just in time," said Uncle Bob. "We are about to kick off."

"Will we win?" asked Jackie.

"Hard to say; we're up against some local lads we've never played before. And playing in Dublin makes the match a home game for them, so I would think they have the advantage, but never say never."

"Are the Manchester scouts here?"

"The rumor is yes, and Liverpool, and perhaps a few other clubs are represented. Fennelly doesn't recognize any of them, but that's the rumor. I think they may be standing over there, on the other sideline."

A few of the players' family and friends had made the trip from Fethard to support their team; they stood in clumps on either side of Uncle Bob. The supporters of the Dublin team stood on the side indicated by Uncle Bob.

"That's not fair," said Jackie. "They can't stand there with the enemy. They're supposed to be in neutral territory."

"Oh, don't you worry, they won't show favoritism. They're just here to judge the form of the players – Come on Mattie, Jeff."

The Ref blew his whistle to start the game. If there had been any doubt that the boys from Fethard could hold their own it was dispatched within the first five minutes, as Mattie picked up a pass from Jeff and raced down the right wing before he cut inside, sped around two defenders, and coolly slotted the ball under the charging goalkeeper and into the net.

The Fethard supporters leapt in unison punched the air and cheered.

"Woo Hoo," cried Jackie and jumped up and down.

Alex picked up her head and took notice.

"Good start, lads, good start," cried Fennelly.

"Well done, Mattie," cried Uncle Bob.

As the game continued it became apparent that Fethard more than matched their opponents. They controlled all areas of the field, and it was only a matter of time before they added to their goal tally. Their second goal came in the crucial moments just before half time when Mattie floated a corner kick towards the back of the penalty area and Andy Brennan bullied his way above the defenders to head the ball home.

"Hello, girls," Brennan shouted to Alex and Jackie. "See that? Sheer brilliance. Worth coming all the way from America to see me play, admit it."

"Brennan, get back and cover," yelled Fennelly.

The half time whistle sounded. Fennelly called the players to a huddle to discuss tactics.

"So far, so good, lads; that second goal has knocked the wind out of their sails, but we mustn't let up."

"The game is in the bag," said Jeff. "Send Tommy out for the second half and let him get his medal."

"Not yet, O'Rourke. Let's put the game beyond their reach first. Besides, those scouts have come to see you, not Tommy Powers. You've done well so far, but they'll want to see how you handle the entire game."

The second half unfolded much as the first had done. Jeff dominated the mid field, shut down all threats from the Dubliners and set up the counter attacks with a stream of accurate passes. With ten minutes to go, Fethard had added two more goals to their tally.

"Send on Tommy," Jeff yelled at Fennelly.

"Not yet, keep playing, crush them," Fennelly yelled back.

Five minutes later Jeff added a fifth goal, a lightening strike of a volley from outside the penalty area.

"That's it, well done, Jeff," cried Fennelly.

"Send on Tommy," repeated Jeff.

"No, keep playing."

The ball came out of play near the Fethard supporters. As Andy Brennan picked up the ball for the throw-in, Jeff approached Fennelly.

"Come on, Boss, we've won. Send Tommy in for the last minute."

"Get back out there," screamed Fennelly.

"I'm done. I need to come off. Send Tommy on to replace me."

"O'Rourke, I'll decide who to take off and who to play."

Jeff put his hands on his hips and looked to his family as if to seek guidance. Their expressions told him that they could not help him. He felt all alone in the world.

"Take the throw or there'll be a yellow card for time-wasting," commanded the Ref.

"O'Rourke, get on that pitch," demanded Fennelly.

Jeff squared up to Fennelly and looked him in the eye. "No, Boss, I'm done for the day." He removed his shirt. "You may as well send in Tommy, or you'll finish the game with ten men."

"Over my dead body," said Fennelly.

Mattie ran over. "What's up? Come on we only have five minutes left."

"Fennelly won't let Tommy play," explained Jeff. "So, I've quit."

"Right, yellow card," said the Ref.

"Mattie, go out and finish the game," demanded Fennelly.

"If Jeff's quit, then so have I," said Mattie and also removed his shirt.

"Have you gone mad?" cried Fennelly.

Andy Brennan ambled over. "Might have known; you O'Rourke brothers were always trouble."

"Don't mess with me, Andy," said Jeff. "If Tommy can't play then I won't play, simple as that. Go and finish your game and get your medal but leave me out of it."

Andy Brennan threw the ball at Jeff's chest and smiled. "Whatever you say, Captain." He removed his shirt. "Guess I'm done for the day as well."

"What's going on?" demanded the Ref. "Play the rest of this match or forfeit it."

"You three are finished," cried Fennelly. "You'll never play soccer for me again. Okay, the rest of you get out there and hold them for the final five minutes."

But the rest of the team simply walked from the field, one by one, and removed their shirts.

"If you can't field at least eight players, the match is awarded to Dublin," warned the Ref.

"Get on that pitch," pleaded Fennelly. "There are scouts watching. You won't get your medals if you don't get back on that pitch."

"There's more important things than medals," said Jeff as he walked away.

The Crusader

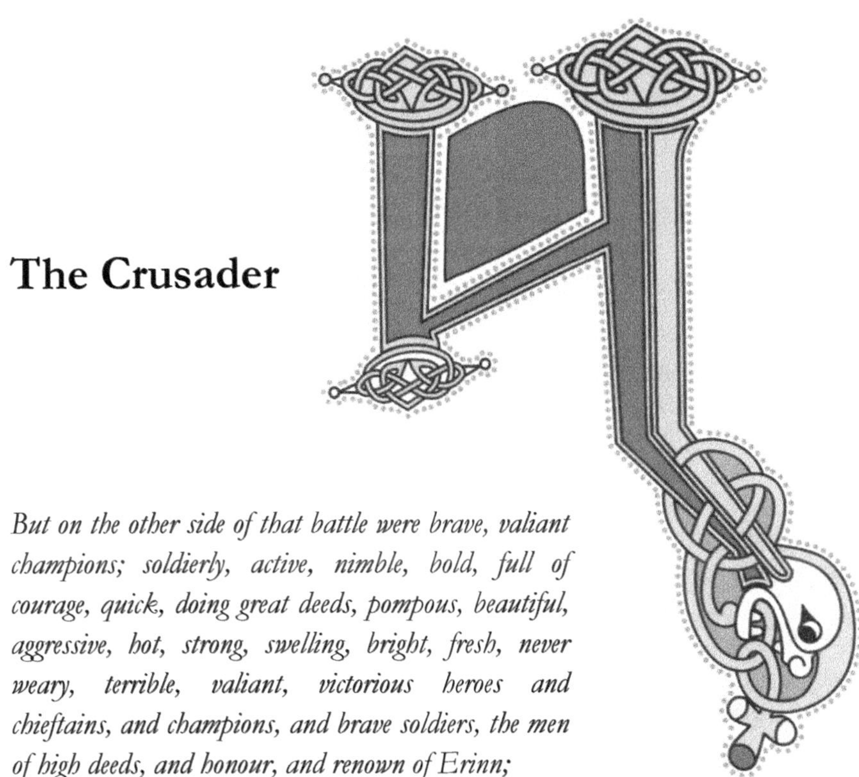

But on the other side of that battle were brave, valiant champions; soldierly, active, nimble, bold, full of courage, quick, doing great deeds, pompous, beautiful, aggressive, hot, strong, swelling, bright, fresh, never weary, terrible, valiant, victorious heroes and chieftains, and champions, and brave soldiers, the men of high deeds, and honour, and renown of Erinn;

Cogadh Gaedhel Re Gallaibh:
(The war of the Gaedhil with the Gaill)
Or
The Invasions of Ireland by the Danes and Other Norsemen

From the *Book of Leinster*, circa 1160,
English translation by J. H. Todd, 1867

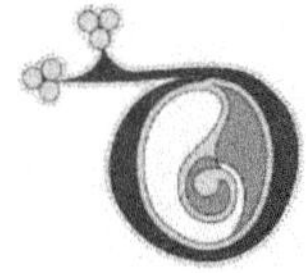**"D**isappeared? What do you mean, *disappeared?"* yelled King Silkbeard.

"The prince thought that he heard the cries of Princess Estrid ahead in the darkness," replied Snorri. "He ran to aid her. In his haste to reach the princess, we could not keep up with him. We last saw him by the cottages to the east, near the river, but a thick fog descended, and we lost him. We called out, but he did not reply."

"What kind of magic is this?"

"What news of my sister?" interrupted Prince Anwud of Norway.

"Alas, no news," admitted Snorri.

"Silkbeard, what treachery is this?" demanded Prince Anwud. "My father shall hear of it."

"No treachery," yelled King Silkbeard, even louder. "Unless it is the Irish. I knew I should have skewered that monk. It is obvious that the Irish took the princess to lure my son. I will make them pay with their heads. Search again, search everywhere. Tear down the walls if you must. Oh, and Snorri, unleash the Berserkers. Prepare for battle."

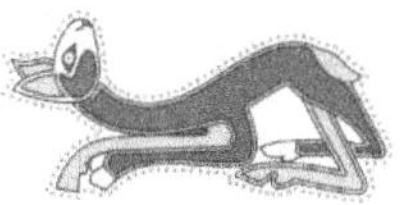

Evening sank over Dublin in hues of orange sunlight, which turned to pastel shades of violet as it bounced of the grey stone buildings and green lawns. Jackie had insisted on some souvenir shopping and dragged Mattie along with her. Alex and Jeff, not in a shopping mood, sat on the grass of Library Square at Trinity College. Because of the ongoing investigation of the theft of the Book of Kells, the Library remained closed to the public and the Gardaí held the hundreds of amateur detectives at bay. In spite of the activity and the crowd, to Alex and Jeff, Library Square seemed the quietest, loneliest place on earth.

"Why did you do it?" asked Alex.

"Because it was the right thing to do," replied Jeff.

"Some people would say it was a stupid thing to do."

"Some people can say what they like. I'm the only one who knows."

"Are you? What makes you so certain? You probably blew a great chance to play professional soccer for Manchester United. People would give an arm for a chance like that, and you just threw it away. Some would say that it was wrong to waste your talents."

"Some people again. You mean you."

"Okay, yes, I think it's wrong to waste your talents. You could have made a difference. Mattie said you were the best soccer player in Tipperary. You could have been brilliant."

"No, not really."

"Don't be modest."

"I'm being realistic. Do you know how hard it is to rise to the top of a profession? Whether it's soccer, or another sport, or music, or acting, it takes more than talent."

"I know: dedication, commitment, hard work, blah, blah; you had all that."

"You left something out."

"What?"

"You have to want it. You have to want it more than anything else in the world. You have to dream about it. You have to be willing to sacrifice everything to it, your friends and your family. I wasn't willing to do that."

"So, you proved. I understand that you wouldn't want to sacrifice your family and friends. Your mom is very proud of you. But for Tommy Powers?"

"Tommy is my friend."

"Yes, but Tommy is not a soccer player. He was useless at it. Today was a chance for you to show the scouts how good a player you were. I'm sorry, but I agree with Fennelly. Tommy shouldn't have played; he wasn't good enough."

"Then what of friendship."

"Tommy is your friend; he would have understood. He would have cheered your success. You blew your chance, and he's still a rubbish soccer player. Nothing has changed except you blew it."

"I think you've got it backwards."

"Sorry?"

"You think it's all about me when it isn't."

"Please explain."

"I'm not sure I know how, but I'll try. Let's suppose I was good enough to land a trial at Manchester United. Let's suppose I impressed them, and they signed me."

"Which, from what I've heard, you could have done."

"At some point, sacrifice would have reared its ugly head. If it wasn't Tommy today, it would have been Mattie tomorrow, or someone or something the day after that. I've known a long time that I'll never make a professional soccer player, that desire just isn't in me. Tommy on the other hand . . ."

"What about Tommy?"

"You think he's useless because he's no good at soccer, because he's a bit shy and awkward. But I've known him all my life and I believe of all the boys in Fethard, he's the one who's going to surprise us."

"Tommy Powers?"

"Don't let the exterior fool you. He's as smart as they come. He'll end up here at Trinity one day, no doubt about it. There's something special in him. I don't think he knows it yet, but I see it. One day, he'll make Fethard proud of him."

"So that makes what you did even more stupid. He doesn't need your help."

"I don't think so. I think one day, we'll be proud of Tommy because he was proud of us. One day, he'll look back at how his mates did the right thing, even when it was the stupid thing, and that in turn will make him do the right thing when his time comes."

"Is doing the right thing so important?"

"For me, yes."

"You know this puts me in an awkward position."

"Why?"

"Well, if you did the right thing, and Jackie did the right thing, then that puts pressure on me."

"What pressure?"

"I've really known it all along, though I fought it as much as I could. I thought I could be selfish, but it's not working out that way. It's time for me to do the right thing. And I'm going to need your help."

"Will I like it?"

"Don't you trust your cousin?"

"Is that a dare? You sound like Jackie."

"It's not a dare. It's a tradition."
"Well . . . okay. What do we have to do?"
"Tonight, after dinner, we have to return what was taken."

Dinner proved a surprisingly upbeat affair, courtesy of a local restaurant near the hotel, amid the hustle and bustle of Temple Bar. Such was the mood that even the tourist-centric food failed to disappoint Jeff. Aunt Róisín positively beamed with pride at the earlier, noble actions of her two sons, but then she didn't understand the importance of soccer. Uncle Bob, who did understand the importance of soccer, took it all in his stride. On the other hand, Uncle Bob expressed that had the boys' offenses been committed during a game of Gaelic football, he may not have remained so calm.

Jackie and Mattie, fresh from their shopping expedition, laughed and joked.

"You two are cheery, tonight," observed Aunt Róisín.

"There's something in the air," said Jackie. "I can feel it."

"And the sun is shining," added Uncle Bob.

"Oh, don't worry," said Jackie. "I think that may be about to change. I think Dublin is as magical as the rest of Ireland. What's that song, cockles and mussels?"

"You mean Molly Malone," answered Mattie.

"Yes, that's the one."

"In Dublin's Fair City,
Where the girls are so pretty,
I first set my eyes on sweet Molly Malone,
As she wheel'd her wheel barrow,
Through streets broad and narrow,
Crying cockles and mussels alive, alive o!"

Sang Jackie, Mattie and Uncle Bob in harmony.

"Alive, alive o!"

Came the reply which only Jackie could hear, and her smile grew even wider.

Alex smiled too, albeit a smile of grim resolve rather than joy. She had determined to do the right thing and damn the consequences, happy to have ended her fight with uncertainty. She looked at Jeff and wondered if he knew that his sacrifice wasn't only for Tommy Powers.

Dinner dragged on through dessert and coffee, and they followed it with a leisurely stroll in the warm, night air, through Temple Bar and alongside the Liffey. Normally, the sisters would have been impatient to ditch the aunt and uncle and set their plans in motion, but tonight, they felt they had all the time in the world, so they walked and talked, joked, and laughed.

"Hey, Mattie," said Jackie. "Why can't you borrow money from a leprechaun?"

"Don't answer, Mattie," said Alex. "It's a trick."

"I don't know," answered Mattie.

"Because he's a little short," said Jackie.

"Boo!" said Mattie.

"I did warn you," said Alex. "Jackie, save the jokes for later."

"Can't do that," said Jackie.

"Why not?" asked Mattie.

"Because you'll be Dublin over with laughter."

"Boo!" said Mattie.

After they had put the elders to bed, the four cousins met in the girls' hotel room to discuss plans.

"Alex has decided to return what was taken," said Jeff.

"I knew that she would," said Jackie. "That's why I went shopping."

"I confess I have no idea what you two are talking about. What does Alex returning things have to do with your shopping."

"Mattie, pass me the bag." Jackie pointed to the brown plastic bag which stood on the dresser.

"And I have no idea what they're talking about, either," confessed Mattie.

"What did you buy?" asked Alex.

Jackie reached into the bag and pulled out a torch.

"A flashlight? You bought a flashlight?"

"Two of them actually . . . and," Jackie reached into the bag a second time and pulled out a long double handed tool which resembled a pair of shears.

"What are those?"

"Bolt cutters."

"Would someone please explain to the less enlightened members of the O'Rourke clan just what is going on?" demanded Jeff.

"I was with Jackie when she brought them, and I still have no idea. Do you know how hard it is to get bolt cutters in central Dublin?"

"How did you know?" Alex asked Jackie.

"Well, it was obvious, wasn't it?" replied Jackie "As soon as you saw it, you knew, and I knew what you had to do. So, I thought the flashlights and bolt cutters would come in handy."

"What's obvious? Saw what? I'm starting to pull my hair out now," said Jeff.

"I don't know if we should take the boys with us," said Alex. "I wouldn't want to get them into trouble."

"What trouble?" insisted Jeff.

"Too late to leave us behind," said Mattie. "We're already accomplices."

"Please, one last time," pleaded Jeff. "Why do you need flashlights and bolt cutters?"

"So we can break in," explained Jackie. "Duh!"

"Break in where?"

"St. Michan's Church."

"You're joking, right?"

"Well, actually, it's the crypt we want to break into," said Alex.

"You're not going to steal a mummy are you?"

"Why would we do that?"

"You tell me – I have no idea what is going through your head."

"We have to break into the crypt because that is where the Sword is."

"The Sword of Nuada?"

"By Jove you've got it. I knew you'd catch up to us sooner or later," said Jackie.

"Are you certain?"

Alex nodded her head. "The mummy known as the Crusader is Prince Oleif. He was holding the Sword. This won't be over until the fairies have their Sword, but it's still protected by Viking magic. We have to get the Sword and return it to the fairies."

"Why us?"

"Because we are the Ua Ruairc. We started this and only we can finish it. Do the right thing you said. Well, nothing will be right again until the fairies get their Sword back."

"You're crazy."

"Sounds reasonable to me, Bro," said Mattie.

"You're all crazy."

"Are you coming or not?" demanded Alex.

Jeff scratched his head. "I guess I'm crazy too."

"Okay, over the fence," whispered Jackie.

"No way; there's spikes," objected Jeff.

"Spikes are easy; tell him Alex."

"No, spikes are a piece of cake," agreed Alex. "You just have to roll on landing so you don't hurt yourself."

"You speak from experience? You've broken into many graveyards, have you?"

"Er, once or twice."

"You're addicted to graveyards at night? That's a pretty bad habit you've got."

"But I swear it's a habit I can break any time I want. Come on, over the top."

"Not here. In case you hadn't noticed, that's a tram stop over there with dozens of witnesses."

"What's 'round the back?"

"The Old Jameson Distillery and the Bow Street Courthouse," said Mattie.

"Courthouse," groaned Jeff. "That will be convenient if we're caught."

"We won't get caught. Come on," said Jackie.

The cousins walked as nonchalantly as they could to Bow Street.

The back of the church property was bounded by a wall. The top of the wall was overrun with a combination of hedgerow and ivy.

"I'll go first," said Alex. "Mattie, cup your hands and lift me up."

"Wait a minute," insisted Jeff.

"Now what? There aren't any people around."

"There might be surveillance cameras."

"What on earth for? Who'd want to break into a graveyard?"

"Well, us for one."

"Stop being a wimp. What's the worst that could happen? If there are cameras, no one will recognize us any way, we're not from around here."

"And if we get caught, we'll just say our insane cousins from San Diego made us do it," said Mattie. "Everyone will see the truth of it."

"Okay, be quick and be quiet."

Mattie cupped his hands and Jackie stepped up and over the wall. Alex quickly followed. Jeff took the third spot.

"Hey, what about me?" Mattie whispered when he realized that no one remained to help him climb over the wall.

"Just stay there," whispered Jackie from the other side of the wall. "We'll come back for you when we're done . . . try to be inconspicuous. Blend in."

"How am I supposed to blend in? I'm not made of brick."

"Just try, okay. We won't be long."

Jeff and the sisters scurried amongst the headstones to the crypt doors, where Jackie produced the bolt cutters and handed it to Jeff.

"Cut off the padlock," she ordered.

"Why me?" argued Jeff.

"Because you're the big, strong man, that's why. You wouldn't expect us weak, little girls to have the strength to do that, would you?"

Jeff squeezed the handles of the bolt cutters. His efforts had no effect. He tried harder, until the sweat poured down his face, the veins in his neck bulged and the muscles in his arms ached. "It's . . . no . . . good . . . it . . . won't . . . budge," he panted, but just as he decided to admit defeat, the lock yielded.

"There's a good boy," said Jackie. "Now, wait here and keep lookout, while me and Alex go get the Sword."

Jackie handed a flashlight to Alex, and they entered the crypt. The flashlights lit up the vaults and coffins, and the sisters crept forward until they reached the end vault. The light from their flashlights settled on the mummy of Prince Oleif. Alex's hand shook so much that she almost dropped her flashlight.

"Are you sure that you're up to this, Sis?" Jackie asked Alex.

"I'll be okay," answered Alex. "It's just unsettling to see him this way; after a thousand years."

"I understand. I'll just grab the Sword and we can get out of here."

"No," said Alex. "I'll do it."

Alex inched towards Prince Oleif. The Sword rested across his chest, held in place by his left hand and arm. Alex tried to ease the Sword out of the prince's clasp. As the Sword moved up, the prince's hand and arm moved up also.

"It's stuck," Alex whispered.

"You'll have to open his fingers," Jackie whispered in reply.

Alex reached out for the prince's forefinger and lifted. She heard a sickening crack.

"Oh, God," cried Alex. "I've snapped his finger off. Oh, God!"

"Don't panic."

"I can't do this."

"I'll be right there, don't panic."

Behind Jackie, without warning, a light appeared. Jackie jumped and turned. Dread started to rise in her body, but she quickly recognized the light which emanated from the fairy horse, Lämmy.

"What's happening? What's happening? OMG," panicked Alex.

"Lämmy, what are you doing here?" asked Jackie.

"Alive, alive o!"

"Not now, Lämmy, we're busy."

"Alive, alive o!"

"What's happening?" cried Alex. She still had contact with the now four-fingered hand of the Mummy Prince Oleif. It moved. Alex looked down. Prince Oleif opened his eyes.

"Estrid, my love," he whispered.

"Aaghh," screamed Alex.

In a single movement, Alex dropped the prince's hand and finger, rose, turned, ran over Jackie, and exited from the vault. Although not conscious of her actions, she carried the Sword.

"Alex, slow down," cried Jackie and ran after her.

Jeff had heard Alex's scream and ventured into the crypt to help. Alex bowled by him. Jackie quickly appeared. "What is it?" he cried.

"Explain later," answered Jackie as she ran.

Alex ran to the iron double gate at the front of the church grounds, pushed them open, and ran out to the street.

"Oh, will you look at that," said Jackie. "The gates must have been unlocked all the time. Come on, we'd better catch her before she hurts herself."

Alex ran across the Father Mathew Bridge and came to rest, out of breath and crying, at the Monument on Lower Exchange Street which honored the Viking presence in Dublin, Áth Cliath. If anyone had thought to help or accost a damsel in distress, the great big sword which she carried acted as a deterrent. Jackie and Jeff, having first rounded up Mattie, found her there.

"Sorry," said Alex. "Got a little bit emotional there."

"That's okay, Sis. You got the Sword. That was the main thing."

"Oh, yes, here," said Alex and handed the Sword to Jackie. "What shall you do with it?"

"Er, all of you wait here; I'm not sure this will work."

Jackie scanned the riverbank for the nearest bridge, the Grattan Bridge, and walked on to it. She stopped halfway across and called out.

"Are you there? I have something for you."

The traffic on the bridge, both car and foot, which was light enough to begin with at that time of the night, disappeared completely and Jackie stood alone.

Then the warm glow of Lämmy appeared at the north end of the bridge.

"That was very naughty of you," said Jackie. "You scared poor Alex half to death."

"And I will follow who follows me."

"Yes, you will. I've followed you around long enough, I think. And you followed me to Dublin. Well, it's done. I have it. Go fetch the Tuatha Dé Danann."

Queen Eeviin appeared beside the fairy horse.

"I've got your Sword."

"Do not mock a dying race, Jackie of the Ua Ruairc," said Queen Eeviin.

"Don't be such a drama queen. I've come to give you your Sword back."

"Without our song, the Sword is but history."

"I've come to give you your song back as well."

"How?"

"You never trusted me, did you? That's all it required, a little bit of trust. I am the Joy Bringer." Jackie walked to the queen. "Here, take your Sword . . ."

The queen took the Sword.

". . . Now, repeat after me, '*Restored by the Sword.*'"

Queen Eeviin spoke the line.

"Feeling better now?" asked Jackie.

"How may we honor you, Jackie of the Ua Ruairc?" sang Queen Eeviin.

Jackie heard the song taken up all around her. It rose from the river and the buildings. The harmonies crashed over her, not sad this time, but full of joy.

Behind them, at the south end of the bridge, the air stirred and crackled, and an old man appeared. His robes, staff, pointy hat, and long white beard instantly made Jackie want to cry out, '*Gandalf*', but Queen Eeviin sang first.

"Odin, scourge of the Tuatha Dé Danann."

"Eeviin Grey Rock," replied Odin. "Why come you here to your place of banishment?"

"Banished no more, Viking. We come to claim what is ours."

"On the fields of Clontarf, a thousand years ago, you came begging at our gates. You were vanquished then and forbidden to enter the stronghold of Dublin. You are forbidden still. The Tuatha Dé Danann are still beggars. Go away from here."

"The Tuatha Dé Danann kneel to no one. At Clontarf, we merely paused. The battle is not yet won or lost."

"Go grovel in the dirt. You are naught but phantoms for the weak and feeble minded."

"Your people, the Vikings, have long since departed. You have stayed too long, Wooden Man. The children of the Tuatha Dé Danann, the Irish, now rule in Dublin. We will have it returned to us."

"You and whose army?"

Queen Eeviin unsheathed the Sword of Nuada and held it high. "By the blood of our ancestors, you will fall before the Sword that is returned. Rise up, oh Tuatha Dé Danann, rise up . . ."

As she sang, the queen grew in stature until she towered above Jackie. Fairy lights began to appear beside her and transform into equally large, beautiful, wonderful, terrifying warriors.

". . . Rise up the mighty Púca and trample your enemies into the dust."

At the queen's side, Lämmy grew and grew. Its color changed from pure white to jet black. Its wings changed from delicate gossamer to tough dragon skin. It breathed sulfur from its nostrils.

". . . Rise up Grey Man and spread your deathly cloak."

A mist floated from the Liffey, enveloped the bridge, and hid Jackie from the view of Alex and the cousins.

"I call on all to strike the Viking gods from our land."

"Then war be on you," cried Odin. "Thor, Loki, look to your defenses. Frey and Freya, show no mercy. Sif, Hel and Idun to me. Let the Valkyrie have bones to harvest."

Odin threw off his cap and cloak, as his godly brothers and sisters arrived in battle dress, then he struck the ground with his staff. A lightning bolt reached out to the night sky.

Queen Eeviin raised the Sword of Nuada, charged at Odin and struck a mighty blow against the Viking god. Odin stood his ground, unflinching, and deflected the Sword with his staff. The clash reverberated around the buildings and streets. Jackie cupped her ears with her hands to shield them against the pain. Unnoticed in this commotion, a small metal object fell from Odin's belt and came to rest on the Bridge.

Following their leaders, the two armies charged and came together in a deafening roar above Jackie's head. They twirled around in a cloud of thunder and lightning. The cloud rose and spread out over Dublin. Lightning struck and knocked out power to parts of the city. Thunder rolled and broke windows with its force. The heavens glowed with fire. In a thousand years Ireland had never seen such a storm.

Jackie turned to walk back across the bridge to her family. As she did, a flash of light reflected from metal caught her eye. She stooped down and retrieved the object which Odin had dropped. It appeared to be a key, its handle carved with animals: a deer, a bear, and a fox. On the bit were carved three Norse letters. Not expecting that Odin would return any time soon to claim his lost key, Jackie pocketed it for safe keeping and then walked to her family.

"I don't think I've ever seen them look happier," she said. "As Lina Lamont said in *Singin' in the Rain*, '*if I've brought a little joy into their humdrum lives, it makes me feel as though my hard work ain't been in vain for nothing.*'"

"Who do you think will win the battle?" asked Mattie.

"Don't know. It'll probably end in a draw. Battles never seem to change anything." A lightning bolt struck the lamp post next to them. "Looks like it might rain."

"Come on," said Alex. "There's still lots to do."

"What are you talking about?" asked Jeff.

"We have to return what was taken."

"But you just did that. The fairies got their Sword back."

"Oh, that wasn't the only thing taken."

"But . . ."

"No time to argue. First, we have to go back to the hotel and get the Book of Kells and the drinking horn."

"Then what?"

"Then we have to find some Banshees."

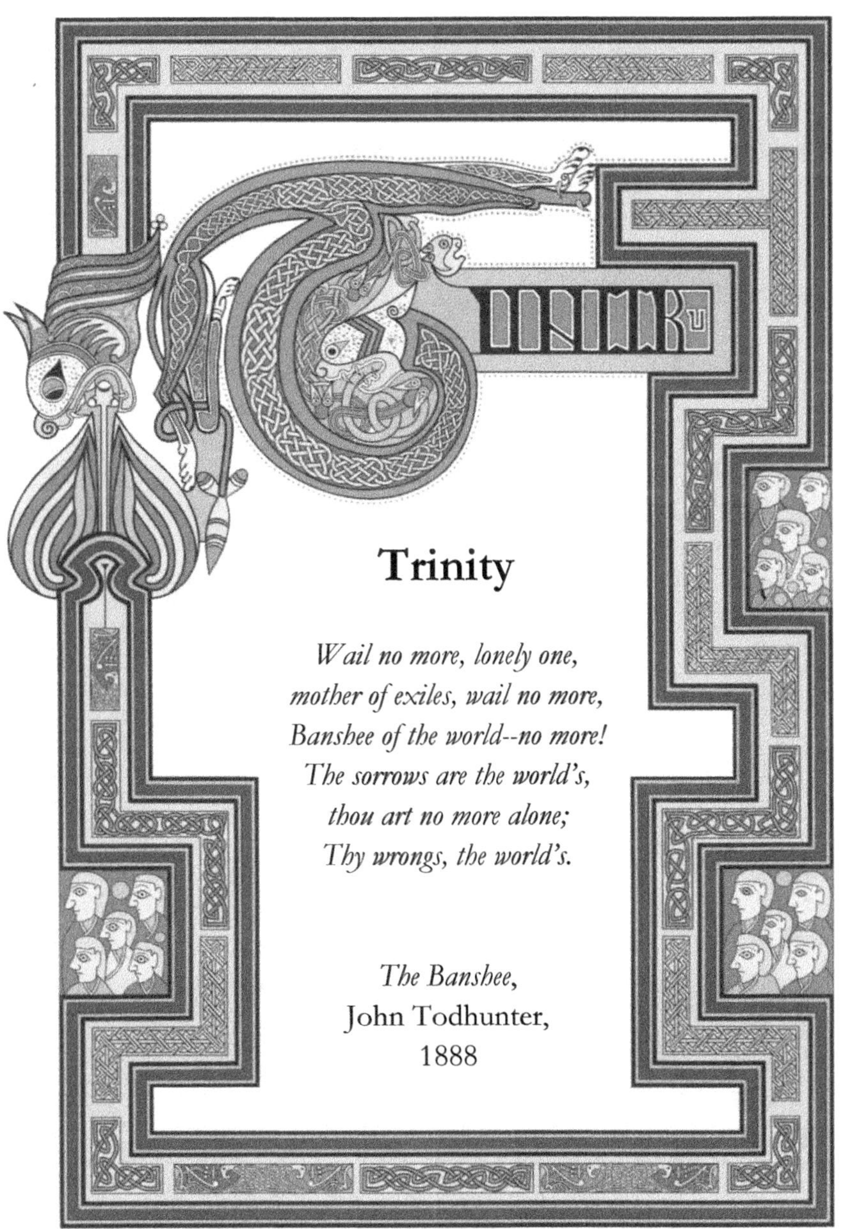

Trinity

Wail no more, lonely one,
mother of exiles, wail no more,
Banshee of the world--no more!
The sorrows are the world's,
thou art no more alone;
Thy wrongs, the world's.

The Banshee,
John Todhunter,
1888

As the battle which raged in the skies over Dublin kept the citizens hidden indoors, the cousins once more stood at the gates of St. Michan's Church. The church and surrounding area lay in darkness because of the power outage, but the constant, violent flashes of lightening overhead lit up the buildings and emphasized the shadows in a manner which reminded Jackie of her favorite monster movies from Universal Studios. The Church gates stood open.

"You don't have to do this," said Jackie. "If it's too hard, I can go talk to him."

"No," said Alex. "I got him into this mess; I'll go."

Alex walked towards the crypt and turned on her flashlight. She found the Mummy Prince Oleif huddled in a corner of his vault. He sobbed gently.

"I'm sorry," whispered Alex.

"I waited and I waited," cried the Mummy. "But you did not come back. Snorri warned me of your witchcraft. Why did you do this to me?"

"I didn't think you'd end up here. What happened?"

"We were to be wed, but you ran away. I searched for you. I ordered my men to search in different directions, so that we could cover more ground. I was alone, but I did not believe I was in danger, not in the heart of Dublin. I searched amongst the huts. I entered the Banshee' cottage and saw you. But the Banshees cried, and you vanished. The Banshees bring death, like the Valkyrie, but I did not die. '*You must not cry for him,*' you ordered. So, I did not die, but was transformed into what you see before you. You condemned me to this living hell."

"I didn't mean to, I swear. I just didn't want to see you die."

"I was a Viking; I lived for death. Now I am not even a man."

"I didn't know this would happen to you. I just didn't think it through."

"I should have died at Clontarf. My destiny was to die proudly with the Ravens in my arms. I would have gone to Valhalla. I would have seen the great halls of Asgard."

"You can still go, it's not too late."

"I am condemned as a coward who ran from battle. I will not dishonor Valhalla with my presence."

"It's not too late. Come with me."

"Why should I?"

"Trust me. What have you got to lose? You think your honor was taken from you, but you can get it back."

"Leave me to my sorrow."

"I can't do that. Remember what you said to me? You said the golden-braided girl was worth more than Ireland. If you believe that, you must come with me. If you don't, you'll stay in this crypt in dishonor for another thousand years while tourists stare at you and shake your hand for good luck. Is that what you want? But if you come with me, you will be a Viking again, you will hold the Ravens. Once, you were willing to give your kingdoms for me, what are you willing to give now."

"Will I see Valhalla?"

"I promise."

The Mummy stood up. "You can restore my honor?"

"You never lost it."

"Then I will follow."

Alex held out her hand for the Mummy to take. He grasped it with his four fingers, and she led him from the crypt and introduced him to the others.

"Er, this is Prince Oleif."

"Hello, Prince, nice to meet you," said Jackie.

The boys merely nodded slightly and then backed away from the well preserved but dusty thousand-year-old Viking.

"Where to?" asked Jackie.

"The house of the Banshees," said Alex. "If I remember my geography, it should be over by Dublin Castle somewhere."

And halfway between Dublin Castle and the Liffey, Alex recognized the house for which they searched. The small wattle and daub cottage of long ago had been replaced over the centuries, with wood, then stone and brick, but Alex recognized the aura it emitted.

"Wait out here," she ordered the boys.

"Why do we always have to wait outside?" complained Mattie.

"They're Banshees; you wouldn't want to scare them, would you? Remember what happened to Kevin Grogan."

"Oh, yes, right, we'll wait out here then, shall we?"

"Good idea."

Alex and Jackie walked to the front door of the house. Alex still held the Mummy's hand and gently guided him. The door opened before they could knock on it and they entered. A group of Banshees stood before them. Alex recognized the woman and child.

"Which one is the Queen of Slievenamon?" whispered Alex.

"I am," replied the queen as she stepped from the shadows.

"Prince Oleif, I'd like you to meet Princess Estrid."

The Mummy's eyes widened, and his mouth opened.

"I do not understand," he said.

"I told you I wasn't Princess Estrid, but you wouldn't believe me. Here is your real bride."

"My Lady." The prince took Estrid's hand and kissed it.

"You have returned the Sword?" asked Princess Estrid.

"Yes," answered Jackie. Thunder and lightning rolled overhead. "As you can probably tell."

"Are you ready to return the other things which were taken?"

"I'm ready," said Alex.

"We three shall drink from the horn."

"What about me?" asked Jackie.

"You must remain."

"Oh, that's so not fair."

"Nevertheless, you must remain. Hold up the horn."

Next to Princess Estrid, a Banshee produced a jug and poured some liquid into the horn.

"What are we drinking?" asked Alex.

"It is honey-mead."

"Oh, one more thing; the Book of Kells, that should also be returned."

"As you wish. All in your possession will go with you."

"Okay." Alex took the Book from her sister. "Time to do this thing."

"Oh, wait," said Jackie. "Before you go."

Jackie walked up to Princess Estrid and whispered in her ear. The princess's eyes widened, and tears fell from them. She stifled a cry before she smiled and bowed to Jackie.

The princess then turned to Alex. "Now drink," she said.

Alex sipped from the horn. Then Princess Estrid held the horn to the Mummy's mouth. And finally, she sipped herself.

"Now, say with me."

"Unharmed go forth."

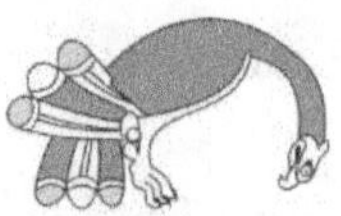

To Alex, it seemed as if everything around her changed while she remained stationary. The brick walls transformed to wattle and daub. Some Banshees disappeared; others appeared in their place. The girl with red hair remained, but her clothes changed. The Mummy transformed into a handsome young man with long blond hair, dressed in the clothes of a Viking.

"Princess Estrid?" cried Brother Oswald.

"Hello Oswald," smiled Alex. "I almost forgot. When you go back to Kells, you need to take this with you."

"The Book . . . I . . . er . . . But how?"

"Long story - doesn't matter. Just promise me you'll take care of it, okay?"

"With my life."

"Oh, and I have to give these back to you." From her pocket, Alex retrieved the two small Celtic letters.

"But those are a gift for your wedding."

"Yes, except the wedding is cancelled."

"Still, a gift freely given should not be returned."

Alex looked at Princess Estrid for confirmation. The Banshee nodded. "Freely given and freely accepted."

"Thank you, Oswald, I shall cherish them . . ."

As she put the metal discs back in her pocket, the door to the wattle hut burst open and through it lurched the figure of Fergal Ua Ruairc, sword in hand and a snarling wolfhound at his heels.

"Ah ha," he began. "I's found you's . . ."

Before he could finish his sentence, the startled Banshees cried out and Fergal fell dead to the floor. The hound turned and fled.

"Ahh," cried Alex as life escaped Fergal's body and entered the Banshees.

"Oh dear," said Brother Oswald.

Shook by the sight of death, Alex turned to Prince Oleif and stuttered. "I'm sorry, I really can't marry you. I return your ring." The Ring of Thor slipped easily from her finger, and she handed it to the prince.

"You must hurry," insisted Princess Estrid. "Others will be here soon. You know what you must do."

"I don't think I can," cried Alex.

"You must."

"Why me?"

"You are still a Banshee, though you deny it."

"I know that. I just pretended so that Jackie wouldn't worry."

"You asked that your sister Banshees not cry for him. We honored your request. You took his death from him. Only you can return it. You must cry for him. That is what it means to be a Banshee."

"I can't do it. I don't want him to die."

Prince Oleif took up Alex's hand. "There are worse things than death, My Love. Please return my honor."

"But you'll die today, out there in a dirty, bloody field."

"There is no finer death for a Viking than on the battlefield."

"No, you should marry Princess Estrid and live happily ever after. I can't do it. I won't do it."

From outside came the sounds of Snorri and the other Vikings in search of their prince and princess. In a matter of minutes, if Alex did not act, others would join Fergal Ua Ruairc in death.

"Let me go," smiled Prince Oleif. "I would give my kingdoms for the golden-braided girl. I would give my life. What would she give in return? You can show me no greater love."

The tears streamed down Alex's face. "No, no, no!" she wept. Then she summoned all the strength she possessed and pushed the prince away from her. And still she cried, "No!" until the sorrow overwhelmed her, and she tilted back her head and howled. And she felt the life force of Prince Oleif enter her. And she filled with pain and sadness. Her Banshee cry reached Snorri and his search party and caused them to cower in terror. It echoed though the streets of Dublin and out over the river and beyond the trees, and on the hillsides, in the camps of Brian Bóruma, and at sea, on the Viking longships, they heard the Banshee cry.

Then she fell to the floor and sobbed.

Princess Estrid knelt beside her to comfort her. "It is done. You must drink from the horn and return to your time. I shall remain as his companion and wife until our end."

She held the horn to Alex's trembling lips and forced Alex to sip.

"Unharmed return."

On her return, Alex instantly collapsed in a heap on the floor of the Banshee house and Jackie ran to her.

"Alex, Alex! What have you done to her?" she demanded.

"Our sister is returned," said the child with the red hair.

"What do you mean, your sister?"

"The Sisterhood will take care of Alex now." The child took up the horn and drank from it.

"Unharmed back home."

The horn disappeared.

"No, she's not a Banshee," cried Jackie. "We cast a spell to undo that."

"The spell failed. You did not use hair of the Banshee."

"Yes, but that's just a technicality. We said the spell and she came back."

"She came back because she was now a Banshee and free to walk where we walk. The spell failed."

"No, I won't accept that. Alex, you must get up. Come on, let's get out of here."

"Alex belongs to us now."

"No, keep away from her."

Jackie dragged her sister to the door and flung it open. On the doorstep stood Queen Eeviin. She appeared peaceful and beautiful, but something about her demeanor forced the Banshees to shrink back.

"How may we honor you, Jackie of the Ua Ruairc?" sang Queen Eeviin.

"The Banshees want to keep Alex."

"That is easy to remedy." The queen reached forward, plucked a hair from Alex's head, and sang.

"To the hair of the Banshee,
The song of the Faerie."

"There, your sister is restored," sang the queen.

"She's no longer a Banshee?"

"She is human again, but she should rest until her strength returns."

"Thank you. Wait a minute? Shouldn't you be fighting Odin?"

"We have banished Odin to the ice from whence he came. Prince Oleif was the last Viking in Dublin. When he died, the Viking magic which held this place also died. Then Odin and his cohorts had no stomach for the wrath of the mighty Tuatha Dé Danann. We have vanquished them and taken their treasure in compensation for our troubles." She looked serenely at the Banshees. "Good day, Sisters, are the Sisterhood not also compensated?"

The Banshees bowed but remained silent.

Jackie suddenly realized the silence had spread everywhere. She looked skyward. The storm had passed.

"Take your sister," sang the queen. "The realms of Faerie and Banshee no longer have power over you."

"Where's my sister?" roared Prince Anwud of Norway and he threw a bottle of wine at the nearest slave.

"Where's my son?" bellowed King Silkbeard. He threw a plate of chicken against a wall, this time in anger.

The Vikings shrugged their shoulders and shuffled from foot to foot. Royalty should be handled with kid gloves at the best of times, but royalty in a temper never bodes well for the people closest.

"Here I am, Father," cried Prince Oleif from the entrance to the mead hall. "I see you missed me." The prince sauntered to the fire pit. A woman walked at his side.

"Where in Asgard have you been?" shouted King Silkbeard. "We've got some Irish to slay or had you forgotten?"

"It's a bit of a long story. I'll tell you later if I get a chance. No, I'd not forgotten. Had to take care of some business first."

"Who's the lady?"

"This is no lady; this is my wife. Ha, ha, get it . . .?"

The king and other Vikings stared blankly.

". . . It's what is called a joke. No? Never mind, it will be funny one day."

Snorri grunted. "You should stick to love poetry, My Lord, and leave the jokes to the jesters."

"Snorri, my friend," said Prince Oleif. "One day the poets will write a saga about you. But for now, I've got the wedding horn, you fetch the goat and the honey-mead. Estrid and I are late for our wedding. And then bring me those Ravens."

The morning of the sisters' last full day in Ireland found the sky full of big, grey, ominous clouds. Jackie had showered and dressed, but Alex, still in her pajamas, lay on her bed and glumly stared at the TV.

"Expect rain at any minute" warned the weatherman.

Alex looked out of the window and sighed.

Throughout Ireland, people talked about the storm in the night. It had downed trees, smashed windows, overturned cars, and sunk boats, and many parts of Dublin remained without power. And although the weatherman denied it, many speculated that the storm must have been a hurricane, tornado, or tsunami, or some devilish combination of all three. Others smiled at their uneducated friends' childish notions. These wiser heads gently postulated the simpler explanation that the fairies must have played a part in it.

But the storm was not the only major news story that day. For the broadcasters also reported a development which concerned the Book of Kells. It had been found unharmed. It had been found in the Trinity College Library, exactly where it should have been all the time. The Gardaí could not explain it, because they had scrupulously watched all entrances and exits since its disappearance.

In additional news, they reported that teenagers had tried to break into the crypt of St. Michan's Church. Unfortunately, damage to the surveillance tape during the storm made identification of the intruders impossible. Fortunately, the celebrated collection of mummies remained undamaged, although the church sexton was at a loss to explain the discovery of an extra mummified finger on the floor of the Crusader's vault. Video footage of the Crusader Mummy flashed on the TV screen.

"I know him," observed Alex. "It's Fergal Ua Ruairc, famous at last."

"Let's go down for breakfast," said Jackie. "We are running out of chances for the full Irish experience."

"I'm not that hungry."

"How about just some juice and soda bread then?"

"No, really, I'm not hungry. You go down. I'll send some texts."

Even though Alex had escaped her Banshee future, Jackie could see that the pain and sadness of the experience remained within her.

"Let's go for a walk to build up your appetite."

"I'm not in the mood for a walk. I'm still tired from last night."

"Humor me."

Alex sighed. "Okay, let me dress. I'll shower when we get back."

The sisters left the hotel and walked toward Trinity College. Gardaí barricades were still in position and all access to the Library was prohibited. They walked the perimeter of the college and sought an unmanned entrance but failed to find one.

"They got their Book back. Why stop people going in now?" complained Alex.

"Want to see the Book?" asked Jackie.

"Love to, but unless you can make us invisible, there's no way we'll get by the police."

"Can't make us invisible, but I can do something just as good." Jackie opened her purse and pulled out the leaf she had taken from the Tree. "I figured out why the Tree grows in the pub."

"Why?"

"It's not just the fairies who sang to me. I guess I suspected all along, but I was only certain after I realized that Lämmy could still sing when the Tuatha Dé Danann couldn't. I figured there still had to be magic around for that to happen. And I wondered where the song came from. Then I realized that the song came from the trees. What the fairies had done was learn how to tap into that magic. But the fairies don't own the trees. They were here long before the Tuatha Dé Danann arrived. The trees here are magical, but it's not fairy magic, it's deeper than that. The trees are the real guardians of Ireland. They are watching out for everything. They watch over all things in Ireland: the fairies, the humans, even the Vikings. That's why it's wrong to cut them down."

"You took a leaf from the Tree. Was that a smart thing to do?"

"At first, I thought the fairies had set us up. Then I thought it was the Banshees. Everyone thinks that they're calling the shots, but they're not. Everyone thinks that their ideas are their own. So, the fairies thought they were using us. And the Banshees thought they were using us. But now I realize it was the Tree all along. The Tree wanted to put things right. To them, we're all just like squabbling children. The Tree grew in the Gatehouse to bring the Tuatha Dé Danann, the Banshees and the Ua Ruairc together, so we could end this squabble. I thought Queen Eeviin told me to go to the Queen of Slievenamon, but it wasn't her, it was the Tree that directed everything. Lämmy was sent by the Tree to guide us."

"Well, that's all very clever, but you didn't answer my question. And I don't see how it gets us inside the library to see the Book of Kells."

"The very first thing Lämmy sang to me, '*The child of woman wishes for song, but cannot sing in harmony. The child of man wishes for dreams, but cannot cast the spell of sleep.*'"

"What about it?"

"I can do it, Alex, I can do it. I can sing in harmony with the Tree, and I can cast the spell of sleep."

"When did this happen?"

"After we cast the spell to free you from the Banshee thing, I don't know if the Tree intended it to happen or if everything just got messed up, but the fairy song didn't just disappear. It was transferred to me. Remember we needed the spell and a charm, and you didn't know what the charm was. I was the charm, the Child of the Charm. '*And if the child so dares to see.*'"

"See what?"

"'*And I will follow who follows me.*' What it means is that the Tree has given me an understanding of its magic, and the power to use it."

"You're a fairy?"

"It's better than being a Banshee. Do you want to see the Book?"

"Yes."

"Okay, I'll need a tree."

"They're all on the other side of the fence."

"No, I just need a leaf or a branch; something I can touch. Here, this will do."

Jackie took the leaf and placed it against the leaf of an overhanging oak. The bark of the oak began to peel back until an opening to its interior appeared. The opening enlarged until it pushed aside the railings of the fence and formed a hole large enough to accommodate them. A tunnel ran from the hole, its end obscured by darkness.

All around the park and streets, people slowed down and stopped. Traffic came to a standstill. The birds stopped their flight in mid-air. The wind stopped blowing.

"Jackie, what's happening?"

"Don't worry. It's the spell of sleep. It's a space-time thing. Time does not exist inside the Tree magic. And there's more to it than meets the eye. The branches and roots spread out to all parts of Ireland. It's a gigantic network. That's how the fairies and Banshees travel. That's how you travelled to Queen Eeviin's palace from Dublin. And it's how we are going to get into Trinity College Library."

The sisters stepped into the passage which had formed before them.

"Which way?" asked Alex.

"Just walk; the Tree knows where you want to go. Oh look, we're here."

Before them stood a wooden door which opened at the merest touch. The door opened on to the Long Room of the Library, lined with old books and white, marble busts of deceased dignitaries. People stood about them, frozen in time. They walked the length of the Long Room and descended a flight of stairs. There before them, under glass and bathed in a soft, gentle glow, lay the Book of Kells.

"It really is beautiful," said Jackie.

"Yes . . . but . . . it's so sad," said Alex and she began to cry.

"I'm sorry, I shouldn't have brought you here," said Jackie. "It was a dumb idea."

"No, it's okay. It's just . . . can I have a few minutes by myself."

"Sure, I'll go back upstairs and wait for you there."

Jackie returned to the Long Room.

"All right," she said. "I know you are watching us. You can come out now."

Lämmy and Queen Eeviin materialized.

"How may we honor you, Jackie of the Ua Ruairc?" sang the queen.

"I'm ready to make my wish," answered Jackie.

"And what do you wish?"

"Return what was taken."

"You could wish for anything, long life, wealth, power Are you certain that is your wish?"

"She's my sister, how could I wish for anything else. What's inside her, what she's feeling . . . that's not normal sadness. It's Banshee sadness, she can't live with that. I want my sister back, as she was before the pain took her."

"If we grant your wish, she will be returned to innocence. You alone will carry the burden of her experience. That is the price you must pay."

"I know."

"You must forfeit all power over magical things. You must return the fairy song. That is the price you must pay."

"I know."

"We know what you sang to the Queen of Slievenamon, for the spell you cast shaped not just your sister or the Tuatha Dé Danann."

"'*The song of the Faerie replaced by the Word,*'" quoted Jackie.

"And the Word is Joy." Queen Eeviin bowed low. "You are a rare and magical creature, Joy Bringer of the Ua Ruairc. You honor us and we shall honor you. Your wish is granted."

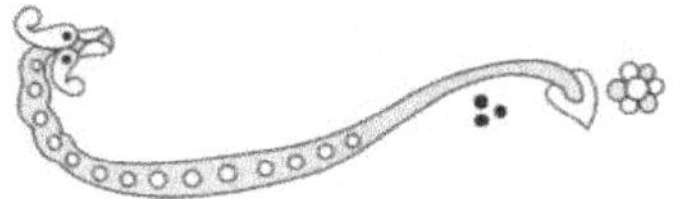

"Jackie, come on," cried Alex as she banged on the bathroom door. "We'll be late for breakfast. I'm hungry."

"I'll be right there." Jackie replied with a mouthful of toothpaste.

"Come on, we only have one more day in Ireland. I have to shop for something that matches my Celtic earrings. I don't know where you found them, but thank you, they're perfect. And we have to get presents for Mattie and Jeff and Uncle Bob and Aunt Róisín."

"You're in a good mood this morning. I said I'll be right there."

"I slept like a log. I think I'm in the mood for the full Irish breakfast this morning. Who knows when we'll be back this way again? Hey, Jackie, I heard a joke: when is an Irish Potato not an Irish Potato? When it's a French Fry."

"Leave the jokes to us professionals, okay," cried Jackie.

Alex backed away from the bathroom door and began to hum Molly Malone. Beyond Alex and the general noise which bubbled up from the streets of Temple Bar, Jackie the Joy Bringer heard singing. She looked out of the bathroom window and smiled.

"Tá sé ag cur báistí," she said.

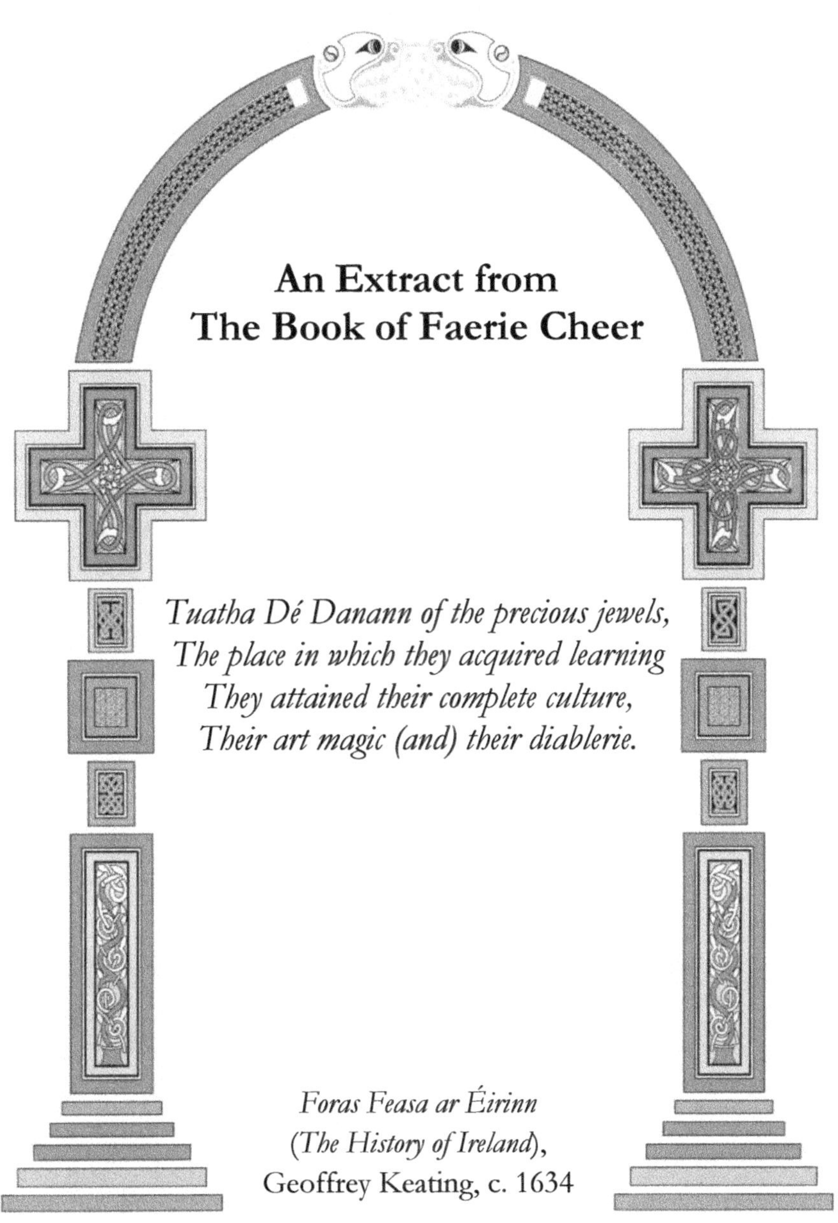

An Extract from
The Book of Faerie Cheer

Tuatha Dé Danann of the precious jewels,
The place in which they acquired learning
They attained their complete culture,
Their art magic (and) their diablerie.

Foras Feasa ar Éirinn
(The History of Ireland),
Geoffrey Keating, c. 1634

An extract from the Book of Faerie Cheer

Author's Note: The *Book of Faerie Cheer* tells the tale of the second golden age of the Tuatha Dé Danann, after their victory over the Norse gods at the Battle of Grattan Bridge (also known as the Second Battle of Clontarf), and how the fifth jewel of the Tuatha Dé Danann was lost and regained.

This extract is taken from my own translation of the anonymously written manuscript. The only known original copy of the book was lost under suspicious circumstances, in the Irish Sea, whilst on a ferry from Dublin to Holyhead, Wales. The official story tells that a freak wave hit the ferry during a snowstorm, just as the book was being inspected near an open porthole, and the book was swept overboard. I say, suspicious, because of the following facts: the manuscript was allegedly being transported to All Souls College, Oxford for forensic testing to verify its age, but the college has no records or correspondence which confirm they expected delivery of the book; the voyage occurred in August, a most unlikely time of the year for snow, and the porthole identified in the reports was not designed to open. In addition, Mr. John Ayres, assigned by the courier company, and entrusted with the protection of the book during its journey, could provide no reasonable explanation why he had removed the priceless manuscript from the security of its transport box. Indeed, Mr. Ayres could provide no explanation at all, for he had seemingly been struck dumb by the episode and was declared unfit to testify at the inquiry. Whether his insanity was a cause or consequence of his gross dereliction of duty, we cannot say.

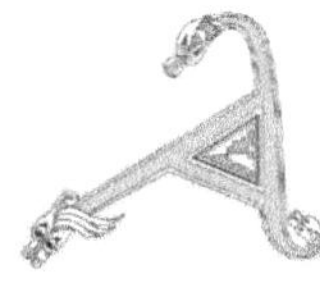

And with the vanquishment of the Norsemen, the Sidhe assembled for rejoice at the Enchanted Palace of the Three Trees, where Queen Eeviin of the Grey Rock gave welcome and bid them bring forth the five treasures of Tuatha Dé Danann from the five cities, according to the ancient rituals.

"Bring forth the Cauldron of Dagda, our bounty from the sea of Murias, under the golden star," sang Queen Eeviin. "Bring forth and our wounds shall be healed. Bring forth and our thirst shall be quenched."

The Cauldron was placed center and all who did appear there at the Enchanted Palace drank from it and had their fill.

"Now let us dust the snow from the Lia Fail of Failias and bring it forth," commanded Queen Eeviin.

Then the sacred stone was placed before Queen Eeviin, but ever silent in later years of the Irish kings of men, it still would not speak.

So, Queen Eeviin called next for the Spear of Lugh, and the Children of Danu did praise the shining spear with song.

Next the good Queen Eeviin commanded on them that from sun flamed Findias should be brought forth the Sword of Nuada, which yet gave excellent service at the Bridge of Grattan.

An extract from the Book of Faerie Cheer

"Kings, queens, Vikings, now again we warn you all not to seek to wield it, for you will ever be denied," sang Queen Eeviin.

And a silence befell the throne room of the Enchanted Palace as the guardians of the Sword unsheathed the pride of Nuada and held it high so that it glinted in the magical light. And the Tuatha Dé Danann did look again in awe upon their sacred jewel.

"Now," commanded Queen Eeviin. "From Dublin's Fair City bring forth the Treasure Chest of Odin, taken as tribute from the hands of our defeated enemy, so that the might and majesty of the Sidhe be acknowledged by all. Bring forth the Chest."

And upon the queen's command, four of the Tuatha Dé Danann entered the hall, bearing on their shoulders a great wooden chest, carved on all sides with woodland creatures. They placed the Chest at the queen's feet.

"Bring forth the key to unlock the Chest of Odin," commanded Queen Eeviin.

"Majestic and Terrible Queen," they cried. "Woe upon woe and sorrow upon sorrow! For the Key of Odin is taken by the daughters of the Ua Ruairc."

"Oh, bugger!" sang Queen Eeviin.

"Fecking Americans!" sang the Tuatha Dé Danann.

Lines 517-631, *The Book of Faerie Cheer*,
anon, date unknown, translated by T. Weston

* 9 7 8 0 9 8 5 0 3 6 1 1 9 *